TELL ME A STORY

LACEY BLACK

KAYLEE RYAN

COPYRIGHT

It is intended for adult readers.

Cover Designer: Just Write Creations
Editor: Hot Tree Editing
Proofreading: Deaton Author Services, Sandra Shipman, Kara Hildebrand, and Jo Thompson

CHAPTER
ONE

BROCK

"Once upon a time," I start, and the group, my best friend, Caleb, and some of my new teammates, erupt in laughter.

We're sitting outside around the fire at Caleb's house, which is my house now, too, since I've been traded to the Kansas City Ramblers. When you're traded in the professional football league, there is no time to shop around for a house. Training camp started two days later. I had no choice but to get my ass to Kansas City. Thankfully, Caleb was all too willing to let me stay with him.

I was drafted to the Chicago Thunder right out of college. I was butthurt when they traded me, but that's the thing about a career in professional sports. It's business, not personal. The Thunder needed a quarterback and did what they had to do to make that happen. As I sit here with my best friend since freshman year of college and my new teammates, I can't find it in me to be mad. I miss my old teammates, I miss my old team, but damn, it's going to be nice playing on the same side of the field as my best friend again.

"Fuck off," Caleb says, trying to hide his smile.

"No, don't stop," Jeff, the left tackle for my new team, says, holding his stomach.

"There were three of them," I continue. "They were all over him, and his drunk ass tells them to drop their panties. I kid you not. All three did just that right there in the middle of the bar." I grin when I see Caleb cover his face with his hands. He lived up to the hype of the football player, being, well, a player in college. Hell, we all did.

"Damn," Dominic, one of the defensive linemen, speaks up. "Sounds like I went to the wrong college."

"What about the time you hooked up with the cheerleader on the back of the bus?" Caleb tries to goad me, but we both know it won't work.

"Good times," I say, holding up my beer in salute, making him laugh. "There is no shame in my game," I tell them. "I was single. Nothing wrong with a little action."

"Not when it's where we can all hear her," Caleb accuses.

I shrug. "You know damn well that if she or any of the cheerleaders wanted to ride your cock, you'd have done the same thing." A chorus of agreement pipes up around me, including from Caleb.

Sex is a beautiful thing, and there is no shame in having lots of it. Two rules. Both of you need to be single, and always wrap it before you tap it. I'm not really a relationship kind of guy. I've got women throwing themselves at me daily, and I'm gone a lot. I know some of the guys make it work and are happy even. However, there are just as many that end in divorce. I may not be one for relationships. However, if I ever do find the one, if I ever take the plunge and settle down, she's going to be it for me. I'll make damn sure she knows how much she means to me. I refuse to be a statistic of a pro athlete and end up divorced. That shit is fucked-up. I've seen it happen too many times. Besides, I was raised by a single mom. I know the toll it takes on not only the parents but the child.

"Do they think that's what we want?" Alan, an offensive lineman, asks. "They have to know that letting us fuck them whenever wherever does not make them wife material."

"You looking to wife up, Jones?" Caleb questions, calling him by his last name.

"Yeah, I mean, isn't that how life works? You meet someone worth taking home, you marry them, have a house full of babies, and live happily ever after, and all that shit?"

"Jones here is the resident romantic of the Ramblers," Caleb explains.

"Nothing wrong with a little romance," Jeff chimes in. "That doesn't mean you have to wife them."

"Why put forth the effort if they're not worth having around for the long haul?" Alan asks.

"Smart man." Dominic points at him with his water bottle that looks like a mini version in his large hands. "And if they're not wife material, we don't have to put in the effort. There are too many warm and willing football groupies to have to even try." I see him shrug through the light of the fire.

We're jaded, like most pro athletes, from the scandals and the jersey chasers who try to latch on to us for fame, or as their meal ticket. I'm sure if there were women around to hear this conversation, they'd be appalled at our reasoning, but it's our reality. The one that we live day in and day out. You know those rumors you hear about fans sneaking into celebrities' and athletes' homes lying naked in their beds? Yeah, that shit really happens. Never to me, but I did have a woman drop her trench coat as I approached my car in the lot one night after an away game. She was buck naked, standing there begging me to take her. I didn't, in case you were wondering. I was exhausted from the game and the long-ass flight home. I just wanted a shower to rinse off the travel and my bed.

My own father was a loser, as was my best friend's dad. He played in the league, a damn good player too, but he played just as hard off the field as he did on. It's not just the women, but the parties too. There are some guys who live for that shit.

"None of you are married or attached?" I ask my new teammates. A variety of "nope, no, nah, and not me" greets my ears.

"What about you?"

"Unattached," I tell them. Don't get me wrong, I'm not opposed to settling down, but it's hard to find someone who's worthy of taking home to your momma when you're on the road or at practice six to seven months out of the year. I don't indulge in the groupies as much as I did in college, or hell, even when I was first drafted. That shit gets old fast. I'm not a saint. I still have the casual hookup, but they know the score, and they're good with it. They want to say that they slept with Brock Williams. I'm bragging rights for them.

Gotta love the life of a professional athlete.

Most of the guys in committed relationships met their girl in college and some in high school. They've been with them before they became a household name. I wasn't that guy. That's fine. I have five, maybe six years left to play. Football is hard as hell on your body. Maybe then, once I'm no longer in the limelight, I might find a nice girl and settle down.

"This has been real, fellas," Hank, the center says, standing from his Adirondack chair. "I'm heading home."

That starts a chain reaction as all the guys stand and say their good-byes. "I'm glad you're here, brother," Caleb says, leaning his head back against his chair and staring up at the night sky. "Going to be a good season with us on the same team." He holds his hand out for me to bump, and I don't disappoint, making a fist and pressing it against his.

"Yeah," I agree. "The guys all seem nice. I expected training camp to be a bitch, but everyone was pretty chill."

"They are," he agrees. He starts to say something else when his phone rings. "It's Joey," he says, referring to his little sister. "Hey, sis," he answers.

I've met Josephine Henderson a handful of times while we were in college. She's four or so years younger than us, so she was graduating from high school as we were leaving college. She's a cute girl, if my memory serves me correctly.

"You have a key. Just come on in. You know where your room is." He pauses. "Do you need me to come and get you?" Another pause. "Are you sure?"

My curiosity is piqued for sure. It sounds like Josephine, or Joey as Caleb calls her, might be coming for a visit.

"All right. I'll see you in a few days."

"Everything all right?" I ask.

"Yeah, I think so. That was my sister. She's coming to visit."

"Unplanned?"

He nods. "That's not like her, but she said she just needs a break. We both know that our dad and her mom aren't good options."

"Definitely not," I agree. Their family history is messy and all kinds of complicated. Caleb and Josephine have the same father but different mothers. The two of them have forged their own little tight-knit family that excludes their parents.

"What's she doing these days?" I ask him.

"She works at some big-wig advertising firm in Springfield. She's wicked smart with all that marketing shit." He finishes off his water before placing the lid back on the bottle. "I hate that she's two and a half hours away, but she loves what she does, and she's damn good at it. She's moved up the ladder pretty quickly in the short amount of time that she's been there. She started right out of college, and now she's a junior something or other. Don't tell her I can't remember her job title," he jokes.

"Good for her."

"I think I'm going to call it a night."

"You getting old on me, Henderson?" I call him out, using his last name.

"Fuck off." He laughs. "I'll see your ugly mug in the morning." With that, he stands and heads toward the back door.

"Night, my man," I say with a wave. I should probably head inside as well, but it's nice out, and the fire is still blazing. The last several weeks have been hectic from getting traded and starting training camp with a new team two days later. It took some time to get into the groove with my new teammates on the field, well, everyone except for Caleb. He and I just work together like a well-oiled machine. Now, here I am, a few days away from the first preseason game of the year.

It's going to be weird for me not to wear a Thunder jersey, but so far, the trade has been good. I do need to find my own place to live, but Caleb insists that my staying with him is fine. I agreed to stay through the season. I'll have more time once the season is over to look at houses and decide where I want to live. I also still need to sell my place in Chicago. It's on the market, but as of right now, no takers. It's in a private gated community, so maybe one of the new recruits to the

Thunder will be interested. Hell, half of my neighbors were my Thunder teammates.

I don't know how long I'm out here staring at the stars when my phone rings. Fishing the phone out of my pocket, I see my mom's name. "Hello."

"Brock, is everything okay?"

Her mom-dar is always on full alert. "Yeah. I'm just sitting out here around the fire. The guys left, and Caleb went to bed. I'm just relaxing."

"Good. How was the training camp? I only got to talk to you for a little bit the other day."

My mother's "little bit" was actually almost an hour. "It was good. The team is tight. Took some time to mesh with everyone, but we finally found our groove."

"Oh, good. I was worried about how that was going to play out."

"What are you doing up this late?" I ask, pulling the phone away from my ear so I can check the time.

"I worked a late shift. I just got home. I was hoping I would get lucky and you'd still be up."

"Mom." I sigh. "I've told you that you can quit that job. Let me take care of you."

"I will do no such thing, Brock Andrew Williams," she scolds.

I know she means business when she does the full name drop. "Stubborn." My tone is teasing, even though we both know I'm serious. I had to fight tooth and nail to buy her the house she lives in. She threw a fit, and I hated to threaten to have her old house torn down so she wouldn't have a choice to get her to cave.

"That's your money, son."

"Mom. You busted your ass to keep me in gear and to get me to games and practices from the time I was five years old. I have more money than I can spend in my lifetime. I've invested well. Let me do this for you."

"Nope. Not going to happen. Have you met any nice girls? You could give me a grandchild, you know," she says, only half teasing.

"I promise you, if I ever happen to come across someone I think is worthy of your time, you will be the first to know." I don't tell her what she already knows, which is that there is a very slim chance of that happening. Not in the next few years. "How was your shift?" I ask to change the subject. Mom is an ER nurse at the local county hospital in Indiana, where I grew up.

"It was slow for once. You know, not a lot of action in this small town of ours."

"How's Howard?" I inquire. Howard is my mom's boyfriend for all intents and purposes. She calls him her "man friend," but they've been "friends" exclusively for about six years now. He's a great guy who treats her right. That's all that I can ask for.

"He's doing well. He's still coming with me this weekend. Is that okay?"

"You know it is. I have two tickets waiting at the booth for the both of you."

"You nervous? First game with your new team?"

"A little, if I'm being honest. We have the preseason to work out the kinks. I think it's more excitement to be on the field with Caleb again and to see where we can take the Ramblers this season than anything."

"I sure did love to watch the two of you play together in college."

"The A team." I laugh.

"Most definitely," she agrees. "All right, well, I won't keep you. I just wanted to check in on you."

"Now the truth comes out," I tease.

"I'm your mother, Brock. I will never not want to check in on you. I don't care if you're twenty-nine or fifty-nine. If there is still breath left in my lungs, and I'm able, I'll be checking on you. When you have kids, you'll understand."

"Love you, Mom." I ignore the kids comment this time. I know she wants to be a grandma, but I'm not sure that will ever happen. I work all the damn time, and in my line of work, it's hard to know who is with you for you, and who just wants your fame and money.

"Love you too, son. I can't wait to see you next weekend."

"Dinner after the game?"

"Yes. Howard and I are driving there on Saturday and not coming home until Monday. I can't wait to hug you."

I chuckle at her reply. She's told me that since the day I left for college, whenever any time passed without seeing her. "Have a safe trip. Are you sure I can't buy you a plane ticket? Howard too?"

"Don't be silly. It's not that far. We're both excited about the road trip.

"I won't get to see you after the game since there will be meetings, but I'm happy that you can be there. The team's public relations rep has me booked."

"You might not get to see me, but I'll see you. More than that you'll know that Howard and I are there. I haven't missed a season opener yet, and I'm not about to start. I Love you."

"Love you too," I reply and end the call. The fire has burned down to nothing but hot embers, so it's time to call it a night. Quietly, or as quietly as I can for a six-foot-four, two-hundred-and-fifty-pound guy, I head into the house, locking the door behind me, before making my way to my room.

The last two days have been hard to sleep at night, living in a new place. I was here two nights several weeks ago before leaving for training camp. This is all still going to take some time to get used to. However, I'm exhausted after two nights of little rest. Thankfully, it's not long after my head hits the pillow that I drift off to sleep.

CHAPTER
TWO

Joey

It's midafternoon as I let myself into my brother's house, disabling his alarm system with the security code. It's one I'll never forget—it's my birthday. This place is absolutely amazing. Caleb's four-bedroom, five-bath home sits on a large corner lot in a gated community and looks like it's fresh off a magazine cover. He scored the property a few years back when the housing market was struggling, and interest rates were low. Now, he has a solid investment that he'll easily be able sell, if he should ever need to.

I pray he never does.

I've gotten used to having him within driving distance. Sure, there's a real possibility he could be traded at any point and be forced to move to New York, Texas, or even California, but so far we've been lucky. I don't know what I'd do if he had to move. My brother may be my half sibling by blood, but he's my everything. If I ever need anything, it's Caleb I go to. Not my dad, and definitely not my mom.

Caleb and I share the same father, but our mothers are night and day different. Caleb's mom baked him cookies and read him bedtime stories, while my mom was too busy trying to find her next sugar daddy to even worry about what I was going to eat or how I was going to get to ballet class.

I was the result of an affair. My dad was a professional football player who got caught up in the hype, the attention, and the women. He met my mom at a club after a game, and nine months later, I came along. As well as an epic scandal. Caleb's mom stayed, even after the affair came to light, at least for a while. She ended up walking away—with half Dad's net worth, mind you—after more allegations of cheating hit the gossip rags.

Through all the drama of my childhood and being the kid of a professional athlete, I always had Caleb to lean on. He kept me grounded. Being four years older than me, I always looked up to him. What's best, he never got mad at me for following him around and trying to hang out with him and his friends.

Caleb has a lot of friends. Always had. He's so charismatic and outgoing, with a heart of gold who would do anything for anyone. That's part of the reason he bought this place. Over the years, he's had several teammates crash in the guest room from time to time, especially at the start of a season.

When I called him two nights ago and told him I was coming for a visit, he didn't question it. He never does——just makes sure my bedroom is ready for me. He's at practice now, having returned from training camp a few days ago. My plan is to take my things upstairs and maybe start dinner. He should be home in a few hours, and knowing my brother, he has a fridge full of healthy options to choose from.

I drop my purse onto the chair and set my cat carrier on the coffee table. An inpatient meow echoes through the room. "I know, I know, Hermione. Let's go find your litterbox." My gray and white cat rubs against the table before stretching her legs and trailing behind me as I head to the laundry room. There, I find the empty litterbox I keep here for when we visit.

Hermione stays close while I add fresh litter and fill a dish with dry food. When she heads inside to do her business, I take the water bowl to the kitchen sink and fill it up. Once it's placed next to the food, I go in search of my own beverage. The fridge has tons of water, some fruit juice, Gatorade, and a few bottles of beer. I know Caleb will rarely indulge once training starts, but he's known to have one here or there, and usually with his teammates.

I let Hermione check out the house while I go upstairs to unload my bag. I'm not even sure what I have, really. I just started throwing clothes into my small duffle bag and my carry-on suitcase. When I left, I didn't care what I brought. I wanted my stuff as far away from Springfield as possible.

Away from Skylar.

But let's not cloud a normally bright, sunny day with thoughts of that douche canoe.

Once my clothes are placed inside the dresser or hanging in the closet, I make my way down to the kitchen. With Hermione walking circles around my ankles, I open the refrigerator to see what I can throw together for dinner. Caleb would insist on ordering in, but I actually like to cook, and seeing that I live alone, it feels good to come here and put together a big meal. Plus, my brother eats for three, so there's never any leftovers.

I pair my phone to his Bluetooth system in the kitchen and crank up my favorite old-school boy bands. Backstreet Boys, NSYNC, 98 Degrees, NKOTB, I got them all loaded up in my Boy Bander playlist. I find chicken breasts and spinach and decide to make a stuffed chicken with creamy spinach sauce. While the oven is preheating, I take care of butterflying the meat and filling each one with a slice of mozzarella cheese, then browning them in a skillet for a few minutes. I whip up a basic creamy white sauce, add the chopped spinach, and even some parmesan.

Knowing my brother likes carbs, I cook up a few cups of instant white rice and wait for the chicken to finish. Once it's done, I add the meat to the white sauce and let it simmer and place a few slices of garlic bread into the oven. The clock tells me he should be home any minute, so I help myself to one of the beers he has in the fridge and wait.

Finally, I see the keypad on the wall flash, alerting me that someone is entering the house. I smile instantly, happy to see my brother for the first time in almost two months. With my busy work schedule, I just haven't been able to get away like I used to.

I'm belting out some Backstreet Boys, singing about playing games with my heart, and shaking what my mama gave me as I stir the sauce. Just as I turn to set the table, I notice a shadow in the doorway. I glance over and scream, nearly dropping the plates I just snagged from the counter. The man moves fast, like a jungle cat, quick and eerily silent. I try to jump back, but he's on me, grabbing my arm to keep me from going down at the same time his other hand reaches for the plates, so they don't shatter on the floor.

"Easy there, Sunshine."

I pull back, shocked. It's been years since I heard that endearment and only one man who used it.

Brock Williams.

I remember the night perfectly. I was visiting my brother with my dad and his then-girlfriend, Cleo. It was a Friday night and Caleb had a big, televised game the next day. We were staying at a huge luxurious hotel, like we always did when Dad was there, and I was getting into the elevator to go down to the pool. There was already a guy there, but he paid me no attention as the door started to close.

We started the ride down in silence before he said, "You're Josephine, right?"

I glanced over, finally taking in his impossibly tall and toned features. As a senior in high school, I had seen my share of good-looking guys, but this one was nothing like the high school boys I was used to. He was all man.

"Yes," I squeaked out over my too-dry throat. "But my friends call me Joey."

He smiled, and it was breathtaking. "I'm Brock, Caleb's friend."

My brother's original roommate turned best friend in college. I'd heard his name many times over the last four years. They played together, lived together, and did everything that didn't involve football together. Both seniors at State, everyone knew they were headed for the draft, and rightfully so. My brother was an amazing kicker, while Brock excelled at the tight end position.

And if that part was as fit as the rest of him, I was sure tight end was extremely fitting.

We'd run into each other a handful of times over the years, but really, football was never my thing. I went to games when I was required to but didn't really pay attention, cheering when the crowd around me did so. At the end of the game, when I hugged my brother and congratulated him on a great game, he'd just smile. He knew. I had no clue what the score was or even if they won or lost.

"Nice to see you again," I finally replied as the numbers dropped on the elevator.

I felt his eyes on me and did my best not to fidget nervously. I'd always noticed Brock the few times I was around him. I mean, who wouldn't. But being in the elevator with him, I was very much aware of his presence. Not only was he incredibly large and toned, but he smelled amazing. Like he just got out of the shower. Clean, with maybe a hint of sandalwood.

I never forgot that scent.

When the elevator dinged and the doors started to open, he said, "Have a nice swim, Sunshine."

I stopped in my tracks and glanced over my shoulder with a curious gaze. He just looked down, the faintest hint of a grin on his lips, as he stared at my butt. He walked around me, threw me a wink, and disappeared. When my eyes dropped, I realized I was wearing my bright yellow bikini with smiling suns all over it under a see-through pink swim cover. It was my first "adult" bathing suit, one that concealed all the necessary parts, yet left little to the imagination. My mom picked it out, not surprisingly, and it was nothing like the one-piece or tankini-style I had worn up until that point in my high school life.

And Brock Williams had noticed me.

I died right there, at the age of eighteen years old, in an elevator car.

Now, I'm standing in my brother's kitchen and catch the same familiar scent. Clean, with a hint of sandalwood. "You all right? I didn't mean to startle you," he says, setting the plates down on the table, yet still holding me in his arms.

"I'm... fine." I try clearing my throat, but the thickness is still there.

At twenty-nine, Brock is just as fit and muscular as he was at twenty-two, and I'm not just talking about his arms and chest. There are *other* things that are not quite hard, yet no mistaking it through a pair of nylon basketball shorts as it's pressed into my side.

After a few very long seconds, he finally helps right me, leaving me standing on my own two feet. I'm actually surprised they're still holding me up. My legs feel like Jell-O. "What are you doing here? Where's Caleb?" I ask, trying to glance around his impossibly tall shoulders and not finding my brother.

"He'll be here shortly. The special teams coach wanted a word with him after practice," Brock replies, still standing somewhat close.

I carefully walk the rest of the way to the table, making sure my legs do what they're supposed to do, and set the table, only to realize I may be a plate short. "Are you staying for dinner?" I ask, glancing back at him over my shoulder.

He flashes me a quick grin. "I wouldn't say no to that. What'd ya make? It smells amazing."

"Stuffed chicken with creamy spinach sauce," I answer, retrieving another plate and turning off the music.

"Damn, I'm gonna have to work extra hard in the gym living here, aren't I?" he replies with a chuckle.

I stop, silverware in hand, and stare at him. "You're staying here?"

He meets my gaze and nods. "Yeah, I got traded right before training camp. I'm crashing here with Caleb for a bit."

"Oh." My mind races. I was planning to talk to my brother tonight about staying with him for a while. Of course, he's going to want to know why I up and quit my job with no notice at all and practically ran from Springfield, but maybe now isn't the best time. He has a houseguest. Sure, he has plenty of room, but I don't want to impose.

"Where'd ya go there?"

His question pulls me from my own head.

"Sorry," I reply, covering my worries with a laugh. "Just thinking."

Just then, the alarm beeps and the front door opens. "Something smells amazing!"

I instantly grin and throw myself into my brother's outstretched arms the moment he walks into the kitchen.

"There she is," he whispers, enveloping me in a tight hug. "It's been too long."

"It has," I reply as he sets my feet back down on the floor. "I made dinner."

"You didn't have to. I could have ordered something, you know that," Caleb says, grabbing three bottles of water from the refrigerator before taking a seat.

"I know, but I wanted to cook. I like it," I state with a shrug.

We sit down, Brock taking the seat directly across from me, and I swear I can feel his eyes on me the entire time. The guys both take hearty helpings of both rice and the chicken and dive right in. They make appreciative little noises while devouring their food, grabbing seconds before I'm even halfway through my chicken breast.

"So, how long are you here for?" Caleb asks, while piling the food on his plate.

"Ummm... I don't know. Two days, maybe three?" I mutter, avoiding his watchful eye.

He doesn't say anything, but I can tell he's staring at me. Caleb and I have been close our entire lives, and if anyone can read me, it's him. "You're welcome to stay as long as you need to. Brock's here, but we'll be busy with practice, so you'll have the place to yourself most of the day."

I swallow my food and reply, "Thanks."

When I glance up, both of them are watching me. My brother clears his throat and says, "You'll tell me later what's going on."

And I will. I tell him everything. I'd just rather not share my humiliation in front of his hot friend.

I nod and am grateful when they change the subject. The guys start talking about practice, about who's stepping up in a big way and who's not carrying their weight. They discuss their first regular season game against the Miami Sharks, and how their defense is going to have to work hard to close the gaps created by Miami's strong O-line.

Once dinner's complete, Brock jumps up and starts collecting the dirty dishes. "I'll take care of these, since you cooked," he offers.

"Oh, you don't have to do that. I don't mind, really. You probably have something to do."

He just grins, perfectly straight, white teeth on full display. Damn, this man is really handsome. "Not really. We're just planning to relax tonight. We've got a team workout first thing in the morning before double practices."

I nod, jumping in and helping. I rinse, while Brock places the dirty dishes in the dishwasher. At least twice, our fingers touch as I hand over the item. Eighteen-year-old me would get all flustered and excited, while twenty-five-year-old me is just rolling her eyes.

No way will I ever act on any attraction with an athlete, especially not a football player. Did you know the divorce rate for a professional athlete is sixty-to-eighty percent? I googled that when I was ten and overheard things like alimony and infidelity thrown around like candy when my dad's second marriage failed. I watched women come in and out of his life in a revolving-door manner for years, and that was just his side of the genetics coin. My mom was worse, always looking for her next payout.

Yeah, there's no way I'd ever let myself get caught up in the hype.

Public relationships rarely work out.

Especially with football players.

CHAPTER
THREE

BROCK

I can sense that she wants to talk to Caleb, and she doesn't want me to witness it. I get it. He's her brother, and she trusts him. There is something in her eyes... a sadness, maybe? I can't really describe it, but I know she's not my Sunshine. Well, she's not mine, but you know that. I mean, she's not her usual happy-go-lucky self. Even when younger and blushing in the elevator, there was still this light about her.

Standing here, helping her wash dishes, is torture. Torture because Josephine Henderson is a fucking knockout. Her long dark hair, eyes that remind me of chocolate, and a body made to bring a man like me to his knees. If I had to guess, she's about a foot shorter than my six-foot-four, and maybe a buck twenty? She's tiny compared to me, and I have this urge to scoop her up in my arms just because I can. She'd give me hell for it, I'm sure. She's not the only one who would give me hell. I'm sure if Caleb knew the thoughts racing through my mind about his little sister, he'd kick my ass. Not that I blame him.

"Thank you again for your help. You really didn't have to."

"Thank you for dinner. It was delicious. Dishes is the least I can do for a home-cooked meal." I'm not just being nice. The food was incredible. A vision of coming home to her and her cooking every night flashes through my mind. I shake out of my thoughts. I don't know what the hell that's about, but I'm not going there. Not with her.

"Yeah, unlike my brother," she says just as Caleb enters the kitchen. He's wearing nothing but a pair of shorts, and his hair is still wet from his shower.

"Hey, I was being productive." He points at his sister. "You and I need to chat, and I thought you'd appreciate me not smelling like a locker room."

"Ew, Caleb. Did you not shower after practice?" Joey wrinkles her nose, and it's cute as hell.

"Always do, but it's never the same as showering at home."

I nod. "He's got a point. In fact, I think I'll do that myself. Joey, thanks again for dinner." I wait for her to look at me, just to get one more glimpse at those big brown eyes before I retreat to my room, giving the siblings some time. "I'll see your ugly mug bright and early," I tell Caleb as I walk past him for the stairs.

After a quick shower, I'm sliding under the covers and staring up at the shadows on the ceiling. Life has been a tornado of events the past several weeks, and I can't help but feel as though there are more changes to come. Something in my gut tells me that me being traded wasn't the only way my world is going to be shaken. I can't explain why I feel this way, only that I do.

After twenty minutes of staring at nothing, I grab my phone from the nightstand and scroll through the local real estate listings. I'm not in a huge rush to find a place, but at the same time, I wonder if I will ever feel settled if I don't. I know buying a home during the season isn't the ideal situation, but if I find my dream home here in Kansas City, then I can't pass it up.

Nothing stands out at me after an hour of searching, and I know if I don't get my ass to sleep, I'm going to be dragging at practice in the morning. Placing my phone back on the charger, I close my eyes and eventually drift off to sleep.

———

I'm up and dressed for practice before Caleb, so I decide to make us some breakfast. Pulling the ingredients for ham and cheese omelets out of the fridge, I get to work. Luckily, we have two hours of watching film before we ever touch the field, so our breakfast will have plenty of time to settle. There is nothing worse than sitting through film starving to death. Okay, maybe not starving, but you get the picture.

"I knew it was a good idea for you to live here," Caleb says, walking into the kitchen.

"Well, someone needs to feed your lazy ass." I chuckle. I slide our omelets onto our plates and start another.

"Man, you're going to regret that second one once we hit the field," Caleb says before shoving a huge bite into his mouth.

"This one is for Joey. That's the least I could do after she made dinner last night."

He points his fork at me. "Good plan. Maybe she'll stay a little longer and make us home-cooked meals every night."

"She good?" I ask. I know there is something going on with her. My gut tells me she's not here just for a visit. Her eyes tell me the same thing. She just seems off to me. Not at all the girl I remember.

"Yeah." He nods. "She didn't really say much. Just that she might stay a little longer than planned."

"Can she do that? I mean with her job?"

"She said she can. I can't turn her away. She's my sister."

"I'd never ask you to do that. I can go if you think it makes her uncomfortable."

"No. It's all good. I just... are you good with her being here?"

"Caleb, this is your house. She's your family. I have no right to say who can and cannot stay in your home."

He nods. "I know. I'm just all out of sorts right now. There's something going on, but she hasn't told me. She said she was exhausted from the drive last night and wanted to go to bed. She promised to talk to me tonight."

"You have any idea what it might be?"

"No idea, man. I just hope it's not our parents. Her mom is a fucking joke, and well, you know my dad."

I grimace. From the stories I've been told and from the things I've witnessed on my own, he's right. Nothing good comes from Joey's mom and their dad. "Let's hope that's not the case."

"Thanks for this." He stands and places his empty plate in the dishwasher.

"You have paper so I can write her a note?" I ask, pointing to the omelet that's still sitting in the cast iron pan.

"Just text her."

"I don't have her number."

"Easy fix." He pulls his phone out of his pocket, and a few moments later, I get a message. "Now you do." He moves to walk out of the kitchen. "I'll drive today. We leave in ten," he calls over his shoulder.

Scarfing down the rest of my breakfast, I place my plate in the dishwasher and then begin to pull open drawers looking for paper. Don't get me wrong, I'm all about modern technology, but for some reason, I want to write her a note. It's more personal, and I don't know. I just feel like she needs that. Whatever it is that's going on with her, I feel like she needs the personal connection.

Finding a small notebook and a pen in the drawer next to the fridge, I scribble her a note.

Joey,

Thanks for dinner. Breakfast is on me.
Check the oven.

Brock

I place the note on the center of the counter before placing foil over the cast iron pan and sticking it in the oven. The oven isn't heated up, but it will help contain the heat of the pan. Hopefully, it's still good by the time she wakes up.

"I looked at some houses last night online," I tell Caleb once we're in his truck and on our way to the stadium.

"Yeah? Find anything?"

"Not really."

"You don't have to rush into finding a place. I thought you were just going to stay with me until the season was over?"

"That's still the plan. I just feel... unsettled."

"That's to be expected moving cities and starting a new team in a matter of forty-eight hours. You've been thrust into this huge life-altering change. You need to give yourself some time to adjust."

"Maybe." I know he's right. However, what I don't tell him is that I feel different. It's as if this move and the trade changed me somehow. I'd never admit it out loud because it sounds crazy enough in my head.

"I can hook you up with the realtor I used to buy my place. Maybe you can give her a call, tell her what you're looking for, and she can keep an eye out," Caleb suggests.

"If I knew what I was looking for, that would be a great plan," I tell him.

He laughs. "You'll get there, man. For now, my home is yours. Take all the time you need."

"I appreciate that." Caleb is the brother I never had. Growing up, I would beg my parents for a brother. I was even desperate enough to tell them a sister would be fine too. It never happened. As I got older, I learned that my parents tried to give me siblings, but it wasn't in the cards for them. They would have had a house full if they were able. I might not be settling down anytime soon, but if and when I get there, I definitely want at least two kids. The only child in me says I want more than that, but that's something I'll have to discuss with my hypothetical future wife. If and when I ever find her.

———

Two hours of film, two hours of practice, an hour lunch, followed by two hours in the weight room, and I'm dead on my feet. I want to go home, shower again, and fall into bed. Caleb must feel the same because we're both quiet on the way home. When we pull into his driveway and I see Joey's car, I perk up a little. Just the thought of seeing her has the exhaustion lifting, and is that hope welling in my chest?

Grabbing our gym bags, we head inside. The house is quiet, as if no one is home.

"Joey!" Caleb calls out.

"In here!" she calls back.

I follow him as he makes his way to the huge living room. There is where we find her. She's sitting on the couch, under a blanket I'm sure to ward off the chill of the air conditioning. She's in some kind of shirt that's hanging off her shoulder, exposing her bright red bra strap, and her hair is in a messy knot on top of her head. She has on a pair of glasses that do nothing to hide her gorgeous chocolate eyes. In fact, they're sexy as fuck on her. I can't stop staring at her, and I know this image of her is one I will never forget. She's relaxed, casual, and without a doubt the most stunning woman I've ever laid eyes on.

"Hey, I didn't expect the two of you home so soon." She places her reading device down on the couch and stands.

I clench my fists at my sides when I see the tiny skin-tight shorts she's wearing. Are they even shorts? Her shirt is cut off and shows off her toned belly, and my cock twitches in my pants. I swallow hard. I have to get out of this room.

"I'm going to shower and take a nap." I don't wait for either of them to try and talk me out of it. With long strides, I make my way upstairs into my room, shutting and locking the door for good measure. It's not like she's going to come into my room and try to seduce me. My cock swells, liking that theory.

Dropping my bag, I strip out of my clothes and head to the bathroom to take a cold shower. Closing my eyes, I let the ice-cold spray do its job, but then thoughts of her creamy skin on her exposed neck and shoulder pop into my mind, and I could be sitting in the waters of Antarctica, and it wouldn't help.

Turning off the water, I towel off, slipping into some boxer briefs, a pair of gym shorts, and a T-shirt. I unlock the door because the idea that she would come to me is crazy. I don't know why all of a sudden, she's got me twisted in my feelings.

Lying down on my bed, I try to take a nap, but all I do is toss and turn. An hour later, I'm still wide awake, and I know it's time to stop hiding. Quietly, I open my bedroom door, and the house is silent. I take a deep breath, slowly exhaling as I make my way past her bedroom door. It's open, but I refuse to look. Holding strong with willpower I never knew that I possessed, I've almost made it when I hear her call my name.

"Brock?"

I freeze. I debate on ignoring her, but let's be honest. There is no ignoring Josephine Henderson. Instead, I take two steps backward and turn to look into her room. She's sitting on the bed, in that same tempting outfit, same glasses, and same messy hair, and her reading device in her hand.

"Hey, I wanted to thank you for breakfast." She reaches over into her nightstand drawer and pulls out the note that I left for her. My heart thunders in my chest. She kept it? "This too. It was sweet of you."

"You're welcome," I reply, my voice gravelly.

"I wanted to text you, but I don't have your number."

"You want my number?" I ask her.

"Is that weird? I mean, I know you're Caleb's best friend, but we're roommates, at least for while I'm here. Makes sense, right?"

"Caleb gave me yours this morning," I confess, just to see her reaction.

The hint of a smile tilts her lips. "Yeah? Well, then I think it's only fair that I get yours as well."

Reaching into my pocket for my phone, I swipe the screen and type out a message.

Me: Hey, it's Brock.

I hit Send, and her phone pings with an alert. She grins as her fingers fly across her screen.

·   ·   ·

Joey: Thank you for breakfast. It was delicious.

I laugh out loud when I read the message. "You already told me that."

"I know, but if I had your number, that's what I would have sent you." She shrugs.

I nod, trying to think of something else to say just so that I can keep talking to her. "What are you reading?" As soon as the words are out of my mouth, a blush coats her cheeks.

"Romance."

"Yeah? Is it any good?"

She nods, her blush growing redder by the minute. "You're blushing." She covers her face with her hands, and now I'm even more intrigued. So much so that I take one, two, three steps into her room. "What are you reading, Joey?"

"There is nothing wrong with my choice of reading," she defends.

"I didn't say there was. I just asked you what you were reading." She doesn't answer, so I step farther into the room, and I'm able to grab her reading device before she can stop me. My eyes skim the pages, and I read aloud. "I beg for his hard cock, as he thrusts inside me for the first time." Letting my hands fall to my sides, I lock my eyes on hers. "Joey?" My voice is gruff.

"It's romance. It's a love story, and sex is a part of life. There is nothing wrong with sex," she repeats, as she fumbles over her words.

My cock that was only semi-hard for her earlier is hard as steel, and I don't care that she knows it. Reaching down, I adjust myself, and her eyes grow wide when she sees why.

"My book turns you on?"

"No."

"Brock, that's—" She points at my dick. "I know what turned on looks like."

"It's not your book."

"Then what is it?"

"It's you." The words are out of my mouth before I can stop them. "You talking about romance and love, and—" I swallow hard. "Sex."

"Me?" The surprise in her voice is evident.

"You, Joey. This is all for you." I don't know what the fuck I'm doing. She's Caleb's little sister, and that alone makes her off-limits, but I can't seem to stop myself where she's concerned.

"What are you guys doing?" Caleb asks from behind me.

I can't turn to face him, or he's going to see exactly what I was thinking about doing to his little sister. "Talking books." I hold up what I know now is a Kindle.

"Did he tell you he's a closet reader? The guys used to give him shit for it in college." Caleb chuckles.

"We hadn't gotten that far," Joey tells him.

"Oh, yeah. Read all the time on the way to and from games. I know he doesn't look the part, but this one, he's smart as hell. Anyway," Caleb changes the subject, "let's go grab something to eat. I'm starving."

"I can make something," Joey offers.

"Nah, tonight's on me."

"Can we order in? I'm not really dressed to go out." She looks down at her outfit, and I want to say no shit, but I bite my tongue.

"Yeah, we can do that. How's Chinese?"

"Good," Joey and I reply at the same time.

"I'm on it," Caleb says, backing out of the room. His heavy footfalls echo as he makes his way downstairs.

Stepping next to her bed, I hand her Kindle back to her and lean over so we're eye to eye. We're so close, it would take minimal effort for me to lean in and kiss her. "You're gorgeous, Joey, but when you blush like that…" I shake my head, trying to find the words to describe it. "You take my breath away." Knowing I need to get some distance between us, I stand, turn on my heel, and head back to my room. Sitting on the bed, I run through my stats once, twice, three times before my cock finally deflates. Something definitely feels different, and my gut tells me it's Josephine Henderson.

CHAPTER
FOUR

Joey

"What the hell is that?"

I stop in the doorway and look down, watching as my cat skirts the outside of the living room before making her way slowly to where Brock sits on the couch. "That's Hermione."

"What's a Hermione?"

I roll my eyes and take the opposite end of the couch, crossing my legs. "That's my cat. You knew I had a cat."

"I did not. Where the hell has she been?" Brock asks.

I shrug, watching as my adorable gray and white feline rubs against Brock's legs.

"My room. She hides under my bed until I fall asleep and then tries to suffocate me by lying on my face," Caleb grumbles from the recliner.

Brock doesn't miss a beat. "First time I've heard you bitch about a little pussy on your face."

The pun rolls off his tongue easily, and I can't stop the bark of giggles that erupts from my mouth. I try to cover it with a cough, but it's no use. The teenage boy in me found his inappropriate comment completely hilarious.

"Finally! Someone who finds me funny," Brock declares, waving his hand in my direction.

"That's because she just doesn't know you yet. Give it time. She'll be tired of your sick, twisted jokes too," my brother states, kicking up the recliner. "Food should be here in ten. Whatcha guys wanna watch?"

"*Harry Potter*. Obviously Brock hasn't seen it," I reply, glancing at him out of the corner of my eye.

"I thought those were for kids."

"Ugh! They are most definitely not just for kids. I gave the books to Caleb a few years ago for Christmas. I'll knock the dust off and let you read them. I'm sure they haven't even been opened," I say, glancing his way and finding his gaze intently focused on me.

"Thanks. I'll read them." Something in the way he states that lets me know he will.

The alarm sounds, letting us know someone's here. Caleb jumps up, pulls money from his wallet, and heads to the front door. When he returns, he has three bags of cartons and a big smile on his face. "I may have gone overboard."

"Don't care. I'm starving," I say, reaching for the bags to help.

While I lay everything out on the coffee table, my brother retrieves plates and forks. "What do you want to drink?" he hollers from the kitchen.

Brock glances at me, question in his gorgeous blue eyes. They're not dark like sapphires but more light blue, like the ocean. "Oh, uh, just water."

"Two waters!" he yells to Caleb, who returns a few minutes later with what we need.

I grab a plate for an egg roll, crab Rangoon, and a spear of teriyaki chicken, and then one of the cartons of vegetable low mein.

When I get positioned on my corner of the couch, Brock asks, "You aren't even going to share? Just take the whole carton, huh?"

Caleb laughs as I move the food away from his roaming eyes. "Joey doesn't share food."

I can't help but laugh at his *Friends* quip, but mostly because it's true. "This is my absolute favorite dish. That's why Caleb orders two, so he can have some. If you'd like some of this delicious vegetable low mein, you're gonna have to share his," I state, pointing my chopstick toward my brother.

Brock gives me sad, wounded eyes. "I'm hurt you wouldn't share with me," he says, dumping the contents of several cartons on his plate. He's loaded up with more food than I could even think about consuming, but it's honestly no different than my brother's plate. It's piled high too.

"You'll learn to not get so offended when Joey refuses to share. She can't help she's cold-hearted," my brother teases with a huge grin.

"Says the big loser who can't eat his food with chopsticks," I mumble, shoveling my first bite of my precious low mein into my mouth.

Brock barks out a laugh. "Don't hold back, Joey."

"So Caleb's the only dummy who can't use chopsticks?" I ask, watching Brock eat rice and orange chicken without so much as dropping a single piece.

"If you're going to be mean, I'll take my food into another room." Caleb says.

"Then you don't get seconds," Brock replies, pointing a stick toward his friend.

"Fine, take her side. Just for that, I get to pick the movie."

That doesn't bother me. Caleb usually picks what we watch, mostly because I like about anything. He settles on *Lethal Weapon*, which is actually one I enjoy. Even though it has horribly cheesy dramatic music, like all eighties action movies, I still enjoy this series. I mean, Mel Gibson and Danny Glover are amazing together.

When most of the food is gone, Brock jumps up and clears away the leftovers, taking them to the fridge. I join him, searching for a pen. Just as I find one on the counter, Brock asks, "What're you doing?"

I write my name in capital letters across the top. "Making sure no one eats my food." He cracks up and shakes his head. "What? It'll make a great breakfast. Fry an egg and throw it in there, and voilà. Breakfast is served."

He pops a hip against the counter and smiles. "Maybe I'll join you."

I mimic his stance and cross my arms over my chest. There's no missing the way his eyes zero in on my bare shoulder. I'm barely able to hide the smirk that plays on my lips. "What time do you have to leave?"

"Nine."

Turning and heading toward the doorway leading back to the living room, I glance over my shoulder and say, "Be down at eight, tight end."

I'm not only referring to his football position.

I flop down on the couch and grab the throw blanket I was curled up with earlier. Brock returns a few minutes later and has a seat, using the coffee table as a footrest. We make it halfway through the movie before I need to stretch my legs. When I do, I accidentally kick into Brock's side.

I quickly pull back, an apology on the tip of my tongue, but am surprised when he grabs ahold of my foot. I don't really know what to expect, but Brock Williams digging his thumbs into the arch of my foot isn't it. The most amazing sensations course through my veins, and I almost moan in pure euphoria. He presses hard, hitting all my nerve endings and pressure points, while wrapping his large hands around my foot.

Holy hell, his hands are big.

Long fingers glide effortlessly across my ankles as he massages and manipulates the muscles I didn't even realize were in need of a little attention. In fact, if he went searching, I'd bet he'd find a lot of other muscles that could use his expert hands.

And maybe other parts of his body too.

I turn to look at the man who's still an enigma to me and find him watching the movie. He appears so focused and casual, leaning back on the couch, his feet still kicked up on the table. Only I know how looks are deceiving. His attention may be on the screen, but his hands are still very busy, kneading and rubbing my foot. Apparently, Brock doesn't have an aversion to feet.

When he finishes giving me the little orgasmic rubdown—still referring to my feet, by the way, though I wouldn't be against... you know—he sets my foot down and slips it back beneath my blanket. I'm about to pull it back when he grabs the other foot and does the exact same thing.

Pure. Bliss.

If this were a movie I'd never seen before, I would have had no idea what happened. My mind isn't focused on Riggs and Murtaugh as they track down a drug dealer at a Christmas tree farm. Oh, no. I'm held in complete rapture by the man opposite me on my brother's sofa.

Brock is still a complete unknown factor to me. Sure, he's gorgeous. I'd have to be dead not to see it. A quick Google search this morning confirmed he was traded to Kansas City from the Chicago Thunder, who were so desperate for a quarterback, they traded a two-time Pro Bowler at the top of his game to get it.

Of course, there were other things I found out while doing a little online searching. One was the fact he's never had a serious girlfriend. At least not anyone the tabloid media could find. Apparently, he liked to party and had the reputation of a playboy back in Chicago. I can't fault him for that. At least he's not married while running around like a dog in heat, like my dad was.

The other thing I discovered was he's a big donor to a children's charity. He contributes a hefty chunk of change every year and attends their big charity gala in Chicago. There were tons of pictures online, including some on the organization's website. Brock looked positively stunning in a tuxedo, always with some model-thin girl in a dress sized for a child draped over his arm.

After Brock massages my left foot, he sets it down on his thigh and rests his hand on my leg. Even though it's the most comfortable position in the world, I'm hyperaware of the fact he's touching me.

And I like it.

If Caleb notices, he doesn't say a word.

At some point, Hermione decided to curl up with the man at the end of the couch and lies in the small space between my feet and Brock's chest. He moves his hand, not the one resting on my leg, but the other one, and starts to pet her, making her purr in happiness.

Yeah, even my feline can appreciate the pure pleasure at being touched by Brock.

When the movie ends, I practically jump up, needing to put a little distance between myself and the man who apparently has the ability to make my brain stop working. It's still early, but I don't care. I need to get off this couch, or else I'm liable to say or do something I shouldn't.

Like invite him to my bedroom.

"Well, I'm going to turn in early. Thanks for dinner," I say to my brother, making a hasty exit.

"You're welcome," he says, watching me intently. "You know, we still need to have that talk," he adds quietly.

I reply with a small smile, "I know, and we will. Promise."

Caleb stares at me for a few long seconds before nodding. "Okay. Night."

"Night." I risk a quick glance to where Brock sits, and all thought goes out the window when my eyes meet his. His hands are behind his head and he's just watching me, the slightest smirk playing on his lips, as if he knows what he does to me. I throw him a wave and practically run to my room.

The only problem is now I'm restless. I can feel his hands on my legs, on my feet. It makes me itchy, but not in a bad way. In the very nice, very sexy way. In fact, all I can think about is his big hands, and that very impressive erection he didn't even try to hide earlier this afternoon.

I get comfy on the bed and try to read, but after a while, that proves to be fruitless. It's another sex scene, and all I can hear is Brock's voice as he read the excerpt earlier. My skin is flushed, my body humming with desire.

Shooting up out of bed, I pace my room, running through every excuse in the world why I should not sneak down the hall and knock on his door. This is so out of character for me. Usually I'm a third date kind of girl. Maybe a nice kiss at the end of the first date, but never any further. I don't picture myself climbing a man and riding him like a cowgirl at the rodeo, yet here I am, imagining just that.

My walls start to close in on me. Maybe a nice little walk would do me good. I slip on my shoes and quietly leave my room, telling myself not to look down the hall. Nothing good could come from glancing toward that particular bedroom.

Except maybe a few mind-blowing orgasms.

I pass my brother's bedroom and notice the door closed as I make my retreat downstairs. First stop is the kitchen to grab a cold drink. My blood feels like it's boiling as it races through my veins, no doubt due to the naughty pictures parading through my head. I find myself wandering to the back room, where Caleb has his game system set up on a large television. There, I find a single bookshelf along one wall with a few trinkets, framed photographs, and books. All things I gave him.

The first hardback I come across is the one I was looking for. *Harry Potter and the Sorcerer's Stone.* I'm surprise it's not dusty, but then again, my brother pays someone to clean for him on a weekly basis, so it shouldn't really come as a shock.

I take the book to the kitchen and go straight to the drawer where I know he keeps pens and notepads. I quickly jot down a message and slip it inside the cover. Before I leave the kitchen, I poke my head into the laundry room and make sure Hermione's food and water is full before I grab a bottle of juice and return upstairs.

My eyes immediately scout the doors. Caleb's is still closed, and I'm sure Hermione is in there, ready to pounce every time he moves his leg. The other guest bedroom door is open, even though I told myself I wasn't going to look, and while it stands ajar, the one directly across the hall is not. That's my brother's home gym.

Without even giving them direction, my legs carry me toward the closed door. I can hear rapid thumping and can picture Brock running on the treadmill. Honestly, that surprises me a little, considering how exhausted they were when they got home from practice.

Not wanting to disturb him, I turn to retreat to my own room when I realize I'm still holding the book. Instead of giving it to him tomorrow, I slip into the room with the open door, my senses completely overcome with his woodsy, masculine scent. It's so heady, it makes me pause where I stand and just inhale.

Like a creeper.

A quick look around tells me he's a fairly neat guy. The closet doors are shut, and the dresser appears organized and tidy. There's a pair of shorts folded on the chair and some slip-on shoes beneath it, and all I can think is this isn't the bachelor room I expected to see. I mean, there's a reason my brother has a housekeeper.

Needing to get the hell out of here before he finds me naked in his bed—according to the internet, that's happened more than once—I set the book on his pillow and I leave. Once I'm back in my own room, I shut the door and take a deep sigh in relief.

Of course, my room doesn't smell nearly as yummy as his did.

I force myself to get into my own bed, grab my e-reader, and try to relax. I skip through the sex scene knowing it won't do any good to read it in my current state and stay up until the book is finished. Only then do I finally feel tired enough to fall asleep.

Until I remember Brock's meeting me in the kitchen at eight to make breakfast.

Maybe I won't be getting much sleep after all.

CHAPTER
FIVE

BROCK

I slept like shit. This time it had nothing to do with being in a new place and everything to do with my new roommate. When I got back to my room last night, there was a book on my pillow with a note.

Brock,

For a rainy day

Joey

It was simple as far as notes go, but it smelled like her. Yes, I smelled the fucking piece of paper like a creeper. It took everything in me not to go to her and thank her. There are a million ideas racing through my mind as to how I can properly *thank her*. Instead, I lie in bed staring up at the shadows on the ceiling, thinking about her silky-smooth skin underneath my fingertips. Fuck me, but I couldn't help but touch her when she was that close. It was a risk with Caleb sitting in the same room with us, but it was one I was gladly willing to take.

She's intoxicating.

Hence the reason I can't stop thinking about her. Glancing at the clock, I see it's quarter past seven. I still have forty-five minutes before I'm supposed to meet Joey downstairs for breakfast. Tossing the covers off, I strip out of my boxer briefs and head to the shower. I don't wait for the water to heat, hoping that the ice-cold jolt will cure this hard-on that I have for her. It turns out luck isn't on my side today. In fact, the more I think about her, the harder I get. Knowing I can't stand close to her and make breakfast like this, I take matters into my own hands.

Bracing one hand on the shower wall, while the other slides between my legs to grip my cock, I tug roughly from root to tip. I close my eyes and she's all I can see. My hand moves faster and faster until I feel the tingles in my spine. Her name is a murmur on my lips as I blow all over the shower wall. Hanging my head, I let the water rain down on me. The water is finally warm, but I feel cold. Empty. I can't help but think that if Joey were here with me, we'd both be warm.

Shaking out of my thoughts, I quickly wash off and spray down the wall with the detachable showerhead before climbing out and wrapping a towel around my waist. I'm quick to dress, just some boxer briefs, a pair of gym shorts, and a Ramblers T-shirt. Grabbing my phone, I make my way downstairs.

"Morning, sleepyhead," Joey's chipper voice greets me.

"You're early," I say, stepping around the counter just to be closer to her. I stop next to the stove where she's frying bacon. With my back to the counter, I rest against the edge, crossing my ankles. I'm trying to appear to be unaffected, but I have no idea if it's working. I've never had to pretend that a woman didn't turn me inside out. Joey's the first and only to do so.

I grip the counter beside me, and I'm sure on the outside I look unaffected, but my nails are digging into the granite countertop, all from the extreme effort of trying not to touch her. I really want to touch her. My fingers ache, not from my grip but from the need to feel her soft skin.

"I couldn't sleep."

"Everything okay?" I release my grip on the counter and turn to face her. Her hair has fallen out of her bun, and a strand has caught in her eyelash. I don't even think before I reach out and tuck the errant strand behind her ear. Her hair feels like silk.

"Yeah, everything's good." She smiles, but it's not her usual sunshine smile.

"You know that you can talk to me, right? I won't spill to your brother." This time her smile is genuine, and it lights up my fucking world.

"Thank you for that. But I'm good. Promise." She turns her attention back to the stove. "So, I decided on bacon, eggs, and toast? How does that sound?"

"Good," I say, my voice gruff. "What can I do?"

"I think I have it under control. How about you grab yourself a cup of coffee and keep me company."

"You want a cup?" I offer.

She points to a cup on the counter that I somehow missed. Then again, it's not all that surprising when all I see is her. "I'm on my second cup."

"How long have you been up?"

"I'm not really sure. I didn't sleep all that great. I think I came downstairs to read at around six."

I nod even though she's not looking at me. "That's about the time I was watching the shadows dance across the ceiling."

"Did you get my gift?" she asks.

"I did. Thank you."

"Did you read any of it?"

"No, my mind was preoccupied."

"Want to talk about it?"

"You like talking about yourself?" I ask before I can think better of it.

She whips her head around to look at me. "What do you mean?"

Setting my cup on the counter, I move to stand behind her, placing my hands on her hips. "What I mean is exactly what I said. You asked me if I wanted to talk about it, and in case you don't realize it, the thing that kept me from sleeping was you. So, if you like to talk about yourself, I'm game." I step closer, aligning my front to her back. "I thought we were making breakfast together?" I ask.

Keeping one hand on her waist, the other travels from her shoulder down her arm until my hand is resting over hers, and we're flipping the bacon together. The feel of her body pressed against mine is exquisite torture that I would endure every single day if given the opportunity.

My eyes focus on her slender neck, and I know that I have to taste her there. Consequences be damned. I lean in closer, and she shivers at the feel of my hot breath against her skin. Just as I'm about to make contact, heavy footfalls on the steps have me moving back to my spot, leaning against the counter. This time my grip is painful as the urge to touch her roars through my veins.

"Something smells good," Caleb says, entering the kitchen.

I wait for the guilt to assault me, but it never comes. Caleb is my best friend and has been since our freshman year of college, but I can't find it in me to feel guilty. Not when it comes to Joey. I love Caleb like a brother, but this sudden pull that his sister has over me is something I can't ignore. It's something I don't want to ignore.

"Bacon, eggs, and toast," Joey tells him. The pitch to her voice is a little higher than normal, but Caleb doesn't seem to notice.

"You know that you don't have to keep cooking for us, right?" Caleb asks her.

Her eyes quickly flash to mine. "I don't mind. It keeps me busy."

"We still need to have that talk," he reminds her.

Worry takes root in my mind. Is she in trouble? Is she hiding out? Did someone hurt her? The thought of anyone laying their hands on her has me seeing red.

"Whoa. You okay, man?" Caleb asks.

"Fine."

"You don't look fine. You look like someone just kicked your puppy."

Joey turns to look at me. "You have a puppy?" she asks.

There's curiosity in her question and something else, something that looks a lot like mischief. "No. No puppy."

"Oh." Her face falls. I want to tell her that I'll skip practice, and we can go get a puppy today—anything she wants. However, before I can even open my mouth, she bursts out laughing.

"You two are gullible." She points at me, then Caleb. "I'm very well aware of the analogy and I didn't take you seriously."

"I thought you were a cat person," Caleb asks her.

"I am, but that's the only pet I was allowed to have at my place. I always wanted a dog growing up."

"I didn't know that," Caleb replies.

Joey shrugs. "Mom never would have let it happen."

"Dad—" Caleb starts, but Joey holds up her hand to stop him.

"Yes, Dad would have bought me a puppy, but Mom would never have let me keep it. One day when I have a house and not an apartment, I'll have a dog. Although I'm not sure Hermione will like that idea as much as I do." She chuckles under her breath.

"Move in with me," Caleb blurts. "You can have a dog. Hell, get three if you want."

"I can't move in with you," she counters. She says the words, but there's something in her voice. Longing maybe? "This is a bachelor pad."

"Yeah." Caleb snorts. "It's a swinging pad. Just look at all the ladies we have to kick out every morning." He gives his sister a pointed look.

"Well, one day, I want to be an aunt. So I hope that you do bring someone home, and I love you, brother, but I don't want to be here to listen to you making me an aunt." She gives him a wide beaming smile, knowing that she's won this conversation.

"Pain in my ass," Caleb says as he walks to her and pulls her into a hug, placing a kiss on top of her head. "But I love you, sis, you know that, right?"

"Yeah, yeah, I love you too, you big lug." She shrugs him off. "Now, don't mess with me unless you want to eat burnt bacon."

"I'm not picky," he tells her. "You're cooking. I'll eat it no matter what it tastes like." He gives her his camera-ready charming smile, and she just shakes her head. "I'm going to go grab a shower. Give me ten," Caleb says, disappearing up the steps.

He's barely gone before I resume my position behind her. This time I wrap my arms around her waist and bury my face in her neck. I don't dare taste her, not as I want. Ten minutes isn't long enough, and I know for certain we'll get caught. I can't do that to her. Caleb is the only family that actually cares about her. Her mom and dad only used her as a pawn. I won't do that to her. However, I will hold her. It's not the same as holding her in my arms while we sleep, but any amount of time I can have her in my arms is a win in my book.

"Thanks for making breakfast," I murmur, my lips next to her ear.

"Y-You're welcome."

I'm still holding her when she starts to pull the bacon from the pan and reach for the eggs. "I'll set the table," I tell her, releasing my hold. Her breath shudders, and she nods. She's just as affected by me as I am by her. Now the question is, what do we do about it?

———

"Thanks for breakfast, sis." Caleb stands and places his plate in the dishwasher. "We have a short practice today since tomorrow is game day. It should be an early one." He pauses and adds, "Oh, I forgot to tell you. I ordered you a new jersey. It should be here today."

"I already have a jersey," she reminds him.

"Yeah, well, now you have another one. Oh, and I got you one of Brock's too." He looks over at me, where I'm still sitting at the kitchen table. "Gotta get my boy's name out there too." He grins.

I grin back at him, but it's not because my best friend is supporting me. It's because he bought his little sister my jersey. The same woman, who in a matter of days, has managed to turn me inside out with need for her. Now, she's going to have my name on her back. Call me a caveman, but that does something to me. It's a feeling I've never felt before. It's new and thrilling and all because of Joey.

"It's your turn to drive," I say, standing. "I just need to run upstairs and grab my wallet." Taking my plate to the sink, I rinse it off and place it in the dishwasher. "Thank you for breakfast, Joey." Her bright eyes sparkle as she nods.

It's insane how badly I want to kiss her. Instead, I back away and race upstairs. In my room, I dig around in the nightstand until I find a scrap piece of paper and a pen. Looking at the paper, it appears to be some kind of instructions for furniture. Turning it over, I write out a quick note on the back.

Joey,

My jersey. I can't stop thinking about you in that and nothing else.
   The things running through my mind...
   Wear it to the game tomorrow?

Have a great day, beautiful.

Brock

It's not exactly romantic, but it's the truth. The moment Caleb mentioned he ordered her my jersey, that's all I can think about. Joey lying on my bed, her hair splayed out over the pillows, and she's wearing nothing except my jersey. Although in my fantasy, it's my actual jersey, not a replica. I want her in the one that I wear. I want her skin to smell like both of us. Reaching into my shorts, I adjust my cock. It looks like it's going to take me longer than a second. I can't go down there like this.

Sitting on the edge of the bed, I close my eyes and run stats. Finally, after a few moments, I'm able to stand. I adjust myself once again and step out into the hallway. I ease open her bedroom door to take the note to her pillow. Folding the paper in half, I place it where she's sure to see it before slowly leaving the room. I take my time making my way back downstairs just to ensure that there is no evidence of what she does to me.

"Caleb's in the car. He's waiting on you," Joey says when I hit the bottom step.

She's standing in the middle of the kitchen, wringing her hands together. Do I make her nervous? "Come here." I open my arms wide, and she hesitates for a split second before walking into my embrace. "I'll see you when I get home."

Tilting her head back, she peers up at me. "I'll be here."

I want to kiss her. It would take nothing, no effort on my part to just lean down a little and press my lips to hers. I desperately want to know if they are as soft as they look. I want to know what she tastes like.

"Have a good practice."

Not able to resist, I lean in and press my lips to the corner of her mouth. When my lips connect with her skin, she sucks in a breath. My lips barely grazed hers, but it was enough for both of us to know we need more. Want more. "I'll see you soon," I say, standing to my full height and releasing her. My cock throbs and I know that I fucked up. Thankfully, I have my gym bag that I can hold in front of me, and Caleb will be in the driver's seat of his car and not in the passenger seat of mine. He's always been one who preferred to drive over riding.

It takes extreme effort to walk away from her, but I manage to put one foot in front of the other and make my way to the garage. Sure enough, Caleb is sitting behind the wheel of his Audi, and I expel a sigh of relief as I climb in the passenger seat.

"I thought I was driving?" I ask.

"Can't help it. I love this car, man. I should have bought one years ago."

"You've had it what, six months now? The new hasn't worn off?"

"Hell no." He laughs. "This is the only woman I need in my life," he says, backing out of the driveway.

A few days ago, I would have agreed with him. Now, I don't think that I can. If he only knew his little sister was tilting my world upside down. I don't know how he would feel, but something tells me I'm going to find out sooner rather than later. Joey is like this magnet, and I can't escape her force. Hell, it's not that I can't. It's that I don't want to. I've never wanted a woman as much as I want her. I glance over at Caleb, aware that this thing with his sister could break us. I don't want to lose him, but I've never felt like this. I owe it to myself and to Joey to see what this is.

We can keep it between us for now. Explore what might be happening, and then bring Caleb in. I just hope he doesn't hate me after.

CHAPTER
SIX

Joey

New Ramblers Tight End Woos Model in Fiji

I stare at the headline posted fifteen minutes ago online, and instantly regret setting up that alert with Brock's name. It was a stupid, juvenile mistake, but I did it in a moment of pure weakness around five this morning when my brain was reeling from lack of sleep and naughty fantasies with the man himself starring in the lead role.

I scan the article, trying to clear the image of Brock and Gisele Sorenson making out on the sandy tropical beach. A friend close to the "couple" is quoted as saying they really hit it off at the wedding of his former teammate and have maintained a long-distance relationship and plan to "meet up again soon."

Well, fuck me running.

The article goes on to say how they met at the beachside nuptials and were inseparable the rest of the trip, spotted enjoying private candlelight dinners, and even sneaking out of each other's seaside suites early in the morning with clothes wrinkled and askew.

Okay. Time to stop reading.

My deceitful eyes go right up to the accompanying photo. There's only one, thankfully, but it's a close-ranged shot, as if the photographer was standing not too far away on the beach. Perhaps from one of those fancy lounge chairs underneath an umbrella. He probably has one of those fruity drinks too with fruit slices and names that contain Caribbean or paradise.

I think back over the last few days, at the looks and the flirting, at the things he said and the way he responded. And by that, I mean getting hard.

All this time, he's been seeing someone?

Sure, Gisele and Brock could have a relationship, even though I haven't seen any signs that lead me to think he has someone he's casually seeing. You know the kind. Hooking up whenever you're in the same city, maybe a few late-night video sessions that end in orgasmic bliss. I've heard all the rumors about him, seen all the headlines. Brock Williams isn't a "relationship" kind of man. He's a "right here, right now, leave you smiling" kind.

This is exactly why I should keep my distance. No casual relationships for me. Even if the man in question is a six-foot-four, two-hundred-and-fifty-pound solid piece of sex on a stick. Like a walking wet dream, only better. He looks positively edible in the photo, all tanned and toned in his black and green swim trunks.

Plus, if I hold my finger up just right, I can completely block Gisele out of the image.

I'm so lost in picking apart the photo I don't even glance down at the screen when my phone starts ringing. "Hello?"

"Josephine."

I close my eyes, chastising myself for the stupid error. Why didn't I check the caller ID? Is it too late to pretend it was my voice mail picking up? Or maybe I'm headed through a tunnel and my call drops?

"I hear you breathing, sweetheart," he says, as if he can hear my thoughts.

I sigh, realizing I'm stuck now. "Hi, Dad. How are you?"

"I'd be a lot better if I didn't have to learn from my son that my daughter is in town for a visit."

Caleb. That backstabbing weasel. "I haven't been here long, I swear."

"Well, I'm happy for that. I'd hate to think my only daughter was avoiding me," he replies with a boisterous laugh, making me cringe.

Good thing he can't see my reaction or he'd know I was doing just that. "How are things going?"

"Excellent. Listen, I'm heading into a meeting with the GM. Meet me at Sully's tonight at seven. I've already made the reservation."

And by that, he means he had his assistant do it.

"I'm not sure what our plans are," I mutter, knowing it's pointless. My dad doesn't hear the word no too often, especially from one of his kids.

"I expect you to be there at seven, Josephine Grace. Tell your brother to come. And the new tight end. My understanding is he's there too. I'll have Marcy change the reservation to five. I'm sure Candi will be able to adjust her schedule."

Great. That means my new stepmom, or as I like to refer to her as wife number four, is going too. I've only met her twice in the eight months she's been married to my dad, but Candi—with an I, as she repeatedly said throughout our first meeting—is exactly half his age. Yep. Wife number four just so happens to be right smack dab in the middle of Caleb and me on the family age chart. Two years older than me, and two years younger than my brother.

Isn't that something special to announce at Christmas dinner?

That's exactly when I found out last December. Right before she shared the names of popular Instagram influencers over our glazed ham, sure to help me learn how to contour my unruly eyebrows.

Yay me.

"Can't wait," I reply, trying to sound upbeat and chipper about tonight's impending doom we'll call family dinner.

"Excellent. See you there. Oh, and wear something nice. You know how the dress code is at Sully's." He doesn't say goodbye, just hangs up the phone. Heaven forbid he take point two seconds to properly sign off.

With another dramatic sigh, I set my phone down on the bed beside me and flop back. Wear something nice? I didn't exactly pack for a fancy dinner out at Sully's when I threw random shit into my luggage and took off for my brother's house.

Hermione makes her presence known, jumping up on the bed and rubbing against my arm. She plops down in the same theatrical fashion I did moments ago and purrs, begging me to pet her.

"I have to go buy a dress, Hermione. I hate shopping," I mutter to my cat as I rub my hand over her soft hair.

She meows, and I'm pretty sure, if she could actually speak, she just told me to get over it and go. My cat has a way with words like that.

"Fine, I'm going," I mumble, making no move to get up.

But first, I'll just pet my kitty for a few more minutes.

———

An hour later, I've dragged my feet long enough, trying to avoid the inevitable. If I don't go now, I'll be late getting back to the house. Late getting ready. Late to dinner. Usually, that wouldn't bother me much, but the last thing I want is for my dad to chastise and humiliate me in front of wife number four, who will probably share great Instagram influencers who can help me work on my tardiness problem, and my brother.

And Brock.

Keys in hand, I head for the front door. Just as I'm about to reach for the handle, the door flies open and in walk the guys. Suddenly, I wish I had been a little quicker in my departure.

"Hey, where you off to?" Caleb asks.

"What? Nowhere," I argue.

He glances down, clearly spotting the keys in my hand, and arches an eyebrow in question. "Nowhere? Just taking your keys for a walk?" he jokes, tossing his own keys onto the couch.

I place my hands on my hips and give him my best glare. "Well, if you must know, because of you, I'm having dinner with our father and wife number four."

My brother has the audacity to look a little embarrassed. "Yeah, sorry about that. He caught me off guard, and I guess I hadn't realized he didn't know you were here."

I sigh, avoiding the intensity of Brock's gaze. I can feel it, like the warmth of a spotlight hitting you in the side of the head. "It's fine, whatever. The good news is you and Mr. Tight End are going too!" I bellow, throwing my arms in the air in victory.

The look on Caleb's face is priceless. "What? Shit," he mumbles. "I see him every day on the field." My brother gets to deal with Dear Old Dad every day, since he's one of the coaches.

"Family dinner for the win, big brother," I sass, holding out my hand for him to give me a high-five.

"You're mean," he grumbles, hitting my hand with a hard, sharp tap.

"Ouch." I try to shake the sting away, but it doesn't work.

"Serves you right for being a smartass. So where are you going? Running way to Cuba to avoid going?"

"A reasonable consideration, but no." I drop my gaze and whisper, "I have to go buy a dress for Sully's."

Caleb gives an Academy Award winning performance, shock written all over his face. "A dress? How will you survive?"

"I don't know, but I'm pretty sure you're buying," I state, holding out my hand.

Brock barks out a laugh, watching our exchange, as Caleb pulls his wallet out of his shorts and hands me his credit card.

"Ohh, the black one. That means shoes and a pedicure too." My poor toes haven't seen paint or any sort of attention in so long, I'm not sure I can even remember when.

"Whatever," he replies with a shrug. "Get what you need."

"Starbucks. Coffee *and* one of those slices of their delicious lemon cake."

He sighs. "What. Ever. Just make sure you're back in time to go. I won't wait on you."

He will. He just likes giving me a hard time.

"I won't make the golden child late for family dinner. I promise."

I extend up on my tiptoes and kiss my brother's scruffy cheek in appreciation. Just as I turn to head for the door, I hear, "I'll go with her."

Well, that makes me pause, because the owner of that voice was *not* my brother. "Oh, that's not necessary," I counter, turning around quickly to continue my protest. However, I didn't realize Brock had moved, so when I turn, I practically face-plant into his chest. His very hard, very muscular, very nice chest.

Oh, the deliciousness of his soap and deodorant hits me square in the face, leaving me a little breathless.

"Well, if I'm the tight end you were referring to, that means I'm going too, and I could use a new dress shirt." He says it so casually, so reasonably.

What the hell? No!

But Brock doesn't hear my mental temper tantrum and opens the door, slipping out as quietly as a mouse.

I glare at my brother. "You're buying me two pairs of shoes now, since I have to entertain your friend."

Caleb grins and shrugs. "Whatever. I'm going to nap while you're gone," he says, turning and heading for his recliner.

"I hope you have nightmares about porcupines!" I yell, running out the door and letting it slam behind me.

As soon as I hit the steps, I start giggling, thinking about the shock and fear on his face. Porcupines are his biggest fear, mostly because he swore one gave him "the look" and chased him when he was ten and his mom took us to the zoo.

It didn't, of course, but I've never let him forget it. He slept with the lights on for weeks after that trip.

"What's so funny?"

Brock's question startles me. I guess I expected him to not be standing so damn close.

"Nothing. Long story," I reply, heading for my car.

When he doesn't follow, I stop and turn around.

"You think we're going in that?" he says.

I turn and look at my car. It's totally sensible, gets great gas mileage, and has a sunroof. "What's wrong with my car?"

"It has four doors."

I roll my eyes, making sure he can see the whites all the way around. "That's a total guy statement."

"Well, I'm a guy, so…"

Brock heads for the garage and gets in his sports car. As he backs it out, I get my first real glimpse at something that probably costs more than my entire year's salary, times two. It's sleek, black, and screams sex.

Part of me wants to throw a fit about my car being passed over for a fancy sports car, but to be honest, I really want to go for a ride. My dad has always had his share of cars that cost a small fortune, but I never really had the itch. My first one at sixteen was a small Mercedes crossover SUV, even after Caleb tried to convince me to get the Audi R8.

The truth was, I never wanted to be one of those spoiled rich girls whose daddy bought them everything under the sun. Yes, I accepted that first car at sixteen, but I also sold it in college and bought a used Toyota Camry. Why? To prove a point.

I could do this on my own.

I didn't need my dad's money or influence.

I was able to secure a job and make sure my bills were paid. Of course, my apartment was paid for by my father. He did the same for my brother after he graduated from college and felt it was the right thing to do for me, even though I tried to refuse. I would have much rather found my own apartment and made monthly rent payments, but he wasn't taking no for an answer. Every "gift" I get from him goes into the bank, and believe me, there have been gifts over the years. Especially around divorce time, when our family name winds up in every gossip rag in the country. That's usually when the past is revived, and everyone focuses on years' worth of headlines featuring my dad's wandering penis.

Slipping inside the car, I barely have time to fasten my seat belt before I'm thrust back into the seat as we jet down the driveway, as if on a runway. He pulls onto the street and easily maneuvers through the subdivision, before hitting one of the main arteries through this part of Kansas City.

"Any idea where you want to go? I'm not sure where the shopping hotspots are located," he says, strumming his thumb against his steering wheel to the beat of the music on the radio.

"There's a small shopping center a few miles up this road. It has a Kohl's there."

He glances my way and grins. "A Kohl's? You think you're going to find something for Sully's at Kohl's?"

I shrug. "Probably not, but that's where I get most of my clothes from, so I'm sure I can find something suitable."

The moment we hit a stoplight, Brock types something into the screen on his dash. It immediately gives him directions, sending us past the shopping center I was referring to and depositing us at some little boutique instead.

"This isn't Kohl's," I state ignorantly as he shuts off the engine.

"I'm aware. Let's go." He jumps out, a little too agilely for a man of his size, and jogs around to get my door. I'm so caught off guard that I just sit here and stare. "You coming?"

Not yet.

My face instantly blushes at the thought racing through my mind that I avert my gaze and try to slip out as gracefully as he did. I, of course—because the universe hates me—get my leg caught on the bottom of the doorframe and practically stumble out of the fancy car. I fully expect Brock to tease me, but he doesn't. Instead, he takes my hand, closes my door, and leads me toward the entrance.

"Come on, Sunshine. We have some shopping to do."

I sigh and drop my shoulders, as if he's dragging me to the electric chair. "Fine, but you better not forget my lemon cake."

Brock snorts. "No worries, love. I got you." He throws me a wink and a sexy little grin and opens the door.

"May I help you?" a perky little blonde with a tight white shirt says the moment we hit the air conditioning.

"We need a dress. For dinner."

"Of course." The woman with the name Sasha on her name tag beams. "And what can I help you with?" she adds, a flirty glimmer in her pretty blue eyes.

"I'll just grab what I need while you help Joey," Brock replies, practically pushing me forward.

"Joey?" Sasha asks, confusion written all over her face.

"Hi. I'm Joey," I mutter, waving my hand in front of her. To be honest, this kind of thing happens all the time when I'm with Caleb. One look at his boyish good looks and the ladies get all loopy. Clearly, Brock has the same potent powers over the female population.

"Of course! Right this way," Sasha replies, throwing one more blinding white smile toward Brock. I'm pretty sure, if it were up to her, she'd be bent over the front counter the moment I slip inside the dressing room.

"Do you have a color in mind?"

I glance around at the dresses of every style and color. "I guess something dark." Maybe it'll help hide me.

I barely even pay attention as she pulls a few dresses for me without even asking my size and thrusts them into one of the rooms. "Try these on and step outside. I'll wait for you here," she says, pointing to the small sitting area.

Sighing, I close the curtain and stare at her selection. I thumb through the first few, hating them instantly. They're low cut and revealing, something I'd never be caught dead wearing. I settle on a simple black dress that hits just below the knees. It has a subtle plunging neckline, which doesn't give a peep show a guy would usually have to pay for.

Resolved to get this over with, I pull open the curtain and step outside, fully expecting to either find Sasha waiting, as she indicated, or seeing her bent over the front counter, as she'd prefer. I find neither.

What I do see is Brock, sitting casually in one of the two wing-backed chairs. "Nope."

"What?" I ask, glancing down at the basic dress.

"It's practically a potato sack. Try again."

I huff out a huge breath. "What if I like this one?" I demand, glancing at myself in the full-length mirror standing off to the side.

"Do you?"

I realize right away that I don't. I hate it. It clings to my body in all the wrong ways and has a shapeless look to it. "No."

"There you go. Next."

I exhale loudly, glancing around and finding Sasha off to the side, refolding dress shirts, and sulk back inside. It goes that way with three more dresses. They're lovely, but not on me. I'm starting to get annoyed and aggravated after the fourth failed dress. "You know what? This is useless. I'm just going to get the potato sack."

Brock stands up and heads for the dressing room, making it feel extremely tiny with his large body towering over me. He thumbs through the remaining garments hanging on the rack, pulling off one in a deep blue and holding it out to me. "This one."

"What?"

"Try this one. If it doesn't look good, you can get the potato sack."

I growl in frustration before snatching the dress from his outstretched hand. When I turn around, he doesn't move, remaining standing in the doorway of the dressing room. "Are you staying?"

Something flashes through his eyes before he slowly shakes his head. He backs out, and I swear he hesitates before pulling the curtain closed. My mind is all sorts of messed up, because it looked like he was about to stay.

And that's just stupid.

Why would someone like Brock Williams go for someone like me when there are women like Sasha and Gisele, with their fancy outfits and hair looking like they just walked out of the salon.

Carefully, I slip on the blue dress, instantly perking up when I spy how well it fits. I slip the single strap over my right shoulder, tuck the exposed bra strap beneath the material of the dress, and zip up the side. When I step back to survey myself in the mirror, I actually gasp.

"Are you coming out?" Brock hollers from the other side of the curtain. "Or am I coming in?"

I take one last look at the dress, loving how it hits just above the knee and how the lace overlay somehow makes the dress look classy and not cheap, considering how tight it is. There's a slight tremble in my hand as I push back the curtain and slowly step out.

"About time, I was just about to come in—" His eyes are wide and his jaw practically dragging on the floor. "—there. You can't wear that."

I glance in the mirror to the side and then turn to check out the back. "Why? Is my ass hanging out?"

"No," he whispers, his voice sounding dry and crackly. "You look... wow."

"Wow?" I ask, finally glancing his way once more. "Good wow, or 'holy shit, I can't believe your friends let you out of the house looking like that' wow?"

"Good," he mutters, clearing his throat. "Very good. That's the dress."

Brock not-so-discreetly adjusts himself before he turns around and starts to walk away. "Hey, where are you going?"

"To pick out a shirt," he announces, but before he gets too far away, I swear I hear him mumble, "before I do something naughty to you in that dressing room."

With a smile on my face, I slip back inside the small changing area and prepare to redress in my street clothes. Yes, this is definitely the dress, and tonight, I might enjoy making Brock Williams swallow his tongue.

CHAPTER
SEVEN

BROCK

My cock is hard. It's not just hard. It's throbbing, painstakingly so, as I walk through the store. When I pulled the deep blue dress out of the rubble of her other options, my only thought was to help her find something other than that damn potato sack. I wasn't thinking, and that's the problem. The dress was sexy, and I knew she would look sexy in it.

The issue? It's not just me who will be looking at her in that dress. It's going to be every fucking male at Sully's. It's going to be every man who is close enough to lay eyes on her. The bigger issue? She's flying solo. It's not like she'll be on my arm. I won't be able to hold my head high knowing that she's mine and that she's going home with me, no matter how badly I wish that were the case.

No, my dumb ass dressed the woman who I can't stop thinking about as a fucking sex goddess, and I don't know how I'm going to handle the attention it's going to bring her. Maybe I'll walk close to her, close enough that everyone with a dick thinks she's mine, but not so close that Caleb or their dad will notice and get suspicious. I feel my shoulders relax just a little with my new plan. It's a far reach as far as ideas go, but I'm going with it.

"Oh, this would look great on you," Sasha, the store associate that greeted us and picked the array of dresses for Joey, says, handing me a bright red shirt. She flutters her eyelashes and gives me a come-hither smile. I know what that smile means. With the simple crook of my finger, I could have her dropping her panties in the dressing room without complaint. However, I don't want Sasha. Sure, she's a looker, but she's not Joey, and Josephine Henderson is the only woman I currently have the headspace for.

"My girl is wearing a deep blue," I say, picking up a shirt that is almost the exact color of the dress Joey chose. Well, that I chose, and she confirmed. Her eyes go wide, and I know it's the "my girl" reference. She knows who I am, and my guess is she also knows I'm unattached. However, I like the way it feels when I call Joey my girl. Like a warm caress on a cool fall night. I like it a whole hell of a lot.

"Oh." Sasha's face is crestfallen, and I have to fight the urge to roll my eyes. She saw me come in with Joey, and I know damn good and well that she saw me hanging out at the dressing rooms with her too.

"Excuse me," I say, turning on my heel and walking away from her. My steps are leisurely as I take the long way back to the dressing rooms. My cock is calmer, but I still need a minute. I've never had a woman affect me the way that Joey does. The more time I'm around her, the more I crave her.

As I turn the corner to head back to where I know she'll be waiting, I pass the jewelry counter. A pair of diamond stud earrings stick out to me, and I find myself pausing to take another look. I'm already imagining Joey wearing them tonight in that killer dress.

"Can I help you with something?" an older gentleman asks.

"I'll take those." I point to the earrings.

He nods. "They're on sale today," he informs me.

"Even better. Can I pay for this here as well?" I ask him, holding up the shirt that I chose to match her dress. That will make us look even more like a couple, and I find my mood brightening even further.

"Of course, sir." He doesn't waste time with small talk as he rings up my purchases. I don't even blink when he tells me the total. All I can think about is seeing the earrings on her. I wonder if I can convince her to wear them tonight? It will go a long way in calming my nerves, knowing that something I chose for her and a gift that I've given her is what she's wearing when all those other tools are looking at her.

I'll have to think of a way to give them to her. If I just hand them to her, the chances of her accepting them are slim to none. She might be Richard Henderson's daughter, but she's not one for handouts. She's not some prima donna, and that draws me to her even more.

"Thank you, Marvel," I say, reading his name tag.

"You're welcome, Mr. Williams." He winks, causing me to laugh. It looks like he recognizes me. I would have never known, with his professionalism of our transaction.

"Do you have a pen and paper?" I ask. I need to get back to Joey, but this won't take long.

"Yes, of course." Marvel reaches into a drawer and hands me a small pad of paper and a pen. I scrawl his name across the paper, thanking him for all his help, and sign my name and my number eighty underneath. I hand him back the paper, and his beaming smile makes the few extra minutes worth it.

"Have a good day, Marvel," I say, turning to leave. His 'thank you' follows me as I eat up the distance between me and the dressing rooms. Between Joey and me.

"Can I have one of those?" a breathless feminine voice asks from behind me.

I pause and look over my shoulder to find Sasha. "Sorry, my girl's waiting." I see the anger in her eyes, and I hate to piss off a fan, but I can't seem to help it where she's concerned. The shop assistant has pushed me to the limit on my bullshit meter. She mumbles something under her breath that I can't quite understand, and I don't even bother to find out.

I reach the dressing rooms to find Joey still in that rocking dress, this time with her hair twisted up and two different shoes on her feet. A silver heel on the left and a black heel on the right.

"Which one?" she asks as I approach her.

"Turn for me." I make a turning motion with my index finger. She rolls those chocolate brown eyes but does as I ask.

I have to bite down on my cheek to keep my groan from slipping. She's a fucking knockout. "Either," I finally manage to reply, once I realize she's staring at me in anticipation.

"Ugh, you're no help," she says.

I watch as she turns from side to side, keeping her eyes on the mirror as she tries to decide. I take a few steps, not stopping until I'm standing directly behind her. Our eyes meet in the mirror. I can see the question in hers, while there is nothing but desire in mine.

This fucking dress.

With my bag in one hand, I slip the other around her waist, resting it on her belly. Her back aligns with my front, and I can't help but notice how perfectly she fits next to me. "It doesn't matter which shoes you pick. You're still going to be the most beautiful woman in the room." Our eyes remain locked. I watch us in the mirror, and her breathing changes, as the rise and fall of her chest quickens.

Bending my head, I place my lips next to her ear. "Close your eyes." This time I don't look in the mirror. I keep my eyes on her and watch as she complies. "Let go of the worry of being in the press. Just feel, Joey. Tell me, what are you feeling right this minute?"

"You," she breathes.

My cock twitches, taking notice of the hitch in her voice and the way her tight little body is pressed up against my own. I swallow hard and ignore her answer. I have no choice in the matter. If we talk about how she feels me, we're going to be arrested for indecent exposure. "Right foot or left foot, babe? Which one feels the best?" I ask her.

"I... don't know."

"Come on. Just feel."

"How do you know I'm worried about the press?"

"Because we're having dinner at Sully's with your father. Caleb and I have been friends for a long time. I can read between the lines. Let go of the worry and the stress of what the press might report. They're going to regardless of what you choose. Choose what's right for you."

"Left," she finally answers.

"Excellent choice. It will bring out the shimmer of the dress." And the shimmer in the diamond earrings I just bought her, but I keep that to myself. Now is not the time to lay all my cards out on the table.

Reluctantly, I drop my arm from her waist and force myself to take a step back. Instantly I miss the heat of her body and the smell of her skin.

Slowly, she turns to face me. Her cheeks are tinted with a slight blush of pink, and the corner of her mouth is tilted in a smile. "Thanks, Brock."

"Anytime, beautiful. Do you have everything you need?" I ask, moving my bag in front of me to hide the steel rod in my pants. Not from her. I know she could feel what she does to me, but the Sashas of the world are lurking, and the last thing I need is my hard cock on the front page of some gossip rag.

"Yes. I'm just going to change out of the dress." She kicks off her shoes and moves to the dressing room.

As she closes the door, I get to work finding the appropriate box that contains the other silver shoe. I make sure they're the same size, not because I'm worried that they're not, but because I need something to do. I need to keep my mind busy to try and forget that she's naked just a few feet away.

Damn. What's this woman doing to me?

A few minutes later, Joey steps out of the dressing room. Her hair is once again falling over her shoulders. I like it either way, but I do miss the sight of her slender neck. Although it's probably for the best. Maybe I can keep from wanting to kiss her there if it's not exposed. That's a big maybe.

"Ready?" she asks brightly.

I hold up my bag. "I already checked out."

"Well then, I better get busy putting Caleb's little black card to good use."

"Where next? Nails? Hair?" I ask her, trailing along behind her. Yes, I look at her ass in those shorts she's wearing. How could I not?

"Nah, I was just giving him a hard time."

I frown at her reply. "You said it had been way too long." I think back to her earlier conversation with her brother. "Your toes," I say, recalling the exact conversation.

"Meh, they'll be fine." She waves me off as she steps forward in line.

"Do we have time?" I ask her.

She steps up to the counter, placing her items gently on the available space. "Do we have time for what?" She glances at me over her shoulder.

"For your toes."

"Really, Brock. It's fine."

It's not fine. She should have nothing but the best, and not just because she has to have dinner with her father, just because she's Joey. "Do we have time?" I ask again.

I watch as she turns her wrist to look at her watch and shakes her head. "Not really. I need to shower and dry my hair, and I think I'm going to curl it. That takes time, and no way am I risking Daddy Dearest's wrath for being late."

I nod in understanding, but I make a mental note to get her a gift certificate to a pedicure. Grabbing her bags and ignoring her protest, I lead her back out to my car.

As soon as we're on the road, my phone rings. "Hey, Mom," I greet after hitting the answer button on the dash. "You're on speaker."

"Oh, I won't keep you. I just wanted to call to check in."

"Doing well," I tell her.

"Good. Good. Well, call me later when you can talk. I want to hear how things are going with the new team."

"I can do that. You doing okay?" I ask.

"I miss my son, but other than that, I'm great." She laughs.

"All right, I'll call you later."

"Love you, Brock."

"Love you too."

"You're close to your mom?" Joey asks.

"Yeah, we're tight. She's cool."

"You're lucky," she says, glancing out the window.

I don't know what to say to that, so I don't say anything. Instead, I reach over and lace her fingers with mine. She lets me hold her hand all the way home.

———

I'm sitting on the bed in my room when I hear the shower turn on in hers. The house is quiet. I'm not sure where Caleb is. My guess is he's catching a quick nap before we leave. I should be doing the same. We had a hard practice today, but I'm too keyed up. The small velvet box that contains the earrings is clutched in my fist as I think of how to give them to her. Sure, I could wait, but I don't want to. I'm all about instant gratification, and call me crazy, because I admit it sounds that way, but I want to see them on her. I want to know that she's wearing something I gave her when we walk into Sully's tonight.

Getting her to accept this is a far reach and even further to get her to wear them tonight, but I have to try. That's when an idea hits me. Reaching into the nightstand, I grab the small tablet of paper and a pen that I put there a few nights ago. Placing the earring box on the bed, I put pen to paper and begin to write.

Once upon a time, there was a princess named Joey. She had big brown eyes and dark brown hair. She was breathtaking. All the men in the land thought so, even Prince Brock. The prince craved her attention, but to no avail. One day he had an idea. He would give the princess jewels so she knew he was thinking about her always. It gave him extreme pleasure deciding on the perfect gift. He chose a pair of diamond stud earrings that he knew would look beautiful on her. He hoped she would accept his gift and wear the jewels. There was nothing in the world that would make him happier.

Princess Joey, these are for you.

Brock

I read over the letter three times before I finally decide it's good enough. Hopefully, she will read my words and accept the earrings without complaint. Folding the letter in half, I scrawl her name on the outside of the paper, grab the box, and slip out of my room. I stand in the hallway listening for Caleb, but the house is silent except for the sound of the shower.

Blocking out the fact that Joey is once again naked and just mere feet away from me... again, I step into her room and place the note and the box on her nightstand next to her phone. Moving back, I stare at the bathroom door, and images of her naked body, wet with soap sliding over her curves, has me reaching into my pants and adjusting myself. This is a constant issue where she's concerned, and I'm going to have to literally take matters into my own hands before we leave tonight. Otherwise, everyone is going to know how she affects me.

Not that I care about that. Not really. But I need to make sure we're both on the same page. We've been dancing around this attraction that sparks between us. Then there's the issue of her brother. Caleb and I have been best friends for years, and I owe it to him to tell him my plans. That is if Joey is on board with it. It's my respect for him that will initiate the conversation, but I'm not asking for his permission. No, this thing between us, this electricity that shocks my system every time she's near, is like nothing I've ever felt before. It's also not something I'm willing to lose or just toss away.

I'm well aware I could lose my best friend over this, but if he felt this connection, if he could only experience what she does to me, he would understand. If not, well, I guess we will cross that bridge when we come to it. If she wants me, I'm hers, at least until we see where this is going to go. Will we crash and burn, or will the embers of the flames stay hot? Either way, my hope is that even if he's not okay with it if things work out between us, he will be.

Eventually.

The water shuts off in the bathroom, and I bolt out of the room and across the hall to mine. Closing the door behind me, I lock it for good measure and strip out of my clothes. Another solo session is in order for me tonight, and it's images of Joey that will be fueling my fantasy.

———

Caleb and I stand at the bottom of the stairs, waiting on Joey. We're both dressed in slacks and dress shirts, with ties. It's irrational, but my chest puffs out just a little bit knowing she and I are going to be matching. Hopefully, Caleb doesn't comment. I can just blame it on a sales associate that wouldn't take no for an answer.

"Joey!" Caleb calls up the steps. "Move it, sister! We're going to be late."

"I'm coming!" she calls back.

I shuffle my stance as my nerves get the better of me. I've never given a woman such a lavish gift. I've never wanted to, and now all I can think about is seeing her in that dress with my earrings in her ears.

"Finally," Caleb says, pulling me out of my thoughts. "Damn, sis, you clean up nice," he says, whistling as she reaches the bottom step.

"Thank you. The two of you look very handsome," she tells us.

"Are we ready?" he asks us.

"All set," I manage to croak. I have to force myself not to stare at the beauty before me. Her hair is down, and I can't see her ears, and the suspense is killing me. It's stupid, and if I were asked to explain my need for her to wear my gift, I couldn't. It's just a need.

"Let's bounce." Caleb twirls his keys on his finger and turns to head for the garage.

"You're beautiful," I tell her. My voice is low and husky, even to my own ears.

"Thank you. Oh, I read your story," she says as she tucks her hair behind her ear. There, like a gleaming beacon, is the diamond stud earring. All I can do is nod. There's a lump in my throat that I can't speak over. My heart hammers in my chest and my hands are clammy. I don't know what's happening to me. I don't understand this feeling, but there is one thing about all of this that I do understand. I want more. I want all she's willing to give me.

Now, I just need to find the balls to tell her and see where we stand.

CHAPTER
EIGHT

Joey

I feel like I'm on fire. My body prickles with awareness, hums with anticipation and desire. It took everything I could to mask my surprise and attraction to Brock as I walked down the stairs and saw him standing in the foyer with my brother. In a shirt nearly an identical color to the dress I'm wearing. All the pep talks in the world about keeping those thoughts of Brock and the crazy desire I feel when he's near fly straight out the window, and it took every ounce of strength I possessed to play it cool and not climb him like a tree.

Now, I'm sitting in the back seat of my brother's SUV with Brock's subtle cologne practically punching me in the vagina. He smells so amazingly yummy that it's taking all my control not to lean forward and lick the side of his neck.

It was a fight just to sit in the back seat. Brock insisted I take the front, but I knew, even with the larger size of Caleb's SUV, the man would be cramped back here. Plus, I thought it would give me the slightest reprieve from the potent sexy vibes seeping from his pores, but man, was I wrong. Sitting behind him is like a direct line straight to my underused female reproductive organs.

My vibrator is definitely going to get a workout later.

As we pull into the valet at Sully's, my nerves instantly rise. I've never really had a great relationship with my parents, by my own choice. They're… difficult. I know normal is a setting on the dryer, but all I've ever wanted was a slice of a "normal life." Parents who weren't tabloid fodder, with paparazzi trailing behind you everywhere you went, hoping to snatch an unflattering photo sure to yield high profits to the right rag mag.

Now, I'm about to be thrust into a forced dinner, where cell phone cameras will surely catch photos of my dad and his new wife looking breathtaking and "so in love," while I'm sitting there, probably shoveling my pasta primavera into my open trap.

My door opens, pulling me from my thoughts, only it's not the valet offering me his hand. It's Brock and his panty-melting smile. Turns out, it's my kryptonite.

Caleb joins us on the sidewalk and offers me his elbow. There's a flash of annoyance and a bit of hesitancy in Brock's face, in his movement, as he slowly holds out my hand so I can place it against my brother's forearm. However, before he lets go completely, I feel him give me a gentle squeeze.

The front doors open by men wearing tuxedos as we enter the restaurant. I've been here before. The last time I visited Caleb, Dad insisted we meet for dinner here. All of my insistence we go to the burger joint down the road fell on deaf ears. "Hendersons are expected to eat at nice restaurants, not at hole-in-the-wall places with cracked plastic red and white checkered tablecloths."

The maître d' greets us with a solemn nod. "Good evening, Mr. Henderson. Your party has arrived. If you follow me, I'll take you to your table."

The walkway to the very back of the room is narrow, so I release Caleb's arm and fall behind him. As I'm walking, I feel a large, warm hand press against my lower back, and it takes every ounce of restraint I possess not to react to the touch. Instead, I focus on putting one foot in front of the other and not tripping in front of a restaurant full of rich and powerful people.

All eyes are on us. Even though I don't dare glance around, I can feel them. Not only is my dad well known, but so are Caleb and Brock. Their faces are front and center in sporting magazines, blogs, and gossip columns more often than I change underwear, so it's no wonder there's a hum of excitement as we walk through the room. There are even a few gasps of delight from ladies nearby. I'm surprised a few pairs of panties aren't thrown in the walkway.

Approaching the intimate table in the back, my father stands and gives us a big smile. He extends his arms and hugs Caleb, slapping him hard enough on the back to catch the attention of anyone whose eyes weren't already on our group. "There're my children," he boasts proudly, as if there were cameras already pointed his way.

Hell, maybe there are.

"Princess." I glance up and offer my dad a small smile. He steps forward and pulls me into his arms, my body completely encompassed by his large body. His familiar cologne wraps around me, a reminder of quick trips into town when I was child, where he'd blow in, throw gifts at me, and then leave again.

"Hi, Dad," I mutter as he places a kiss on my cheek.

"You look beautiful," he replies, stepping back and looking me over with a critical line. "Is this a new dress?"

I feel the blush burn up my neck as images of Brock helping me choose the perfect dress for tonight pepper through my mind. "It is," I reply, clearing my throat.

"It's lovely." Dad turns when a hand with long red fingernails slips through his arm and grips his suit jacket. "Ahh, yes. Candi dear, the kids are here."

I almost snort, considering Candi is two years younger than her husband's oldest child.

"Josephine! Wow, I almost didn't recognize you without a ponytail and Chucks on your feet!" she bellows, certain to draw the attention of everyone in a two-block vicinity.

"Good to see you, Candi," I mumble, watching as her focus is completely drawn over my head. "Brock Williams, I've heard so much about you. It's so wonderful to finally meet you," she says, reaching out her hand and bumping me in the upper arm.

I try not to move, but I'm wobbly in my heels and stumble backward. Fortunately, I'm kept from making a scene, when a pair of strong hands grip my hips and hold me in place. Once I'm steady again, Brock reaches for the extended hand and places a kiss on her knuckles, all while keeping his other hand firmly on my hip. "Pleasure to meet you, Mrs. Henderson."

She blows out a dainty puff of air. "There'll be none of that," she practically coos. "You can call me Candi. With an I," she adds with her trademark giggle.

"Candi," Brock confirms, releasing her hand and taking a step back to grab a chair. He pulls it back, guiding me toward it with the hand still resting on my hip. "Ladies first."

My heart does this weird fluttering thing in my chest as my eyes lock on his. There's this deep, dark intensity I'm not prepared for, and if I'm being honest, I'm not sure if I should be appalled or excited by my schoolgirl reaction. "Thank you," I whisper, taking a seat in the offered chair.

Dad and Candi return to their seats, while Caleb takes the one to my left and Brock to my right. I notice Candi instantly lean to her left, slipping ever so subtly into Brock's personal space, and the movement grates on my nerves even further.

After glasses of water and a bottle of fine wine is delivered to our table, Dad and Caleb immediately start discussing the upcoming season, while Candi does everything she can to engage Brock in conversation about his transfer to the Ramblers. Funny how Dad wanted to have dinner with me yet talks quickly turn to football, which doesn't include me at all.

Typical.

I keep myself busy by browsing the menu. It has everything from the finest steaks to fresh lobster and salmon. Usually I prefer comfort foods like baked lasagna or lobster ravioli to get me through an evening with my father and wife number four, but tonight I might actually take a slab of beef that costs more than my car payment just to get by.

I'm jolted from my thoughts by a thumb gently caressing my back. Casually, I glance to the side to find Brock's arm tossed over my chair back. He looks completely relaxed and positively edible as he leans back in his chair and listens to whatever Stepmommy Dearest is droning on and on about. He glances my way with the briefest of looks, flashing me a hint of a grin that sets my blood pumping and causes my mouth to water, before returning his attention to Candi.

"Josephine?"

"Huh?" I ask, glancing up and finding my father and Candi's gazes riveted on me.

"What?"

"Candi was just asking you how work was going," my dad says before reaching for the bottle of wine.

"Oh, uh, fine." I make sure to avert my gaze to try to mask my features. I've always been a horrible liar, and I know my family—especially Caleb—will see right through me.

"Well, I'm glad you were able to get time away to see us. Family is the most important, you know," my dad boasts proudly, almost making me roll my eyes. Richard Henderson is not someone I'd call a family man.

I slink down in my seat, wishing I were invisible, as Dad pours three glasses of wine. He hands the first to his darling wife and the second to me, before taking a healthy drink from the third glass. I steal a glance at my brother, who's sipping on ice water with lemon. "You're not having wine?"

Dad speaks for his son. "Caleb knows not to drink alcohol during the season. It affects your endurance, your game, and your mind. This way, he won't wind up as some tabloid fodder."

"Or with a baby from a football groupie in nine months," I say, unable to stop the jab from spilling from my lips.

A slight gasp sounds from across the table, most likely from my dad's betrothed, while a chuckle can be heard to my right. You know, that awkward laugh that is quickly covered to sound like a cough? Yeah, that's Brock beside me, making me grin as I chug some of the expensive wine in front of me.

"That was uncalled for," my father reprimands, clearing his throat and returning the conversation to football.

I relax in my chair, eager to just get through this dinner with as few tongue lashings as possible. Just as I bring my glass up to my lips once more, I feel Brock's hand gently squeeze my shoulder. His fingers are warm, his palm slightly rough, and it leaves a wake of tingles behind that seem to go straight to my ovaries.

I risk a quick glance over, only to lock gazes with those mesmerizing blue eyes. Brock gives me a slight grin and a wink before relaxing his hand back on my chair. He may not touch me directly, but I can feel the heat of his skin so very close to my own. Having him so close is messing with me. I can't think. I can't breathe. I can't concentrate on anything around me.

Just him.

How close his hand is.

How badly I wish it were caressing my bare skin.

I have to get through this dinner. Just another hour, and I can retreat to my bedroom and try to forget about the way my body hummed with anticipation and desire.

Yeah, fat chance of that happening.

———

A knock on my door wakes me from my Brock-filled dreams. I glance at the clock and find it's just after eight. Too early when all you have to do is sunbathe by the pool and figure out what you're having for breakfast.

"Joey, you awake?"

I turn toward the door and sit up. "Yeah, I'm up. Come on in," I tell my brother, who hesitantly pushes the door open.

"Sorry to wake you, but I wanted to let you know we're heading out to get ready for the game. I left your ticket on the counter downstairs, as well as a parking pass for the back lot. This way you don't have to worry about the tailgates and fans," he says, leaning against the doorjamb with his large body.

"Oh, thanks."

"I put you midfield so you have a great view, but not so close to the wives and girlfriends that you'll be peppered with questions the entire time. Oh, and you don't have to worry about Candi. She'll be up in the management suites with the other viper wives," he adds with a wink and grin.

"Thanks," I reply, totally appreciating the extra lengths my brother has gone to. He knows I'm not a huge fan of crowds and would much rather not sit beside people who will constantly talk about the players, contracts, and how much money they spend. I'm more of a cheap seats kinda girl. Even if I don't really know what they're hooting and hollering about, it's usually a fun atmosphere.

"I almost forgot," Caleb states, pulling a large bag from behind his back and setting it on the foot of my bed. "Jerseys were delivered this morning."

"Thanks," I reply, making no reach for the bag. Mostly because I'm well concealed beneath the soft down comforter. I'd much rather not scar my brother, considering I'm only wearing panties and a tank top under here.

"All right, we're out. See you after the game."

"Okay. Good luck!" I holler as my brother heads out. He closes my door securely behind him.

Finally, I reach for the bag and pull two large white boxes from within. The first one contains a replica black jersey with a big red number three on the back, the name Henderson printed boldly above it. I smile, so very proud of my brother. It wasn't easy being a former NFL great's son, but my brother has held up well. Even as a young player, he tried to forge his own path, not taking the easier one paved by our dad. When everyone expected him to play quarterback like the infamous Richard Henderson, my brother realized his passion lay in kicking. And he's done well too. Caleb was a Pro-Bowl player last season and has earned several records for the team.

Setting aside the box with my brother's jersey, I reach for the second box, already knowing what it contains. I peel off the top and gaze down at the number eighty jersey staring back at me. While Caleb's is black, this one is white, with black and red numbers and letters. Those letters, of course, spelling out Williams.

As I pull the jersey out of the box, I find a sheet of paper tucked beneath it. A smile instantly spreads across my face as I reach for the note.

. . .

Princess Joey,

Once upon a time, there was a handsome football player. He was at the top of his game, and all the maidens in the land loved him. However, the handsome football player wasn't interested in the other maidens. Oh, no. He had his eyes set on the fairest princess of them all. One day, he presented her with a jersey. One bearing his name and number on the back, and all he could think about was seeing the princess in it. Would she wear it to the game? He couldn't wait to find out.

To be continued...

A smile was already spread across my lips as I set the note aside and grab the jersey, bringing it to my nose and inhaling deeply. There's definitely that new clothes aroma with a hint of plastic, like it was taken out of a plastic bag. But also there, ever so faintly on the fabric, is the scent of man. Musky, clean, and with a touch of sandalwood. I've become all too familiar with it in recent days.

Brock.

I lie down and curl back up with my pillow, the number eighty jersey cradled in my arms. As I close my eyes to catch a few more minutes of rest, I hold the material against my cheek, catching whiffs of the light fragrance of Brock's aftershave. It's what accompanies me as I fall back into more Brock-filled dreams.

CHAPTER
NINE

BROCK

There is nothing like the first game of the season—from the roar of the crowd filling the stadium to the smells of popcorn and nachos that fill the air. Football is its own season in my world. It's not fall. It's football.

Preseason games are a good way to gauge how our team stands up in the league, but at the same time, it's... fun. The fans are on point. The team is pumped to be back on the field. Hell, even the announcers are joyous and overflowing with positive comments of what the season might hold.

Today is all that and more. It's more because I'm on a new team. I'm a Rambler now, and for the first time in years, I'm playing on the same side as my best friend. That alone makes this day great. However, there is a little something that makes it even better. Or should I say, someone?

Joey.

I can't exactly pinpoint how it happened, but she's become... more than just Caleb's little sister. I want her with an intensity that's bigger than football. That's really the only way I know how to explain it. I think about her all the time, and I find myself doing things like lingering in the kitchen just to get a few more minutes of her time.

She's turning me inside out.

"You ready for today?" Caleb asks, taking a seat next to me on the bench.

"Born ready." I flash him a grin.

"Good to have you, brother," he says, clamping a hand down on my shoulder.

"Is that a tear I see?" I goad.

"Fuck off." He laughs, dropping his hand. "I'm just saying. It's been years since we've been on the same team, and it's going to be nice to have you out on that field and not be the enemy."

"I get it." I nod. "It's been too damn long." He looks down at his phone and furrows his brow. "What's up?"

"Nothing. At least, I don't think so. I texted Joey to see if she made it to her seat okay, and I haven't heard from her yet."

"I'm sure she's just stocking up on snacks," I say the words as I reach for my phone just in case by some chain of events, she sent me a message and not her brother. I fight not to let my disappointment show when there are no messages waiting for me.

"Something's going on with her. She keeps telling me that we'll talk, but it's yet to happen."

My heart begins to race as the worry in his voice grips my chest. "You think she's in trouble?"

"No." He's quick to reply. "I just know there's more that she's not telling me. Like how she can take so much time off work."

"I'm sure she'll talk when she's ready."

"Yeah," Caleb agrees.

"Yo, Henderson!" one of our teammates yells as he tosses a football at Caleb's head. He catches it with ease, and they start talking shit to one another. I laugh along with them but sneak a quick message to Joey.

Me: You make it to the stadium all right?

. . .

The three little dots immediately begin to bounce across the screen, which calms my nerves. I let Caleb get me all riled up.

Joey: Yep. Just found my seat.

Her reply is accompanied by a picture of the field.

Me: You supporting team colors?

I stare at the screen, waiting for her reply, and when it comes through, I can't contain my smile. It's a picture of her wearing her brother's jersey, but with both of our numbers painted on her cheek. I try not to let the disappointment show that she chose Caleb's jersey over mine. He is her brother, after all. I'm just his best friend. The guy who can't stop thinking about her. The guy who would give damn near anything for just a fraction of her time.

Me: Beautiful.

It's the truth. Regardless of which jersey she wears, she's still the most beautiful woman I've ever seen, and she needs to hear that as often as possible. Sure, I'm a little disappointed it's not my name scrawled across her back, but that just gives me something to look forward to at our next game.

Joey: Good luck out there.

Me: See you after?

. . .

Joey: Count on it.

Tossing my phone back into my locker, I finish suiting up for the game. I'm ready to kill this first preseason game, so I can see her. Never in a million years did I ever think that I would want to rush the game, but here I am. The need to see her, to be around her, is strong.

———

"Fuck yeah!" Jones thrusts his hands up in the air as we enter the locker room. "Game one with the W baby!" he calls out. The entire locker room erupts in cheers and chants as we celebrate our win. Sure, it's preseason, and it doesn't count toward the playoffs, but damn, if it doesn't feel good regardless—a win is a win.

"Drinks at the Rambler Inn," Dominic Jefferson, a D-lineman, announces.

I make eyes with Caleb, and he just grins and shakes his head. I want him to turn him down because there is nothing that's going to keep me from going back to his place to celebrate with Joey. Sure, I'd like to have her all to myself, but I know that if I ditch, I'm the new guy, not wanting to hang out with my new team. In reality, I'm the new guy who just wants to hang out with his best friend's sister, but I'd rather not announce that either. Not if I can help it. Not yet anyway.

"Can't tonight," Caleb tells Dominic. "My little sister is in town."

"Bring her."

"Nah. Not really her scene. Besides, Brock and I promised her we'd be home for some dinner that she made us."

It's the first I've heard of it, but I'm rolling with it. "Right," I agree. "And pissing her off is not at the top of my list of fun things to do." My comment kind of makes her sound like a diva when she is anything but; however, it works because the guys grumble, but none of them invite themselves over. Caleb catches my eye and gives me a subtle nod. Good. He wasn't feeling it either. Now all I have to do is get him to leave me alone with his sister when we get back to his place.

"You bowing out too?" Dominic asks me.

"Yep. When the lady of the house requests your presence, you make it a point to be there."

"Lady of the house?" He raises his eyebrows.

"She's the closest thing this one's going to get to having a lady of the house." I point at Caleb.

"He's not wrong." Caleb shrugs, taking the jab in stride.

"Fine. You two loners go home and be bored sitting on the couch while the rest of us celebrate with some babes and beers," Dominic comments.

"I'm out too," our quarterback, Bronson Baker, announces. "The youngest isn't feeling well. I told the wife I'd come to relieve her."

By the time we've all showered, a handful of players, mostly the rookies, are headed for drinks while the rest of us head home. I remember a time when I was Dominic and celebrating a night out. Maybe a hookup to warm my bed was the only way I wanted to celebrate. Now, just the thought of the chance of spending a little time with Joey has me rushing Caleb's ass so we can get to my car and get home.

———

"Damn," Caleb mutters when we walk into the house. "Something smells damn good." He drops his bag at the door and stalks into the house. "Joey!" he calls.

"In the kitchen!" her sweet voice calls back.

I discard my bag by the door and follow him into the kitchen. "What's all this?" I can't help but ask as the incredible aroma greets me.

"A celebratory dinner." Joey smiles up at me, and I feel something shift in my chest.

"And what if we would have lost?" Caleb asks with humor in his voice.

"Well, then it would have been a 'pick yourself up and try again' dinner. Now, if you're done questioning me, you can set the table," she tells him, sticking her tongue out.

"Yes, ma'am. What's on the menu?" he asks.

"Lasagna, garlic bread, and salad. Brock, do you mind getting the bowl of salad out of the fridge? And there are a couple of different dressings too, if you don't mind grabbing those as well?"

"On it." I get to work doing as I'm asked. Within a few minutes, the three of us are sitting around the kitchen island with full plates of lasagna and salad.

"This is great, sis. Thanks," Caleb says, barely covering his mouth that's full.

"You're welcome." Joey laughs and hands him a napkin.

"It's delicious," I agree.

"How was the seat?" Caleb asks her.

"Perfect. You know I'd rather be in the crowd than in some stuffy suite."

"Well, that works for now, but once people get wind that you're my sister, that might have to change."

"Why would they?"

"It's not like we hide the fact. Besides, it's only a matter of time until Daddy Dearest summons you to sit with Candi in the suite."

"Ugh. I'm going to have to call in reinforcements for that one." Joey laughs.

"Reinforcements?" I ask.

"Yeah, my best friend, Taylor. Dad loves her, and she's a great buffer with anyone."

"How is Taylor? It's been ages since I've seen her," Caleb asks.

"She's doing well. She's busy working, giving me a hard time for not coming to visit more."

"She's a paralegal, right?" Caleb asks.

"Yes. She works a ton of hours but still finds the time to give me shit."

"Sounds like Taylor." Caleb chuckles.

"Have you seen her? Since you've been here?" I insert myself into the conversation.

"No. However, she did call me on my way to the stadium, and we're going to get together this week."

"Invite her here. I know you hate going out and risking being seen and then dealing with Dad or, even worse, your mom." Caleb shudders.

"Yeah, I just might do that. Maybe I'll have her over for dinner one night."

"We have an away game this Sunday. Cincinnati. You coming?" Caleb asks.

"I wasn't planning on it. Did you want me to?"

"You know that I do. I don't get to see you enough as it is."

Tell me about it. "I have family coming to Cincinnati. You could sit with them," I offer.

"Is Momma Williams going to be there?" Caleb asks. "Wait, more importantly, is she making us her peanut butter cookies?" There is an almost desperate plea to his question.

"Yeah, Mom will be there. I can put in an order for cookies, but you might want to call her yourself to get an extra couple of dozen. I don't plan on sharing," I warn him.

"What about me? I need to try these cookies if they have you two fighting over them." Joey laughs.

"I'll share with you," I tell her. I'm pretty sure there isn't much that I wouldn't give her.

"My mouth is watering." Caleb chuckles. "Joey, you have no idea how good these cookies are. We're talking melt-in-your-mouth peanut-buttery goodness."

"Well, I picked up some cupcakes for dessert. I don't know if it can hold up to Brock's mom's peanut butter cookies, but they'll satisfy your sweet tooth."

"I'm not going to turn away cupcakes either." Caleb stands and moves to place his plate in the dishwasher. "Thanks for this, Joey," he says, dropping a kiss to the top of her head. "It's nice having you here."

"You're welcome." She tilts her head back and smiles up at him.

"And we still need to have that talk." Caleb points at her.

"I know." Her face grows somber. "We will. I promise." Caleb nods, grabs two cupcakes, flashes us a grin, and takes off up the stairs.

"This was delicious. Thank you," I say, standing and rinsing off my plate before placing it into the dishwasher as well.

"Good game today."

"Thanks." I flash her a smile. "I'm glad you were there."

"So, next week, are you sure it's okay if I sit with your family?"

"Definitely. In fact, why don't you bring Taylor? It will just be my mom and dad, and I've got four tickets. That way, you won't feel awkward."

"Are you sure?"

"Call her," I say, sliding her phone across the island where she's still sitting. "I'll clean up while you make plans."

"I don't know if she can get off work."

"Call her, Joey," I urge. "All expenses paid. My treat. In fact, I'll call and get you a room where the team is staying."

"You don't have to do that."

"It's done." I pull my phone out of my pocket and send a message to Miller, my agent. He'll take care of it. I'm not a diva client, and I never ask for much, so he'll know with just this request that it means something. That she means something. Well, he'll think that one of them means something to me.

"Hey, Taylor." I hear her say into the phone.

"Go." I wave her off. "I'll clean up here. Go catch up with your friend."

"Hold on, Tay." She moves the phone away from her mouth. "Are you sure?"

"Positive." I reach out and run my index finger down the side of her cheek. "Go. I've got this."

With a soft smile, she stands and presses her lips against my cheek. "Thank you, Brock." With that, she places the phone back to her ear and disappears up the stairs.

I place my hand where her lips were and relish the feeling while simultaneously kicking my own ass for sending her away. I was hoping to get to spend some time with her tonight, but the smile on her face at the thought of a weekend with her friend was worth it.

Once the kitchen is cleaned, and the leftovers are put away, I turn off the light and make my way to my room. As soon as I step inside, I can smell her, and my eyes scan the room. That's when I see it—the small, folded piece of paper on my pillow. My feet carry me as fast as they can to the paper as I sit down on my bed and open it.

Princess Joey antagonized over which jersey to wear. She wanted to support her brother and the most handsome football player in the land. In the end, Princess Joey wore her brother's number on her back but supported both on her cheek. You see, Princess Joey has all these feelings that she's not sure she should be feeling about the handsome football player. Just being around him makes her heart race and her palms sweaty. She's worried that even though the handsome football player wanted her to wear his jersey, he might not feel the same way.

To be continued…

Folding the letter, I slip it into the nightstand and stand from the bed. I make my way to the hallway and listen for Caleb. The house is quiet, so I slip quietly into Joey's room. She's still on the phone talking softly with, I assume, Taylor.

She gasps when she sees me. "Hey, Tay, I need to call you right back. Yeah, everything is fine. I just have to pee. I'll call you back," she says, ending the call.

It takes four long strides for me to get to her. She's lying back on her mound of pillows, her hair spread out, and at this moment, I need her. Leaning in close, I place my hand against her cheek as our eyes lock. "I feel it, Joey. I feel it deep in my soul. I want you. I want whatever you're willing to give me, beautiful." And with that, I press my lips to hers.

She opens for me, allowing me to taste her. She takes as much as I give as our tongues caress one another. She emits a moan from deep within the back of her throat that has my cock rock-hard. I want nothing more than to climb into this bed with her and devour every inch of her.

Every. Inch.

Instead, I slow the kiss, resting my forehead against hers. "To be continued," I whisper, kissing her one more time before standing to my full height and walking out of her room. My breathing is ragged, as if I've just run a full practice of sprints. I want to hold her, and kiss her and explore her body, but there's time for that. I need to let tonight's revelation sink in. I need to let her process that I want her.

I want all of her.

CHAPTER
TEN

Joey

I've been tossing and turning for hours—*hours*—replaying that kiss.
My sheets are tangled around my legs. My body hums with an awareness I don't think I've ever felt before. I can still feel the press of his lips
against mine, the soft caress of his tongue.

It's maddening.

I want more.

I've been telling myself for days to stay away, but when push
comes to shove, I don't. I *can't*. I'm drawn to him in a way I've never
experienced and have reached an irrefutable conclusion. Even as I
wrote those words, I'd fought it up until the last second, but as pen
pressed to paper, the story started to flow. That's when I accepted what
I was no longer able to deny.

I want him.

But I also can't ignore the Gisele Sorenson tabloid claims I saw. It's
something I'm going to need to find out about before anything else can
happen with Brock.

The clock reads just after two. I've tried some of my go-to bedtime
rituals like reading and writing in a journal. I snuggled my cat, only to

have her slip from my room after a few minutes, most likely seeking out my brother. In the last hour, I've been desperate enough to actually consider using my brother's weight room.

Okay, I'm not *that* desperate.

Yet.

There's only one thing left to try, short of leaving to buy Melatonin or raiding my brother's liquor cabinet.

Orgasms.

I'll admit, my lack of receiving—other than by way of a battery-operated toy hidden in my nightstand—in many months doesn't exactly make me an expert, but it's a tried-and-true remedy, right? Everyone always brags about them. They help everything from your complexion to your mood, so why not your sleep pattern too?

Trying to work up the nerve to actually do *that*, I slip from my bed and peek down the hall. Caleb's door is closed, which means Hermione may have had to settle for the couch, but Brock's is slightly ajar. Images of seeing him standing in my doorway earlier, the desire written clearly on his handsome face, is enough to cause my core to flood with desire.

I close my door, making sure it's latched and locked, before slipping beneath the covers. When I shut my eyes, it's his face I see. It's his lips I feel. The touch may not be his, but he's all I picture as my hand slips beneath the blankets and into the waistband of my panties. My body is already soaked, my panties useless, as I run my fingers over my swollen clit.

A gasp spills from my lips as I press two fingers into my body. I picture Brock's face, imagining it's his hands, his fingers touching me. My nipples tingle against my shirt as my other hand moves up to cup my breasts. I can already feel myself rocketing toward release. My fingers move swiftly, thrusting in and out, as my hips gyrate. One pinch to an oversensitive nipple and the brush of my palm against my clit has me coming.

Hard.

"Brock!" I gasp, trying to bite back my release, but knowing I failed. I don't care. I ride out my orgasm, glorious waves of euphoria rolling through my body. Squeezing my eyes closed, I picture him there, his wide fingers stretching me as he watches me. The look in his eyes is pure predatory, one that can only be described as animalistic.

It's just like the one I saw earlier right before he kissed me.

When my breathing finally slows, I remove my hands from my body and lie completely still. Except for my dry throat, the orgasm seems to have worked wonders. I glance over at my glass, only to realize it's empty. Exhaling dramatically, I slip from my bed and grab the glass before heading to the door.

I throw the lock and quietly pull it open, only to gasp at the sight of someone standing in the hall. He's leaning against the wall, his body tense, and for a minute, I'm afraid someone has broken into my brother's house. Except it's not just someone.

It's Brock.

He steps forward, his eyes wide and his breathing slightly heavy. "Sunshine?"

"Y-Yes?" I ask, my response barely above a whisper.

He takes another step toward me, now close enough I could rest my hand on his bare chest. "I'm going to ask you a question, and I need you to be completely honest with me. Okay?"

I nod, unable to speak words.

Brock draws his hand lightly up my arm, leaving a trail of goose bumps in its wake. When he reaches my shoulder, he moves once more, our bodies now dangerously close. He bends down and runs his nose from my shoulder to my neck, inhaling softly as he goes. I almost groan as my head tilts to the side ever so slightly, giving him access for whatever he has in mind next.

He steps forward again, his hard body now pressed against mine, as he wraps his big hand around my waist, his fingers angled down to cover part of my ass. He tips his head back and meets my burning gaze with one of his own, and only then does he ask his question. "Were you touching yourself in there?"

My eyes widen as embarrassment sweeps in. *He heard me?* Oh my God, this can't be happening. I drop my gaze, praying the carpet opens up and swallows me whole right about now.

His other hand moves to my neck and slowly grazes up until he cups my cheek. "Please look at me. The thought of you in that room, in your bed, touching yourself has me so fucking hard I can't think straight." He takes a deep breath. "So tell me, Sunshine, were you touching yourself?"

Meeting his gaze head-on, I lift my chin and whisper, "Yes."

His blue eyes darken even further until they're a deep navy. "You moaned my name. Were you thinking about me?"

"Yes," I reply right away.

A throaty moan rips from his throat as he closes his eyes. It's almost as if the confirmation was too much. "I can picture it." When they reopen, they burn with an intensity I'm unaccustomed to. "I'm going to picture it for the rest of my life," he adds with a hint of satisfaction in his voice.

Before I can reply, he releases the hold on my jaw and my hip and takes a small step back. I feel the void of his body immediately and almost reach out for him, but Brock retreats more. Glancing down, there's no missing his erection. It tents his shorts dramatically and makes my mouth water.

"Goodnight, Sunshine."

Confusion replaces the desire I felt just moments ago. "Goodnight?"

Nodding, he reaches forward and places a strand of hair behind my ear. "For tonight, yes. When I take you to my bed, I'll need time to savor you, because when we're finally together, you'll be screaming my name all night long, Sunshine. All. Fucking. Night. Long."

His words cause a shiver to sweep through my veins.

I step back, ready to return to my room, when he speaks once more. "Oh, and, Joey?"

I look up and meet his gaze.

Brock reaches for my hand, the one I had used to pleasure myself and have yet to wash. He holds my two fingers, brings them to his mouth, and wraps his lips around them. My body practically detonates all over again as he lightly sucks.

He finally releases them with a pop, a wolfish grin spreading across his face. "Now you can go to bed."

I mumble something incoherent and reach for my door, closing it with a definitive click that cuts me off from Brock. I go ahead and lock it for good measure too. I'm afraid, if I don't, I'll be back in the hallway within seconds, sneaking into his room and discovering exactly what it's like to be worshipped by Brock Williams.

Something tells me I'd never be the same afterward.

But deep down, I know he's right. As much as I'd love to climb into his bed and ride him like an eight-second prized bull, we're not there yet. I've never jumped into someone's bed without at least dinner first. Hell, I've always considered myself dating that individual. But I'm not dating Brock.

Not even close.

Sure, there's this undeniable sexual tension that surrounds us every time we're near, but that doesn't equal a relationship.

So where do we go from here?

He doesn't seem to want a quick fling, which honestly, surprises me a little. Everything I've read, everything I've heard has talked about his playboy ways and the trail of broken hearts he leaves in his wake. That might actually be a good sign. Perhaps we'll be able to explore this crazy chemistry, while getting to know each other better outside of the bedroom first.

Is Brock capable of a relationship?

Am I willing to blur the boundaries of getting physical with him if he's not?

I guess time will tell.

———

Grabbing my book, I slip outside and head for the pool. I'm not much of a sun person, but a little color on my pasty legs wouldn't hurt any.

The guys had an early morning today, first with a team workout, followed by game film of yesterday's preseason game and meetings, which means I didn't see them before they took off. Probably for the best anyway. I'm not sure I could look Brock in the eye without blushing a thousand shades of pink.

By the time I finally went to bed last night, my dreams were plagued with images of Brock as he acted out the words he spoke in the hallway. I woke in the same sweaty, needy state I went to sleep in, which hasn't helped much today. Fortunately, I've been alone, which has helped me get these raging hormones under control.

I lay my beach towel out on a lounge chair and slip my swimsuit cover-up off. When I chose a swimsuit from the few I keep at my brother's, I admit I intentionally chose the yellow and pink two-piece. It's not the same as the one I had years ago when Brock nicknamed me Sunshine, but with the yellow color, it did have a little weight in my decision.

After rubbing on a low SPF sunscreen, I settle into the chair and open my book, only to realize I've reached one of the book's steamy scenes. After the night I had and Brock's words replaying in my head, that's the last thing I need right now, so I choose to skim that part and begin reading at the end of the sex scene.

It's probably better that way for my mental health.

After thirty minutes of sunning my front, I position the lounger flat and flip over. Instead of reading, I close my eyes and relax, soaking in the sun and the quiet surrounding me. It's a soothing feeling, your skin warm from the rays, the light noise of the pool water cycling through, and the faintest breeze kissing your body. It's just what I need to help push a certain football player out of my mind for just a little while.

The next thing I know, I'm startled awake. The sun has changed, which means it's later in the afternoon, and as I crack open my eyes and shift in the lounge chair, I can already tell my back is fried. "Great," I mumble, dropping my head back down to my arm.

"Looks like you could use a pair of hands to help with the sunscreen."

I glance over, shielding my eyes from the sun, and find Brock sitting on the lounger beside me. "I think it's already too late for that."

He tsks. "Day late and a dollar short, like always." His eyes roam my body from head to toe, then slowly back up again. His gaze feels like a caress, one that leaves a trail of desire in its wake. "Your back is pretty red, Sunshine."

I gingerly sit up, not liking the tightness of my skin as I move. "I think you're right. I put sunscreen everywhere but my back because I couldn't reach." Glancing around, I notice he's alone. "Where's Caleb?"

Brock sits on the edge of his seat, turning to face me. "He was called to your dad's office at the end of our team meeting. I'm sure he'll be heading this way soon."

Standing up, I stretch my arms over my head. It isn't until Brock groans in what sounds like pain do I remember what I'm wearing. The now-familiar intensity returns to those blue orbs as he gazes up at me, drinking in my body once more. This is when I'd usually reach for a towel or my cover-up, but something inside me screams to be bold. *Let your inner seductress out.*

Knowing his eyes are glued to me, I turn and head for the shallow end of the in-ground pool, a little extra swing in my step. Of course, I ignore the burn of the concrete on the bottoms of my feet. There's nothing sexy about that.

I step into the water, loving the way it cools my flushed skin. When I reach the bottom, I'm waist-deep, and only then do I glance over my shoulder. Brock is standing beside the lounger, his hands on his hips and the faintest smirk on his face. "Coming in?" I ask, sliding my hands over the top of the water.

He kicks off his flip-flops and rips his shirt up and over his head, throwing it on the lounger. I notice he's already wearing swim trunks, which makes me grin. He walks my way, like a predator stalks his prey, rounds the edge, and heads for the deep end. With one swift motion, he jumps in, making a huge splash that drenches me.

"Hey!" I holler when he returns to the surface.

His smile is so carefree, so happy as he shakes the water from his face and swims my way. I meet him halfway, finally dipping my top half into the warm, clear water. "The water is amazing," I say, dipping my head back and wetting my hair.

"No, the water is nice," he starts, reaching out and wrapping his big hand around my waist. When he pulls me close enough to touch, he adds, "The view is amazing."

I place my hands on his chest and glance down. "Yes, I do believe the view is quite splendid."

He chuckles, pulling me against his body and lifting me. My legs wrap around his waist and my arms around his neck. I can't help but glance back toward the house, just to make sure we're alone. "I've got you, Sunshine. I'll watch the house; you just hold on to me."

So I do. We float together for what feels like forever, each making small talk about our day and even going as far as to discuss what we could make for dinner. It's nice, relaxing, and enjoyable. The perfect way to spend part of the afternoon.

While floating, I finally get up the nerve to ask him the one question I need to ask. "Can I ask you something?"

"You can always ask me anything," he says, his hand rubbing lightly on my arm.

"There have been news stories about you and Gisele Sorenson," I start, and when he opens his mouth, I quickly add, "I don't need the details or anything, but I do need to know if there's something there between you two. I know you're a casual guy, and I wouldn't fault you if there were, but I just need to know where you stand with her." I feel like I'm breathing hard suddenly.

He meets my gaze head-on as he says, "There's absolutely nothing there, Sunshine. Nothing at all. She's a friend of a friend, I swear." He explains how the photo caught a moment that looked like passion, but in reality, it was a quick kiss on the cheek as she came to say goodbye. She was off to have dinner with friends, and after spending time with him and others that afternoon, she was leaving to get ready. "Besides, how can I think about anyone else, when you're all I see?"

My heart flutters in my chest with the force of a hundred butterflies, and I know by the sincerity in his eyes I believe him. "Okay."

We continue to float for a while longer, until what feels like too soon, Brock leans in, pressing his lips to the corner of my mouth. "I've really enjoyed this."

"Me too," I whisper, knowing our time together has come to an end. I hug him tightly and try to ignore the way my nipples pebble against my bikini top.

He slowly lets me go and swims back a few feet. "He's in the kitchen and just spotted the pool gate open."

I nod, moving myself away from Brock, even though it's the last thing I want to do.

It only takes a few minutes before I hear the back door open.

"What's going on out here?" Caleb hollers, stepping through the gate and heading our way.

"Just a little afternoon swimming. How was your meeting with Daddy Dearest?" I ask, slowly floating toward the shallow end where he stands.

He groans. "Fine. He wants to go over a few things he wants me to work on," he states, rolling his eyes. "I know he knows his shit about football, but it's hard to know when it's coming from the coach or the dad side of him."

I head up the steps and meet my brother on the concrete. "Probably a little of both," I say, going up on my tiptoes and kissing his scruffy cheek.

"Where're you goin'?" he asks, kicking off his shoes and plopping down in the lounge chair Brock sat in earlier.

"To rest. I've been out in the sun for a while. I'll be back down later to make dinner." I grab my cover-up and slip it over my head, stealing a quick peek at Brock in the pool. As suspected, his eyes watch my every move.

"You don't need to do that. You're not staying here to cook for us. We can order something."

I wave off his comment. "I already have a plan for dinner. You can buy tomorrow night," I state with a wink.

"Deal. See you in a bit," he replies, shoving his arms behind his head and kicking his feet up.

I glance back to the pool and find Brock leaning against the side of the pool, most likely concealing the erection I felt while we were swimming. "Bye, Brock."

"Later, Joey."

Grabbing my book and phone, I move inside and toward my room. The moment I step over the threshold, I can smell his aftershave. It only takes a moment to spot the note sitting on my pillow.

The handsome prince had the hardest time sleeping last night. Memories of the fair maiden's moans of pleasure and the way she tasted against his lips plagued his thoughts and monopolized his dreams. He even found it difficult to concentrate at work. Things were hard *for the prince, you may say.*

Then he came home, only to find the maiden sunbathing by the pool. He instantly wanted to go to her, to take her in his arms and slowly remove that sinful swimsuit. Yellow, which instantly reminded him of sunshine, and rose pink, a color he wonders if it's similar to that of the maiden's nipples. He can't wait to find out, fantasizes about it actually. Someday soon. It's a discovery he yearns for.

To be continued…

Instantly, I fan my flushed face.

Yeah.

I'm so screwed.

CHAPTER
ELEVEN

BROCK

Today was our first regular season game, and I'm sitting outside on the back deck with a bottle of water that I wish were a beer. I try not to partake in alcohol during the season, not often anyway. Caleb and some of the guys went to a local club, but I opted to stay in. I blamed it on exhaustion. It was easy for him to believe. I have been dragging ass this week, but it has nothing to do with today's game and everything to do with his little sister.

I can't get her out of my fucking head. It's been almost two more weeks of writing notes and stealing moments. She's under my skin, and it's fucking with me. I know she's supposed to be off-limits. I understand that I could potentially lose my best friend over this, but I can't seem to stop. I still sneak into her room and leave her notes, and when I find one in return, it sets my fucking soul on fire.

I want her.

It's more than just me wanting her. I have this carnal need to be with her all the time. She's all I think about, hence the reason I've not been sleeping. How am I supposed to sleep when I know there's a damn good chance she's locked behind her bedroom door, touching herself, thinking about me?

Me.

She's sliding her fingers inside her pussy, wishing it were my cock. Reaching down, I adjust myself, getting hard just thinking about it. Who am I kidding? I stay hard. Just the thought of her gets me hard. And when my mind goes *there*, to that night, well, my cock turns to granite. With each passing day, my control is slipping. I know that I need to decide. Either she's mine, or I need to shut this down.

Luckily for me, I have the house to myself tonight. Joey went to the game with her best friend, Taylor and afterwards they decided to do some shopping and have dinner. She's been gone for hours, yet I can still smell her. It doesn't matter which room of the house I'm in. There is a constant reminder of her. Hell, even sitting out here reminds me of her. I can see us in the pool, her tight nipples pressing against my chest through the thin fabric of her bikini.

And then there are the notes. They get hotter and sexier, and they do nothing to quench my desire for her. Leaning over, I grab the small notebook and pen I brought out with me. Her latest note is lying loosely between the pages. Pulling it out, I use the light from the firepit to read it once again. Before I can get past the first line, the sliding glass door opens, and Joey steps out onto the deck.

"Hi," she says shyly.

"Hi." Placing her note back inside the notebook, I toss it to the ground, the pen going with it, and I move over. "Have a seat." I tap the lounger next to me for her to sit. She kicks off her sandals and climbs next to me. I waste no time wrapping my arm around her and pulling her close.

"How was shopping?"

"Good. It's been a while since Taylor and I just spent an entire day together."

"Did you eat?"

"Yeah, we stopped on the way home." She lifts her head to look at me. "Did you eat?"

"I had some leftovers from last night."

"What did you do today?"

"After the game, I showered and took a nap."

"I thought you were going with Caleb."

"Nah. Not much on going out these days."

"I've noticed. Is there a reason?"

"There's this girl."

"You've met someone?" There is a wobble in her voice. Surely, she knows I'm talking about her.

"Yeah, I've met someone," I say, running my fingers through her hair.

"Do I know her?"

"She's all sunshine."

"Oh, a blonde then."

"Nah, my girl's a brunette with chocolate brown eyes. They sparkle when she's happy or excited." She doesn't say anything to that, and that's okay. I'm content to just hold her in my arms and stare up at the night sky. I know without a doubt this is better than anything Caleb and the guys are getting into.

My eyes grow heavy as the heat from her body seeps into mine. She's finally where she belongs, and my body recognizes that. I need sleep. I'm just about there when a ringing phone has my eyes jolting awake.

"It's mine," she says, digging her phone out of her back pocket. I glance at the screen like the nosy bastard I am and see Caleb's name. "Hello."

"Joey, it's me." Caleb screams so loud I can hear him. "Sorry, it's loud. Can you hear me?" he yells again.

"I can hear you. Where are you?"

"At the club. I just wanted to let you know that I won't be home tonight. I will be back in the afternoon."

"Be safe, and stay out of trouble," she tells him.

"Don't worry about me."

"Don't you have to be at the field tomorrow?" she asks him.

"Nah, Coach gave us the day off."

"Okay."

"Are you home?" he asks.

"Yeah, I just got in."

"Is Brock there?"

"Yes." I reply.

"Good. Let him know he's missing out, will ya?" He laughs. "Gotta go. I'll see you tomorrow."

"Bye," she says, but he's already hung up. "I take it you heard all of that?"

"Yeah, kind of hard not to. I hope they stay out of trouble."

"You and me both," she says, shivering.

"You cold?"

"A little."

"Let's go inside." She stands, and I lean over to grab my notebook. Not because I need it, but because tucked within the pages is a note from her. I've kept every one of them. I walk behind her into the house. She smiles at me over her shoulder and makes her way upstairs. Knowing we're both in for the night, I make sure the back door is locked and the front too before setting the alarm and turning off the lights.

Her door is shut, and I'm tempted to go to her, but she shut it for a reason. She knows it's just the two of us until tomorrow afternoon. So, if she wanted me, she'd have left it open. I try not to be salty about it as I step into my room. The room is dark, but I know my way by now. I head for the nightstand to place my notebook inside. I'm hoping I can get just a few hours' sleep now that she's home and after holding her in my arms.

I strip down to my boxer briefs and turn to climb in bed, and that's when I see her in my bed. "Joey?"

"Is this okay?" she asks hesitantly.

"More than okay," I say, sliding under the covers next to her. She moves closer, settling her head on my chest, and I take full advantage of having her here and wrap my arm around her, holding her close. We're both quiet, but I know she can feel my heart pounding in my chest. She has to. The rapid beat tells me there is no shutting this down. I can't fight this pull she has over me. It's more than just desire.

It's deeper.

Pressing my lips to the top of her head, my body relaxes into the mattress. I close my eyes, willing myself to be a gentleman and go to sleep, while keeping my hands off her. I need to sleep.

"Brock?"

"Yeah, Sunshine?"

"Tell me a story."

"Once upon a time," I say automatically, "there was a man who had his world turned upside from his career. He called his best friend, and his friend offered him a place to stay. Little did the man know that his best friend's sister was going to show up while he was staying there. The sister, she's the most beautiful woman he's ever laid eyes on. As the weeks pass by, the man tries to hide his attraction to her, but it grows by leaps and bounds every day." I pause, getting lost in my own thoughts about Joey and the time I've spent with her since I've been here.

"Keep going," she urges.

"The man, he's torn. He knows that she's supposed to be off-limits, but they share a connection he's never felt before. He struggles with the fact that he could lose his best friend, and maybe even the woman if things go bad."

She wraps her arm around my waist and squeezes. "More."

"The more time he spends with her, the more he realizes that it's not enough. He worries that no amount of time spent with her will ever be enough."

We lie here in complete silence for I don't know how long. I assume she's just as lost in her thoughts as I am. She's not sleeping; instead, she's making lazy circles on my chest with her fingers, and I, well, I can't stop running my hands through her silky strands. I'm exhausted, but I don't want to miss a moment of this time I have alone with her.

Her hand starts to travel south, and my cock turns hard as stone, just waiting for her. She slides her hand over my underwear and sucks in a breath. I won't apologize for my body's reaction to her.

"Joey?"

"Yeah?"

"Tell me a story." It's the first thing I can think of. It's how we communicate, and I need to know what she's thinking.

"Once upon a time, there was a girl. She was having a rough time and needed to get away, so she went to stay with her brother. When she got there, she realized she wasn't the only one who was there." She pauses, running her hand over my cock, driving me crazy. "Her brother's best friend needed a place to stay too. As weeks passed on, the two became close. The man, he made her feel sexy and wanted and beautiful. She'd never really felt that way before."

"More," I say when she stops talking.

"The girl, she found herself in a situation. One that she fought at first, but now, now she can't remember why. You see, the girl started falling for her brother's best friend. Now, she craves him, and she's not quite sure what she should do about it."

She lifts her head to look at me. The soft glow of the moon shining through the window gives me just enough light to make out her silhouette. "I don't know where we go from here."

"Tell me what you want."

"I want you."

"Then you'll have me."

"What about Caleb?" I can hear the concern in her voice. "I don't really care what my dad thinks, even though he is your coach."

"I tried to fight this, Sunshine. Truly, I tried, but I can't. It's not possible. I can't stop wanting you. I'd like to think that he will understand that."

"I don't think we should tell him."

"What?"

"I mean, what if this is just an itch we both need to scratch? There's no point in ruining a long-time friendship for an itch."

"Do you think that's what this is?" I ask her. If I thought my heart was hammering in my chest before, it's a jackhammer now.

"I don't know. I know you don't really do relationships, so…" Her voice trails off.

"I've never done relationships because I've never met someone I wanted to be in one with. You're different."

"How do you know?"

"I know because I can't sleep at night, too busy thinking about you just down the hall. I can't go a single second without thinking about you, and I can't control my body's reaction to you. Can you feel my heart racing? Do you feel how hard I am for you? Those two things, they're out of my control."

"Your cock is hard because I'm lying on you and touching you. As far as your heart racing, there's the fear of getting caught, of losing the friendship that you have with Caleb."

"No. It's not that. I promise you. It's you. It's the thought of you, the smell of your skin, your laugh, your smile. It's you, Joey. You do this to me."

"I still think we should see what this really is before we tell him."

"What do you want this to be? What do you want us to be?"

"I'd rather we see how things turn out together."

"You can talk to me," I tell her. "Tell me how you feel. Tell me what you want. This isn't just about me, Sunshine. It's about both of us."

"And that's precisely why I want us to find out together. We keep it just between us for now and see how it goes."

"If he finds out before we have a chance to tell him, it's going to be worse."

"Then we need to make sure he doesn't find out. We've done okay with that so far." I'm not going to lie, I'm disappointed. I'm not looking forward to telling my best friend that his little sister owns me, but lying to him is even more unappealing. However, she's not ready, and I can wait for her.

"We have," I agree. "But that was before I got the chance to hold you in my arms and fall asleep. That was before I got to wake up next to you the same way."

"You haven't done those things," she reminds me.

"Not yet, but we're changing that tonight."

"Oh, we are, are we?"

"Yes. I'm exhausted. I don't sleep at night, and I can't stop thinking about going to you. Will I find you touching yourself, or will you be sound asleep? It literally keeps me up at night."

"Is that why you look so tired? You haven't been sleeping? I'm sorry."

"You have nothing to be sorry for."

"Maybe I can help you fall asleep."

"Just being here, letting me hold you, that's enough for me to fall asleep."

"Maybe, and you can have that too, but I have a better idea." The next thing I know, she's moving to the foot of the bed and settling between my thighs. I open for her because when the woman of your dreams moves to place her head next to your dick, you do what you have to do to make her more comfortable.

"Lift," she says, pulling at the waistband of my boxer briefs and pulling them over my ass and down my thighs. Her eyes are hungry, and my body shivers at the thought of her mouth on me. While I can't control my physical response to her, I can't seem to control the vise that her tiny hands seem to have wrapped around my heart either.

"You don't have to do this." Her answer is to take the head of my cock into her hot wet mouth. "Fuck," I moan. With each bob of her head, she takes more of me. I grip the sheets to keep from burying my hands in her hair and fucking her mouth. This is her show, and I'm going to let her dictate the ending. Even if it kills me.

She doesn't stop. With each stroke of her hand on my cock her mouth takes me deeper. It's a feeling, unlike anything I've ever felt before. I've had my fair share of blow jobs, and this one is by far the best of my life. I'm smart enough to know it has everything to do with the woman giving it to me.

Not able to take it, I move my hands to her hair. I bury them there, but nothing more. I just need to touch her. I don't push her, letting her keep her pace. "Baby, you have to stop," I tell her as tingles begin to race up my spine. She doesn't stop; in fact, it feels like she doubles her efforts, and her head bobs a little faster, and the jerk of her hand picks up speed. I tap her on the shoulder, warning her that it's time. "Jo—" I pant, not able to get her name past my lips. "Fuck!" I roar as I shoot down her throat. She doesn't move, taking everything I'm giving her.

When she finally moves up my body, I flip her over, holding my weight off her. "My turn." That's the only warning I give her before I'm stripping her naked, and moving my head between her thighs, tossing her legs over my shoulders. With the first swipe of my tongue against her clit, her back arches off the bed, and she cries out my name.

One hand snakes up her body, tweaking her nipple, while I use the other to guide my fingers inside her.

I once thought that when I got her in my bed, I'd take my time with her, but my mouth is frantic, and my hands are relentless in my pursuit of her pleasure. I want to give her what she gave me. I want her to give me her orgasm, and then I'm going to hold her in my arms, and we're going to sleep. When we wake up tomorrow, we can talk more about this and decide what's next. However, tonight, I'm going to devour her pussy until she gives me all she has to give.

"Brock," she pants. "I-I'm so close."

I nip at her clit before sucking it into my mouth, moaning as I do. She arches into me. A moan from somewhere deep inside her fills the room. Her walls clamp around my fingers; she's close. When her hands bury in my hair, and her legs lock around my head like a vise, I know she's there. She calls out my name as I swallow everything her body has to give.

When she's no longer writhing beneath me, I move next to her, pulling her into my arms. Her back is to my front, and I curl my body around hers. Slowly, our breathing evens out, and I can feel sleep settling in. "Goodnight, Sunshine," I whisper, before falling into a deep sleep.

CHAPTER
TWELVE

Joey

I can feel Brock's fingers between my legs, slowly inching their way to where I'm swollen and wet. My thighs automatically spread for him. He brushes his lips over my bare shoulder just as he grazes across my clit. "I'm not sure I'll ever get enough of touching you, Sunshine," he whispers against my ear before nipping at the lobe.

He pushes two fingers inside me. I'm already close, the memories of his mouth on me last night so vivid, even in this dream. And what a glorious dream it is.

My body tightens around his big fingers as he buries them completely inside me. His mouth trails kisses over my skin, his teeth digging into my flesh. His cock presses against my back, hard and heavy with his own desire. Dream Brock is just as big, just as needy as the real man I fell asleep with last night.

I want him just as badly.

My back arches as need floods my veins. I rock my hips, riding his hand. My orgasm is just within reach. I'm so close. It's so real, so perfect, so...

"I love feeling you clamp down on me like this. It's the moment I know you're so close to coming. It drives me wild."

I blink open my eyes, recognizing the walls around me as those of the other guest bedroom. The one Brock is using. The one I crept into last night before he came to bed, only to find me there, waiting.

Realization sets in. Dream Brock and Real Brock are one and the same, but right now, I'm unable to dwell on it. Expert fingers are picking up speed, pushing me closer to release. My ass grinds against his hard length, making him grunt as he flexes forward. Using his palm, he presses against my clit, causing me to detonate like a bomb. Stars burst behind my eyelids as I rock against his hand and grind my ass against him. Brock bites down on my shoulder, pistoning his hips and finding his own release against my back.

He slows his fingers, though doesn't completely remove them. "Next time, it won't be my fingers I slide inside of your wet pussy, Sunshine."

I suck in deep breaths, trying to slow my racing heart. "Why wait?"

Brock's deep chuckle tickles my ears. "Soon, Joey. Very soon." This time, he does pull his fingers from my body and kisses the place on my shoulder he just bit. "Shit, I think I left a mark," he adds, remorse evident in his voice.

I glance at the slightly reddened skin before meeting his gaze. "I liked it."

"I'm sorry," he whispers, placing another tender kiss on my shoulder.

"I'm not."

Finally, he relaxes the worried lines between his eyebrows. "I think we made a mess," he mumbles.

"We? I think that was all you, buddy. Actually, I thought I was dreaming at first," I confess.

"Yeah? You often have dreams about me fingering you and making you come?"

My blush says it all. "Maybe," I reply coyly.

Brock chuckles and lightly slaps me on the ass. "How about you jump in the shower, and I'll start a load of laundry? As much as I hate to wash your scent off my sheets, they're a little soiled," he says, glancing down at the mess he made.

The vixen inside me, I didn't even realize I possessed, glances over my shoulder and murmurs, "You know, I'm pretty soiled too. You should probably join me and help me wash up."

He throws his head back and laughs. "I would, but you and I both know we'd never leave that shower. Besides, I have plans for us today," he replies, climbing from the bed and using the sheet to wipe off his stomach.

"Plans? What kind of plans?"

"The kind that are a surprise. So get up, get dressed, preferably in something that covers you from head to toe so I'm not tempted to stray the course and just bring you back here to ravish, and meet me downstairs when you're ready. I'm going to start laundry and coffee."

He places a hard kiss against my lips as he helps me stand, wiping my back with the sheet before tossing it on the floor. Once he has the bedding gathered, he heads out, leaving me standing naked in his room.

I slip into his bathroom, even though I should just head to my own. The thought of using his shampoo and bodywash is thrilling, almost dangerous. Will someone be able to smell it on my skin? Will Brock?

After a quick shower, I wrap my body in one of the big fluffy towels I insisted Caleb buy, and make my way to my room. I'm saddened to find Brock's room empty, only because I have this wild daydream of walking out and finding him waiting for me. You know, so I can drop the towel.

But that doesn't happen.

Inside my room, I dress quickly in comfortable shorts and a fitted tee and pull my hair up in a wet ponytail. I swipe a little mascara over my lashes, brush my teeth, and grab my comfortable sneakers.

When I reach the kitchen, I'm shocked to find Brock standing there, sipping coffee, and fresh from the shower. He's wearing shorts, a comfy T-shirt, sneakers, and a ballcap on his head. Once he sees me just staring, he pours me a cup of coffee into a travel mug, leaving plenty of room for creamer. "Everything all right?"

I grab the creamer from the refrigerator and meet him at the counter. "I'm just a little surprised to see you already showered."

He shrugs. "I just got down here. When I heard you finish, I slipped into my room and took a quick one myself."

I stop pouring and glance up. "You didn't join me?" There's a tinge of hurt in my voice, one I can't hide.

Brock just grins that gorgeous smile. "If I would have joined you, we wouldn't be down here right now." He picks at a piece of fuzz from my shirt and steps closer, the fresh scent of his bodywash invading my senses. "We'd be upstairs, with no plans to leave the bed for a very, *very* long time."

A little breathlessly, I whisper, "I still don't see the problem."

He snickers and grabs his cup, bringing it to his lips. "Oh, Sunshine. You're going to be the death of me." He polishes off most of his coffee before dumping what's left in the sink. "Let's go. We have somewhere to be."

———

"The zoo?" I ask thirty minutes later, as we pull into the large lot.

"Have you ever been here?" he asks, finding a parking spot about halfway to the front entrance.

I shake my head as bubbles of eager anticipation rise in my chest. "I've always wanted to come, but Caleb always said it wouldn't be enjoyable because he'd be recognized the entire time," I reply, remembering the disappointment I felt each time he told me no.

And my brother rarely tells me no. In fact, it's usually the opposite. But when it comes to us being in large public places together, he's always shied away from the chance of being thrust into the spotlight because he knew I hated it.

"That's why I brought my super-secret disguise with me," Brock replies, pulling his hat down a little lower and offering me a big smile.

"Well, you're going to have to tone down the grin then, Bond, because it gives you away immediately."

"Figures," he states, reaching for his door handle. "Ready?"

I nod with enthusiasm, making him chuckle. When we meet at the trunk of his fancy sports car, he takes my hand and leads me toward the gate. "Are you worried?" I ask, unable to keep from saying the question.

"About?"

"Being recognized."

He stops, well before the short line gaining entrance into the zoo. "No. And if I am, I'll deal with it. Right now, I just want to spend some time with you, getting to know you better. All the rest we can deal with later."

I want to argue. The chances of being recognized are pretty great, even with his ballcap. He's Brock Williams, for heaven's sake. Everyone who knows anything about football knows who he is. He's one of the top Google searches, as fans—well, mostly women—search for those Tommy underwear ads he did a couple of years back. They leave little to the imagination. I would know. I may have searched them out recently too.

"Come on, Sunshine. Let's go enjoy the day."

When we reach the front of the line, Brock hands over cash and takes our two entrance tickets. He doesn't talk but nods his appreciation as we move to the brief security line, which will check my bag. Once that's complete, we step inside and take in the chaotic scene.

Families are everywhere, taking photos of their kids in front of the signs, the fountain, and the exhibit entrances. I can't help but smile. Even though it's a little noisy, it feels completely natural and normal to be surrounded by such madness.

"What do you want to see first?" he asks, drawing my attention toward a large zoo map behind plexiglass.

"I'm not picky," I tell him, reaching down and taking his hand in my own.

Brock nods, a slight smile playing on his lips, as he brings our hands to his lips and kisses my knuckles. "Then let's just wander."

Together, we head for the first path we come to, which happens to lead us to a few of the larger animal exhibits. We stop and take in the zebras, elephants, and rhinos before moving toward the monkey house. He holds open the door, letting me slip inside to the noisy exhibit. Just as the door starts to close, Brock pulls me back against his chest, barely avoiding being run into by two rowdy boys.

"Sorry!" the first one yells as they dart by, exiting the monkey house with a flurry.

"I'm so sorry!" the frazzled mom hollers as she practically runs by, trying to catch up to her kids.

"That was a close one," Brock mutters against my ear, the warmth of his breath fanning across my skin.

I slowly turn in his arms and wrap them around his neck, going up on my tiptoes and kissing his lips. "My hero."

He snorts. "Well, if that's all it takes, I'll save you from screaming, running kids anytime, sweetness." He returns my kiss but keeps it from progressing any farther. Considering we're in public, it's probably for the best.

We continue to hold hands as we walk through the monkey house, identifying as many varieties as we can, with the help of the signs and photos. A few times, I glance at someone and find them staring at us with question in their eyes. As if they're trying to place either him or me, and every time, we just walk away and find something else to see.

Eventually, we make our way toward the area where they keep lions, tigers, and bears. "Did you know bears are one of the most intelligent land animals in North America?" Brock says, as we stroll past the enclosure with two brown bears.

"Really?"

He nods. "They have the largest and most complex brains, in comparison to other land mammals their size."

I stop and offer him a grin. "How do you know that?"

He shrugs, bringing my hand back up to his mouth. "I had to do an oral report on the bear in junior high. It stuck with me."

Stepping forward, I wrap my arms around his waist and rest my face against his chest. "What else do you know about bears?"

"Grizzly bears have a biting force of like 1200 PSI, which is strong enough to crush a bowling ball," he says, resting his arms on my lower back and holding me close.

"Yeah?"

"True story."

We stand here for several long seconds, just wrapped in each other's arms, before separating and continuing through the enclosure. Before we reach the end, a young boy walks up to us. "Excuse me," he says quietly. "Are you Brock Williams?"

A flash of panic crosses Brock's face before he schools all his features. "Me? No way, man."

"You're not? Wow, you look just like him!"

Brock snickers. "Yeah, I hear that a lot."

The young boy's features fall as he slowly turns around. "Darn it. I thought I was meeting my favorite player ever!"

Something flashes in Brock's eyes. "Hey, what's your name?" he asks, crouching down to look at the young boy in the eye.

"Stephen."

"How old are you, Stephen?"

"Ten."

"Well, Stephen, what if I let you in on a little secret?" When the boy eagerly nods, Brock glances around before whispering, "I'm Brock."

His face lights up with pure excitement. "You are?"

"I am."

Confused, he asks, "Why did you tell me you weren't him?"

Brock leans in. "Well, my friend and I were trying to go unrecognized today, but I should have known a big fan like you would realize it was me."

Stephen nods eagerly. "I am a big fan. Big, big fan."

"Well, it was nice to meet you, Stephen."

The boy's eyes are so wide, it's almost comical. "I won't tell anyone I saw you, okay?"

"I appreciate it, Stephen. Hey, do you have something you want me to write on?" he asks, pulling a pen out of his pocket. When the boy produces a napkin with a smear of mustard across it, Brock flips it over and signs his name, adding a personal note to Stephen before handing it back.

"Thank you so much, Mr. Williams. I'll keep this forever," the boy insists.

"Stephen, get over here!" a man hollers from across the enclosure.

"That's my dad, so I better get back over there."

"It was nice to meet you, Stephen."

The child gives him a toothy grin before taking off to where his family waits. When he reaches his dad, he holds up the autograph proudly, the dad's surprised as he glances over to where we stand. Brock waves before taking my hand and leading me away.

"That was sweet of you. Why did you tell him who you were?"

Brock shrugs, linking our fingers together. "When I was a kid, I would have killed to meet some of my favorite athletes. It hit me, while I was telling him I wasn't the person he thought I was, that could have very well happened to me. How sad would I have been if someone I had idolized did that? Even if I don't always want to be recognized, the fact is... I *am* Brock Williams, and I owe it to my young fans to acknowledge them, even on the bad days. They buy my posters, jerseys, and whatnot. They deserve for me to be me."

I smile, gazing up at this incredible man. "You're pretty great, you know that, Brock Williams?"

"Great enough to earn a kiss?" he asks, waggling his eyebrows suggestively.

"Of course." I go up on my tiptoes and press my lips to his.

The kiss is too short, much like I feel they all are at this point, as he pulls back and grins down at me. "Ready to finish our visit?"

"Ready," I confirm, tucking in close to his side and walking down the path.

To where?

I have no clue.

But having him at my side just feels right.

I pray this sensation never goes away.

CHAPTER
THIRTEEN

BROCK

The locker room is loud as hell as my teammates celebrate our second regular season win. We're off to a great start, and the guys are pumped.

"Hotel bar is going to be lit tonight!" Jones says, thrusting his hand in the air. He's buck-ass naked as he declares the plans for tonight.

I shake my head and make my way to the showers. I rush through the process. I'm ready to get to my room, order room service, and call my girl. I have to bite back the smile that wants to break free anytime I think about Joey. She's been "mine" officially for a week now, and although I have to sneak time with her, I wouldn't change it for the world.

In fact, the more time that I spend with her, the harder I fall. We need to talk to Caleb because things between us aren't changing anytime soon. The thought of her no longer being in my life has fear making its way up my spine. Letting Joey go isn't something I'm able to do. Not yet, hell, maybe not ever.

"Where's the fire?" Caleb asks as I rush to shove my shit into my bag.

"What?" I turn to look at him before returning to my task.

"You good, man?" he asks.

No. I need your sister. "Yeah. Just exhausted. Ready for food and sleep." It's not a complete lie, but my real hurry is Joey. She didn't travel to the game, and I miss her something crazy. I need to hear her voice and see her smile.

"You're bailing on drinks again?" he asks, the surprise evident in his voice. "You skipped out last weekend."

"Not feeling it."

"Since when are *you* not feeling it?" he asks.

That's the trouble with best friends, they know you, and it's hard to keep anything from them. I'm not a huge partier, but having a drink with the guys after a game, no matter the loss or win, is something I've never passed up. At least when he finds out about us, he'll see I've changed. That Joey has changed me.

"Now that I think about it, you're not hooking up unless you are being super stealth about it. I know you don't brag about your bedroom activities, but even when we go out, I don't see you chatting up the ladies. What's going on?" He tilts his head to the side, studying me.

For the first time in my life, I'm about to lie to my best friend. I've never lied to him, never kept my truths from him, but I'm about to. For her. The woman I love trumps him every time.

Wait.

What?

The woman I love?

Flashes of our time together filter through my mind, and yeah, I'm in love with her. For the second time in a matter of minutes, I have to bite back my smile. "Just getting used to the new team and all that."

"What better way to get used to the team than to have a drink with the team?" he asks.

Fuck. He's got me there. "Fine," I grumble. I don't see any other way out of this mess.

"My man." He claps me on the shoulder and heads to the shower. Grabbing my phone, I text Joey.

. . .

Me: Caleb's asking questions.

Joey: About us?

Me: No. But he's calling me out for skipping drinks and going straight to my room.

Joey: Oh.

Me: It was either tell him about us or agree to go.

Joey: You need to bond with your team.

Me: I bond with them at practice and games. What I need is you. To see your face and to hear your voice.

Me: Sunshine?

Joey: Give me a minute. I'm busy swooning here.

Me: I miss you.

Joey: I miss you too, big guy. I'll see you when you get home tomorrow.

. . .

Me: Too long.

Joey: Have a good night.

Me: I don't like this.

Joey: It's one night.

Me: One night too long.

Joey: Go celebrate a great game.

Me: You watched?

Joey: Always do.

Me: I'll text you later.

Joey: Have fun.

Caleb appears next to me. "Who are you texting?"

"Just checking in with Mom."

"How is she?"

"Good," I say, guilt churning in my gut. "She said good game." I might as well twist the knife of lies and guilt a little deeper.

Caleb grins. "We kicked ass." He drops his towel and gets dressed.

I avoid eye contact as I pretend to check my emails while he finishes changing.

"Ready?" he asks a few minutes later.

"Let's do it." I stand and follow him out of the locker room. It's not that I don't want to hang out with my teammates. It's that I want to see her and hear her voice more. I'm slowly becoming addicted. It could be something to do with the "I'm in love with her" revelation I came to not minutes ago. I've never been in love, never wanted to spend every waking moment with a woman. Usually, it's shared pleasure, and we go our separate ways. With Joey, it's different. I never want to be away from her.

Ever.

The last few days have about killed me. I don't like leaving her alone. At least when we have home games, I know she's in the stands watching. Yeah, I've got it bad.

"Damn," Jones says, digging his elbow into my side. "Hottie at three o'clock can't take her eyes off you."

I tip the beer bottle to my lips and take a long pull, not bothering to look to my right. There's no point. I know it's not going to be my Joey standing there.

"Here she comes, my man," Caleb says, keeping his voice low. "Watch the master in action." He nods at me.

I try not to take offense to his words because they are true. They *were* true. I've been told my dark hair, blue eyes, and killer smile is a panty dropper. I've always had a way with the ladies and never regretted enjoying the company they provided, at least not until this minute—my stomach rolls at the thought of touching someone who is not Joey. What's worse is that I'm going to have to turn her down in front of my teammates. In front of my best friend. If he didn't think something was up before, he's going to know now.

And I can't tell him.

I know the exact moment the leggy blonde reaches my side, not because of the attraction but because of the panic. Having her so close is wrong. I don't want her next to me. Hell, I don't want her or any other woman who is not Joey next to me.

"Hey, handsome," she says, resting her hand on my arm.

I finish swallowing back my beer and set the bottle on the table. Slowly I turn to look at her, giving her a not interested look. I glance down to where her hand, which has some viper-looking bloodred nails, still rests on my arm. "Not interested." I hear the shock of my teammates, but I ignore them, taking another drink.

"Are you sure about that? You seem stressed. I can make that all go away," she rasps. Her voice sounds like she's smoked one too many packs of cigarettes. Her hand moves up my arm, and I've had enough.

Abruptly, I stand and take a step back from the table. "I'm out." Reaching into my back pocket, I pull out a wad of cash and toss it on the table. I don't make eye contact with my teammates. Instead, I turn and stalk out of the hotel bar and toward the elevator. My body is shaking from anger. I knew better than to go. My reputation is going to make me lose the best fucking thing that's ever happened to me.

As soon as I step into my room, my phone is to my ear, and to my relief, she picks up on the first ring.

"Brock?"

"Sunshine," I breathe, already feeling lighter at just the sound of her voice.

"What's wrong?" When mine is full of panic, hers is full of concern.

"There was a woman."

"Okay." Her tone doesn't change. She's giving nothing away.

"She laid her hand on my arm."

"Okay." The same one-word reply that still tells me jack shit of how she's feeling.

"I didn't like it."

There is silence on the other end of the phone, and then it's her soft laughter filling my ear. "Is there any more to this story?" she asks.

I go on to tell her about the locker room, and the guilt Caleb threw on me, and then the woman from the bar. "I promise you I don't want her. I don't want anyone's hands on me but yours." There's no humor in my voice, even though I can hear it in hers.

The woman tonight freaked me the hell out. One, it's new for me not to give a fuck about the random football groupies. I knew I wasn't interested, but for me to react as I did, that's a big fucking deal, and I know I'm going to have my best friend to answer to. Speaking of, I get a text and pull my phone from my ear. I hit the speakerphone button and open his message, not wanting to miss a second of my call with Joey.

Caleb: You good, man?

Me: Yeah. Just tired. Calling it a night.

I know I have some explaining to do, and I don't know what I'm going to say. I can play the exhaustion card, but that's not going to continue to work. I just hope that Joey decides we can tell him. Soon. I don't know how much longer I can keep this up. The lies are harder to come by when all I want to tell him is that I'm madly in love with his little sister. Sure, that's also a new development, but it's one I'll gladly latch on to.

"Hang up. I'll call you right back." She catches me off guard.

"Jo—" I start, but the line goes dead. "Fuck." Sitting on the edge of the bed, I grip my phone in one hand, waiting for her call, while my other grips my hair. "She's pissed, and I need to be there. I can't—" I start, but before I can finish my thought, my phone rings, and it's a video call from Joey. I fumble with my phone to hit the green button. "Sunshine."

"I wanted to see you." She shrugs.

"I'm sorry," I mutter.

"Hey." Her eyes soften. "You didn't do anything wrong."

"I let her touch me."

"Brock." She smiles. "She put her hand on your arm."

"She's not you."

"I trust you. We have to have that trust with your job."

"I know. I just hate sneaking around. I hate that you're not here with me. I hate that it's been days since I've held you and kissed your lips."

"This is our reality."

"No. If you were mine openly, I'd bring you with me."

"That's not feasible."

"The hell it's not." I say.

"A waste of money."

"No." I shake my head. "It's worth every cent in my bank account."

That earns me another one of her beautiful smiles. The one that lights up her face. "Now you're just talking crazy."

"We have to tell him, Sunshine."

"I know. Just a little longer."

"Okay, baby. If that's what you want." I hate lying to him, but I can't say no to her.

"Were you sleeping?" I ask when I finally calm down to notice she's in bed.

"Just reading." She pulls the phone away, and I can see she's wearing a Ramblers T-shirt.

"Is that mine?"

She points to her chest. "We're both yours."

I can only imagine what my face looks like. Cartoon heart eyes and a gigantic red heart is pulsing in and out of my chest. I swallow thickly as I take in her smile. "This is real—you and me. I'm not just passing the time or playing around. You're important to me." *I love you.* "I want you. Not just for a few days or weeks—" I pause, collecting my thoughts. I'm afraid if I tell her forever, it will scare her away, and I can't have that. "You're mine, Josephine Grace Henderson."

"Are you mine? You're staking your claim. I've told you that I'm yours, but are you mine, Brock?" she challenges.

She knows damn good and well that I'm hers. My girl just wants to hear me say it. "Every piece of me," I tell her. "All that I am is yours."

"Careful, Williams, I might make you fall in love with me." She grins.

I open my mouth to tell her it's too late, but she moves around, dropping her phone. When she reappears on the screen, she's snuggled under the blankets, her glasses no longer perched on her nose.

"You tired?" I ask her.

"Yeah."

"I'll let you go." I say the words reluctantly. I could talk to her all night, but if she's tired, I want her to get her rest. I wonder if it sounds creepy to ask her to just prop the phone up next to her so I can watch her sleep?

"Brock?"

"Yeah, baby?"

"Tell me a story."

My grin takes over my face. Cartoon heart eyes, and big flashy grins, that's what this girl does to me. My girl wants a story, a story she'll get.

"Once upon a time, there was a man. He worked hard for his career, one that was demanding and required a lot of travel. He didn't mind it. He loved it, in fact. That was until suddenly, one day, every-thing changed. It was a gradual change; one he didn't see coming. He met a woman. A woman who made him see the world with fresh eyes. One day the man kissed her, and he knew."

I pause. Her eyes are closed, and I think she's asleep. I take a minute to stare at her like a fucking creeper, but I can't seem to end the call. Not when it gives me the opportunity to get my fill of her.

Slowly her eyes open and lock on mine. "What did he know?"

It takes me a minute to realize she's talking about the story. "He knew that she was going to change his life."

"I was wrong before," she says, her voice low.

"About what?" I ask, my voice just as small.

"You might just make me fall in love with you."

My fucking heart stops. I rub my hand over my chest before reply-ing, "That's the plan, Sunshine."

She smiles. "Night, Brock. Safe flight," she says, covering a yawn.

"Goodnight."

She blows me a kiss, and I do the same, and then the call ends. Plugging my phone in, I stand and make sure the door is locked, turning off the lights. I strip out of my clothes until I'm in nothing but my boxer briefs and climb under the covers. What started as a shit night ended with my girl, and she makes everything better. It's her big brown eyes I see when I close mine.

CHAPTER
FOURTEEN

Joey

A smile breaks out on my face the moment the front door opens and closes. It feels like forever since I've seen him, even though we talked late last night after he got back to his hotel. I've missed him terribly, having become used to him being somewhere nearby. Now, he's home, which makes me incredibly happy, even if I know it'll be somewhat short-lived.

They have another away game next, but this one is even more special. Monday night, live on the biggest sports channel, Kansas City takes on Brock's former team the Chicago Thunder back in the Windy City.

I have yet to go to an away game, even though we thought I was going a few weeks back during preseason. Taylor had a work thing come up, so she had to back out, and I just didn't want to go alone. I actually used that weekend to finalize some of my affairs back in Springfield. I still need to have that conversation with Caleb, but I was able to put him off a little bit, claiming to be working remotely. Plus, it helps he's pretty busy now the season is underway and has no clue what I do during the day.

But now isn't the time for that. My focus is on Brock and next weekend. I plan to fly in Sunday morning, spend the day touring some of the city's biggest sights, and then going to the game Monday. In fact, I'm more eager to go alone than ever. Going solo means I can slip in and out of Brock's room a little easier.

And that's my plan.

We've been dancing around sex for weeks. Hell, he's made me come with his hands and very talented tongue more times than I can count, but we haven't actually gone all the way yet. But that's all about to change. I'm going to Chicago and have big plans for us post-game. Plans that involve no clothes, room service, and a whole box of condoms.

I can't wait.

"Joey?" my brother hollers as he makes his way to the kitchen where I am.

"Hey! Welcome home," I sing, though my excitement falls the moment I see his face. "What's wrong?"

Brock follows behind Caleb, mouthing a quick "I'm sorry."

Sorry? For what?

Panic starts to set in. Did he tell Caleb about us? Did something happen on the plane home? Or worse, after we hung up late last night?

"I got a phone call this morning before the plane took off," Caleb starts, standing in front of me, arms crossed over his chest.

"Okay," I reply, not really sure why he seems so pissed off.

"It was from Debby in Human Resources at Johnson."

That catches my attention. My blood runs cold. Why would Debby be calling Caleb? "What did she want?" I ask, trying to sound casual, but certain I'm failing.

His face is clearly skeptical. "She said she sent a courier with a small box of personal effects they found in your office, or should I say, *former office*, but you didn't live at that address anymore."

I sigh, wishing I didn't have to get into this conversation now, but there's no way around it. I steal a quick glance over my brother's shoulder and see Brock standing there, watching and listening intently.

"What the hell is going on, Joey? You quit your job? When? Why?"

I plop down in the first chair I come to and take a deep breath.

Meeting my brother's intense gaze, I answer, "Right before I came here."

"Came here? As in last month?" He seems genuinely perplexed. "I don't understand."

I close my eyes, picturing the scene I've spent weeks trying to forget. The inappropriate touching, the feel of his body pressed against mine, the forced kiss that caused me to stumble. "I don't work at Johnson anymore," I reply lamely, unable to meet his eyes.

"Why?" he asks, genuinely confused. "You loved that job."

I finally look up and nod, keeping my eyes trained only on his. "Yeah, I did. But something happened."

He comes over and takes a seat across from me. "What happened?"

"I was working on a big pitch for a new online dating site. A few of us had been staying late all week, including Mr. Davis. It was all-hands-on-deck with the team I was on, so it wasn't a surprise when he asked me to meet him in his office when everyone else was heading out late on Friday night."

I can sense him tense before I see it. His soft eyes seem to harden almost immediately. "I'm not going to like this, am I?"

"He asked me to show him what we had so far, so I took the display boards over to his desk. He stepped aside while I laid the boards out and explained where we were at with the campaign. He stood next to me, so close his arm kept brushing against mine. When his hand grazed across my ass, I took a small step away. Only, he followed me, reaching out and touching my arm suggestively."

A growl erupts from the room, surprising me, especially since it didn't come from my brother. Sure, Caleb's eyes are hard with anger, but it's Brock that draws my attention. He's pacing across the kitchen, his hands in his hair, his eyes furious.

"Did he—" Caleb starts, but he can't seem to get the words out.

I quickly shake my head. "No. Nothing like that. When I stepped away again, he followed me. I asked him to kindly step back, and that's when he kissed me. He never grabbed me or hurt me, just pressed his lips to mine as if he had the right to do so. I jerked back, stumbling when my foot hit his garbage can, and fell down. He tried to help me up, but I wouldn't let him. He told me I was clumsy, laughed, and went back to the boards on his desk, as if the kiss didn't happen."

"Tell me you kicked that fucker in the balls and called the cops," my brother seethes.

When I shake my head, I can feel the disappointment rolling off him.

"Why not?" he demands. "That fucker touched you and kissed you. You could sue his ass for sexual assault and own that fucking company right now!"

I sigh, recalling how I agonized over what I should do that entire weekend before ultimately coming to the decision I did. "When I went in on Monday, he called me into his office. He basically told me no one would believe me if I went public with my accusation and if I valued my job, I'd get back to work and not say a word. When I went to my office, I packed up my personal belongings, sent human resources my resignation letter effective immediately, and left."

My brother slides his hands into his hair, his shoulders slumping forward. "I will ruin him."

"He tried to kiss me and then brush it off. There are so many worse things that happen in the world, Caleb. I don't want to cause problems. I don't want to be the focus of a lengthy legal battle. Besides, it's his word against mine, and he has deep pockets."

"I understand where you're coming from here, really I do, but we can't just let him get away with it. He needs to know what he did was wrong, and no one messes with my sister."

A small smile spreads across my face. "I appreciate that, but I've thought a lot about it, and I don't want to do anything. I want to move forward, Caleb. I don't want a scandal. I've had cameras in my face since the day I was born because of one. I refuse to drag myself into one now."

If anyone understands the shit I went through as a kid, it's my brother. He was right there in the mix. Except he wasn't the product of an affair, like me. "Promise me, Caleb. Promise me you won't do anything."

He sags against his chair. "Joey," he whines, clearly not wanting to agree.

"Please."

He looks completely defeated when he closes his eyes and sighs. "Fine." He clears his throat and asks, "So where's all your stuff? The lady said you moved."

"That first weekend you had the preseason away game, I went back and had a friend help me move my stuff into a storage unit. I turned in my keys and came back here. But really, I didn't have a lot. Most of the furniture stayed behind in that fancy place Dad insisted I live in when I started that job. I brought a few bags of clothes and personal things back here."

Caleb runs his hands over his face and exhales loudly. I risk a glance over his shoulder, and the intense look on Brock's face is startling. He looks completely angry, his face a little flushed and the tips of his ears red. When his gaze meets mine, he seems to relax a bit, but not much. Is he mad at me? Because I lied about my job and kept this from him?

"So, I guess that means you're staying here, huh?" Caleb flashes me a smile.

"I want to look for my own place. I don't expect you to put me up for long," I insist, but it falls on deaf ears.

"Bullshit. You can stay as long as you need to. Hell, you can just move in here if you want. It's just me, Joe. Well, me and Brock here, but like I've said before, you know I have plenty of room." Caleb gets up and grabs two bottles of water, handing the first one off to Brock, who is leaning against the counter with his arms crossed, just watching.

I flash my brother a wide grin. "You just want me to stay because I cook better than you," I tell him, getting up from the chair and walking around to where he stands.

He snorts out a laugh and throws his arm around my shoulders. "That's a nice bonus, I'll admit, but you know it's more than that." He meets my gaze. "It's always been you and me against the world."

I nod, my throat thick with emotions, as I wrap my arms around his chest and hug him tight. "Love you, Cay."

"Love you too, pipsqueak." He kisses the crown of my head before stepping back. "All right, I'm going up to unpack and shower. We've got a team workout in the morning and films and meetings all afternoon tomorrow."

"We can throw some burgers on the grill later," I tell him.

"Sounds good." Caleb turns to leave the kitchen, throwing Brock a fist bump on his way by.

The tension from earlier is now gone, but it's only replaced by a new form, and this one feels heavy on the sexual side. I turn to face Brock, truly acknowledging him for the first time since they arrived home. "How was your flight?"

Those piercing blue eyes just stare at me, deep and all-knowing, as if he can see all the way down to my soul. "It was shit, actually. I was worried about you."

With a deep exhale, I step up to where he stands, inhaling the familiar woodsy scent I will forever associate with Brock. There's a hesitancy as I place my hands on his chest and meet his gaze. "I'm sorry. I didn't mean to upset or worry you."

He reaches forward, wrapping his big hand around my back and pulling me into his embrace. "When Caleb got that call right before we boarded the plane, I didn't know what to think. My mind went to some pretty fucked-up places, but the reality may be worse. Knowing someone touched you, even just brushing against your arm, and then kissed you—" He shakes his head and closes his eyes. When he opens them, they blaze with fire, but it doesn't feel angry, nor directed at me. Brock rubs his thumb over my bottom lip as he whispers, "I don't like knowing someone else had their lips on yours, especially when it's not reciprocated."

I shudder out a breath. "I've been kissed before, Brock."

His growl is animalistic and possessive. "Of course you have, Sunshine. You're so beautiful and smart and funny, any guy would be lucky to get the chance to kiss you. Doesn't mean I like it though, or that it should be without your permission."

I wrap my hands around his shoulders and lean into his chest. "I get that, and I do agree. Do you think I like the thought of you kissing those thousands and thousands of women you've been with?"

Brock snorts out a laugh. "Jesus, you have to stop reading the tabloids. Thousands and thousands?"

"Hundreds and hundreds?" I tease, drawing another chuckle from his lips.

When he meets my gaze, he sobers. "I have a past. Everyone does, and I won't deny it. But I get what you're saying. What happened in the past stays there."

I nod. "I know women throw themselves at you. I can't blame them for it, because you're, well, you're hot. Like when that woman in the bar touched your arm. You didn't ask her to, but she did it anyway. That's what happened with my old boss. He initiated something that was uninvited, and I stopped it. I didn't tell anyone because I just didn't want the drama. If it had gone farther, then I would have said something, but a kiss is hardly anything to get worked up about."

He growls again, his hands gripping my back as he holds me close. "I'm going to erase him from your memory."

I can't help but smile. "You already have."

His mouth is powerful, his lips urgent, as he presses his to mine for the first time in three long days. "God, I've been waiting to kiss these lips for what feels like forever," he whispers, sliding his mouth so easily against mine.

"Me too," I reply, rubbing my body against his like a cat in heat.

A thump echoes from upstairs, causing us to separate well before either of us are ready. When we hear my brother's feet descending the stairs, Brock finally releases his hold on my body and gives me an unamused look. "I'm going to have to take another cold shower."

I flash him a quick grin. "Or you could just sneak into my room later tonight after my brother is sleeping."

I turn and go to the fridge just as Caleb returns. "That shower felt fucking wonderful. I hate flying, especially after a long night of post-game celebrating," he announces, wiggling his eyebrows.

"Gross," I mutter, pulling out the platter of patties I made earlier.

"Damn, Joey, those look amazing," my brother says, checking over the food.

"I minced up green onions, mushrooms, and green peppers and mixed it all into the ground beef. Oh, and I found fresh pepper jack cheese at the deli, so I thought we'd throw that on top."

Brock whistles in appreciation. "How about I run up and shower, and then I'll throw them on the grill?"

"You grill, I'll supervise," Caleb declares, grabbing another bottle of water from the fridge.

Brock goes upstairs to shower, and while my brother holds and snuggles my cat that he claims he didn't miss, I take the opportunity to run a clean laundry basket up to my room. The moment I cross the threshold, a familiar scent fills my nostrils. Instantly, I look for the note I know is here somewhere. I find it on my pillow, just like the previous ones left for me.

My heart is practically leaping with joy in my chest as I grab the slip of paper.

Once upon a time, there was this sexy football player who couldn't wait to get home to see the amazing woman who tied him in knots. It had been two horribly long nights since he saw her, and he wanted nothing more than to hold her in his arms. He wanted her in his bed too, but not just for the night. For much longer. He thinks about her day and night, can't seem to stop. The things he wants to do to her when they're alone keep him up at night, especially since he knows how she sounds when she comes. All he wants is her.

All. The. Time.

She's his obsession, and for the first time in his life, he's not scared. In fact, he craves more.

To be continued...

CHAPTER
FIFTEEN

BROCK

Dinner was incredible, and the company even more so. I had to make a conscious effort not to stare at Joey. I wanted more than anything to sit next to her and snuggle up to her. Three days without Joey in my arms is too damn long. Add in the revelation about that dickhead boss of hers, and the temptation to hold her close and never let go is strong.

That's why I called it an early night. I couldn't sit there in the living room having a casual conversation and not pull her onto my lap, wrap my arms around her, and bury my face in her neck. It's not even about sex at this point. Sure, our chemistry is off the fucking charts, but it's more than that with her. I just need to be next to her.

Don't get me started on having to stand in the background while she told her brother and me, by default, what that jackass ex-boss of hers did to her. Sure, it could have been much worse, but he touched her without her permission. Staying calm and not showing the rage inside me in front of Caleb took more control than I thought I possessed. Then Joey wrapped her arms around me, and I got to hold her, and some of the anger slipped away.

Now, here I am, lying in my bed, staring up at the ceiling, waiting for them both to go to their separate rooms. Then there will be more waiting to ensure my best friend is asleep before I can go to her. I'm probably going to hell for this, but I can't stay away. I love her more than I ever thought possible. After her earlier revelations and the fact that I spent three days without her, there is nothing that can keep me away from Joey tonight. Not even the risk of getting caught. In fact, I almost think it would be better if we were caught. Hiding and sneaking around is getting harder and harder when all I want to do is hold her and shout to the world that she's mine.

I'm going to have to talk to her about that.

Heavy footsteps sound as they pound up the stairs. I hear Caleb as he steps into his room and closes the door. Now we wait. Closing my eyes, I pull up the many images of her I have engrained in my mind to hold me over.

My bedroom door creaking open jolts me awake. My eyes pop open as they adjust to the darkness of the room. I hear the door click closed and the lock slide into place.

Joey.

I must have fallen asleep, and my girl came to me. I pull up the covers, inviting her in, and she doesn't disappoint. Joey slithers under the covers and settles in her space, resting against my chest. "I missed you."

"Oh, Sunshine," I whisper. "You have no idea," I say, pulling her a little closer and placing a kiss on the top of her head. Her hands glide over my abs and grip my cock, and as much as I love her hands on me, I don't want that. Not tonight. "Can I just hold you?" I ask her. I would never deny her anything, so if messing around is what she wants, then that's what she'll get, but tonight I need more than that.

"You don't want me?"

"Hey."

She tilts her head up to look at me. I can make out her silhouette, but I can't see her eyes, but I can guess there is worry and maybe a little hurt looking back at me if I could.

"There is nothing in this world that I want more than you. I just missed you so fucking much, and after hearing what you went through, I just need to hold you. I need to know you're here with me. I need to feel your skin against mine and know that you're safe."

"I'm safe. It was a kiss."

"One you didn't want."

"Our past is the past." She tosses my earlier words at me.

"I know, but that doesn't stop me from wanting to stalk to his office and beat the shit out of him. He put his hands on you, Joey. That's not okay."

"It could have been much worse. I pushed him off, he stopped, and I removed myself from the situation."

"I feel sick when I think about what could have happened to you. He needs to be punished."

"Not you too." She sighs. I can hear the sarcasm in the tone of her voice, and it pisses me off.

I move out of her hold and climb out of bed. My feet carry me back and forth over the plush carpet as I pace the distance of the room and back, over and over again.

"Brock?" she whispers. This time it's fear and uncertainty that I hear.

I stop next to the bed, bracing my hands on the mattress. I can make out her form but can't see her features. "He put his hands on you," I grit out. "He threatened you, Joey. The man made you feel as though your only choice was to quit a job that you loved. That's not okay."

"I'm okay." Her voice is soft.

"Thank fuck for that," I say, letting my anger at what she went through take over. I'm well aware that it was minor compared to what it could have been, but he put his hands on what's mine, and he needs to pay for that.

"I don't know why you can't just let this go. I'm here. I'm safe, and nothing happened, not really."

"Why?" I ask in disbelief. "Because when anyone hurts someone I love, I get pissed. Why are you letting this go so easily?" My chest is rising at a rapid pace, and my pulse is thundering in my ears. How can she not see that this is not okay?

"W-What did you say?"

"Forget it." I stand back to my full height and walk toward the window, staring out into the dark of night. How do I make her understand what she means to me? With all this fucking sneaking around, I can't show her that I'm damn proud to call her mine. And I'm hers, and that alone gives me the right to be pissed off about this. I go three days without her, and this bomb is dropped, and she doesn't understand why I can't let it go? Unbelievable.

Bracing my arms on the frame of the window, I bow my head and will myself to calm down. I don't want to be a dick to her. That's not what this is about. I just want her to take this seriously.

It's not until her hands slide around my waist and she rests her head against my back do I feel as though I can take a full deep breath. Neither one of us says a word as we stand here in the darkness, just holding on. Eventually, she slips under my arms so that we're face-to-face.

"Brock?" She's hesitant.

"Yeah, Sunshine?"

"You said that you love me."

My lips twitch with a smile. Dropping my arms from the window, I pull her into my embrace. "More than anything." I hate that I blurted the words out in anger, but it doesn't make my feelings any less true. I didn't even realize I'd said it until now. I replay the last five minutes, and sure enough, I said the words that have threatened to spill from my lips for weeks.

I feel soft hands press against my cheek, which has me dropping my head to look at her. Standing here by the window, with the light of the moon, I can make out her features. She's staring up at me, and in her eyes, I see the love I feel for her reflecting back at me. "I love you too." My chest feels like it might explode from the love I have for this woman. To hear her tell me that she loves me too is a moment I will never forget.

Dropping my hands to the back of her thighs, I lift her into my arms. She doesn't hesitate to wrap her legs around my waist and arms around my neck. "Say it again."

"I love you."

"I love you too, Sunshine. So fucking much." Then I kiss her. I put everything that I have into this kiss. It's hot, wet, passionate, and us. It's everything that I feel for her wrapped up in the mutual pressing of our lips together. Sliding my tongue past her lips, I taste her properly. I let her know how much I missed her these past three days and how much I love her with every stroke of my tongue against hers.

She grinds against me, and my cock throbs at just the thought of pushing into her sweet pussy, but that's not what this night is about. I don't want our first time to be after a fight—if you can even call it that. I still just want to be with her. Hold her and kiss her as if my life depends on it. So, no matter how much my cock protests, I'm not fucking her tonight.

Instead, I carry her to the bed, and I sit. With Joey still on my lap, I keep kissing her. Now that she's straddling me, my hands are free to roam, and roam they do. She moans, a sound from deep within her that has my cock hard as steel. Ignoring the ache, I bury my hands in her hair and kiss her hard.

"Brock?" she whines.

"Not tonight, baby. Not with your brother in the next room. This is all you're getting tonight."

"Fine," she grits out. Her hands press on my chest, pushing me back on the bed. My hands settle on her hips to hold onto her as I move back on the bed. Joey adjusts her position and begins to rock back and forth. She's riding me, taking what she wants, what she needs from me through the thin layer of her silk panties and my boxer briefs. She's seeking her pleasure.

My hands slide under her baggy T-shirt to cup her breasts. I tweak her nipple with my index finger and thumb, and she moans. It's louder than what I'm comfortable with since Caleb is in the room just down the hall. Sitting up, I take her mouth with mine, swallow her moans and cries of pleasure as her orgasm crashes through her.

She buries her face in my neck, and I hold her tightly against my chest. I hold her until her breathing evens out before she climbs off my lap and reaches for my waistband. "Not tonight," I tell her. "Go clean up, Sunshine. I want to hold you." She nods and disappears into the bathroom. She's back in no time and gliding under the covers next to me. She kisses me softly, and that's how we spend the rest of our time until we're both too tired to keep our eyes open.

———————

When my alarm blares at the ass crack of dawn, I reach for her, only to grip cold sheets. Flopping back on the bed, I cover my eyes with my arm and curse the universe. I know she was here. My sheets still smell like her. What I wouldn't give to wake up next to her. I'd snuggle the hell out of her until the very last second.

Like a movie reel, our future plays out in my mind, and I can't wait to have that exact scenario happen every single day. Joey is my future, and last night I told her as much. My confession of love didn't come lightly. When she said them back, that sealed our fate—sealed our forever.

Tossing off the covers, I move to sit on the edge of the bed when a piece of paper on the floor catches my attention. My heart literally skips a fucking beat in hopes it's what I think it is. Standing, I retrieve the piece of paper, and I'm not disappointed.

Once upon a time, there was a girl. Her entire life, she's felt as though she didn't really belong. Being born out of wedlock as the result of an affair, she always felt... misplaced. That is until the girl met a man. A man who changed her life in ways she never knew were possible. This man, he puts her first. He shows her with not only his words but his actions what she means to him. Another first for her, the bone-deep love she feels for him. She knows without a shadow of a doubt that he is the love of her life.

To be continued...

Opening the bottom drawer of my nightstand, I shove the letter into the small box that sits underneath a few T-shirts to hide it from Caleb. Not that he would ever snoop, but better safe than sorry. Standing, I head to the door. I need to see her. I need to tell her that I feel her words. Bone-deep, as she put it. All the way to my fucking soul I feel them.

Opening the door, I hear voices downstairs. "Shit," I mutter. Resting my forehead against the doorframe, I listen to Joey and Caleb as they talk downstairs. Her laughter floats up the stairs and wraps its way around my heart. As if she needed one more string to tie herself to me. We have to tell him. Soon.

Stepping back into my room, I close the door and head to the shower. Not ten minutes later, my feet are pounding down the stairs to join them in the kitchen. Joey has her back to me as she stands in front of the coffee pot. I don't stop until I'm standing beside her, our elbows rubbing as I reach for a coffee cup.

"Morning," she says, her voice still raspy from sleep.

"Good morning, Sunshine." Her eyes widen at my chipper mood, but she doesn't comment. Instead, she makes her way to the table and takes a seat.

"Eggs and toast," Caleb says, pointing at a plate that I assume is made for me.

"Thanks," I say, grabbing the plate and going to sit across from Joey at the table, with Caleb trailing behind, his plate now empty, left on the island, and his cup of coffee in his hand.

"What's got you so chipper?" he asks, taking the seat next to Joey.

"No reason," I reply, shoving a huge bite of eggs into my mouth.

"You sneak a girl in your room last night or something?" Caleb chuckles.

I know it's meant to be a joke, but I choke on my eggs and take a scalding hot sip of my coffee to wash it down. "No." It's a simple one-word reply, but my tone tells him to drop it.

"Well, something's got you in a sunshiny mood today."

This time it's Joey who chokes on her food, and I flash a worried glance toward Caleb. He's watching Joey, concern lacing his features. "You good?" he asks her.

"Yes." She nods. "Eating too fast, I guess." Caleb nods, accepting her excuse, not the least bit suspicious that we both choked on our food in a matter of moments.

"Eat up. We need to head out," Caleb tells me.

"Go on without me. I'll be right behind you."

"You sure?" he asks.

"Yeah. I still have to run upstairs and grab my bag. I'm going to finish this without choking and killing myself, and I'll be right behind you."

"All right." He leans across the table and offers me his fist, and I don't leave him hanging. He stands and kisses the top of Joey's head. "Later, sis," he mumbles, before placing his cup in the sink, grabbing his phone, keys, and bag from the floor, and waves over his shoulder before he's out the door.

"We have to tell him." I say.

"I know."

"The longer we wait, the worse it's going to be."

"I know."

"I missed waking up with you. I found your note."

She smiles. "I missed it too. Soon."

"Very soon, Joey. He's going to be pissed, but once he realizes what you mean to me, he'll get over it."

"And if he doesn't?"

"I hate to think that this would ruin our friendship, but if that's how it plays out, then so be it."

"You don't even care?"

"Of course I care. He's my best friend, but I can't give you up. I refuse to. If it takes losing Caleb in my life as my best friend, then I'll have to deal." I take a sip of coffee. "Besides, you're a permanent part of my life, so he's going to have to see me when he sees you. When he visits, when we get married, when we have kids, he's not going to just forget about me that easily." I smirk, trying to make light of our situation.

"Those are pretty big declarations."

"I love you. That's as big as it gets, and they're not declarations, baby. They're promises for what's to come." Standing, I grab my now-empty plate and cup, and bend to place a kiss on her lips. "I need to go. Love you. Have a good day."

"Love you too." she whispers after me as I turn to go upstairs to grab my bag. I can't stop the grin when I think about the look on her face. Part shock and part love. So much love. We have so much to look forward to. Sure, I hope that Caleb can come to terms with us. I'd like to think once he sees that she's it for me, he'll come around. He may not see at first, but once he witnesses firsthand how much I love her, how could he not?

CHAPTER
SIXTEEN

Joey

The ringing of my cell phone makes me pause from the online help-wanted ads I've been browsing all morning. The moment the guys went to practice, I grabbed my laptop and started searching. I've high-lighted a handful of media company and advertising executive posi-tions; however, I don't really have the experience they're looking for. Sure, I was with Johnson since I graduated from college, even climbed the ladder a few times, but I lack some of the task management and strategic planning duties preferred.

I sigh the moment I see the name on the screen and even consider letting it go to voice mail. However, I know my mom, and she won't stop calling until I answer. And if that doesn't work, she'll show up. That's the last thing I—or Caleb—need.

"Hey, Mom," I say in place of my usual greeting.

"Josephine, sweetheart, how are you? It's been too long!" she yells into the receiver.

"Where are you? Why is the music so loud?" A quick glance at the clock confirms it's just after one o'clock.

Mom laughs. "Sorry, it's so loud here. Tommy and I flew to Jamaica for a few days."

I sit up on my bed, phone clutched in my hand. "Wait, you're in Jamaica? And who is Tommy?"

"Tommy Dunn, my boyfriend."

I blink once, twice, multiple times. "Tommy Dunn? Like from Crash Factor?"

"Yes! That's him. We met at a mutual friend's house the other day, and when we were talking about vacations, we realized neither one of us have ever been to Jamaica! Did you know weed is readily available and super cheap here?"

My head starts to spin. "Mom?" The Caribbean music blasts in the background, making me wonder if she's standing directly beside a speaker.

"I'm here. Tommy too."

"That's great, but did you say you jetted off to a foreign country with a man you just met?"

She scoffs. "Well, technically we just met, but everyone knows Tommy Dunn. It's like we've known each other forever," she replies, her giggles filling the phone line.

I close my eyes and shake my head. I wish I could say this is the first time she's ever done something like this, but that would be a lie. Mom has a habit of hopping on a plane with some random guy, only to have something dramatic happen along the way. He disappears, leaving her with the resort bill. He's unable to hide her from his wife back home. Or my personal favorite, he has a run-in with the law and winds up in jail.

That's happened.

Twice.

"Listen, Mom, I'm in the middle of something, and it sounds like you're busy too," I say the moment I hear a man mumble about taking off her bikini.

"Oh! Yes, of course. The reason I was calling is because I'm coming to see you this weekend."

My heart skids to a stop in my chest. "What?"

"Yes, Tommy has a show Friday night near St. Louis, so I thought I'd drive to Springfield to visit my only daughter."

My stomach drops. "Actually, I'm not home. I'm visiting Caleb for a bit."

"Caleb, huh? How's he doing? How's his dad?"

"*Our* dad is fine. Caleb's fine. I'm not sure when I'll be back to my place yet," I reply, avoiding the whole conversation about moving out.

"Well, I guess I'll just catch up to you another time. Say hello to Caleb and your dad for me. Love you!"

She hangs up before I can reply, finally cutting off the heavy music, and all I feel is a sense of relief. Talking to my mom is taxing. There's always some sort of drama surrounding her, and I hate the way she asks about Dad and Caleb. Mostly because I know she's not just asking out of the goodness of her heart. There's always motive, always an agenda.

Tossing my phone onto the bed, I fire off my last résumé email and prepare to shut down my computer. But an idea hits me, and I pull up the internet browser once more. Caleb mentioned to me which hotel they're staying at in Chicago, so I pull up their website and check availability.

Nothing.

I know they try not to book too many guest rooms when a sporting team is staying with them, but they can't be completely full, can they? Deciding to call, just in case they're not reserving over the internet, I reach for my phone.

"Good afternoon, you've reached the Marriott. How may I help you?"

"I'd like to reserve a room, please."

"Absolutely," the gentleman says. "What dates were you looking for?"

"This weekend. Sunday and Monday night, please."

He pauses. "Let me check on that for you." I can hear him clicking away on the keyboard before he replies, "I'm sorry, we're all booked up for those two nights. May I transfer your call to one of our sister facilities nearby?"

"Uhh, no. Thank you," I mumble, hanging up.

Shit.

How am I supposed to get all sexified with Brock if I can't actually stay in the same hotel? There's no way it would work if I were in a completely different hotel. The chances of someone seeing him or me coming and going are greater, and the last thing we need are questions.

I try a second time, just to see if I can get a room, but that search comes up the same. They say they're all booked for the weekend.

This dilemma leaves me with few choices. I can back out of my weekend away to see Brock, stay at a neighboring hotel, which creates its own set of problems, or make another call. One I know I'll regret, yet it feels like my only real option.

I pull up his contact, my finger hovering over the Call button. With a deep sigh, I touch the screen, the phone ringing.

"Josephine, what a surprise."

"Hi, Dad," I greet, my voice overly sweet.

"We're in the middle of watching game films. I don't have a lot of time," he says, letting me know he's with the team.

"Actually, I needed a favor. I tried to book a room in Chicago at the Marriott where you are staying, but they say they're full. I know they usually keep rooms back for families of players, so I thought I'd see if it were possible to get one of those."

"Nonsense, you can stay with me in my suite."

My eyes almost pop out of my head. I hadn't expected that. "Oh, no, Dad, that's not necessary. I don't want to be in the way," I insist.

"You won't be. You're my daughter. You used to travel with me from time to time as a child."

"I know, Dad, but you'll be so busy helping run the team. You have meetings in your suite all the time, and I don't want to cause disruptions. Plus, I like to read in silence, and we both know when you have coaches and players in and out, it's rarely quiet."

He's silent for a few long seconds, making me wonder if I laid it on a little too thick. Does he see right through me?

"You're right, princess. That makes sense. I'll get you a room away from all of ours, so you have a little more peace and quiet, but still close enough to join us for team events and the game. You can sit in our suite during the game."

"That's not necessary. I love watching from the stands, you know that."

He sighs. "But anything can happen to you in the stands, princess. I don't like knowing you're out there, unprotected."

"I've been attending games for years that way," I remind him. He knows I hate the pomp and circumstance of those fancy suites. The free food is nice, but so is having a big hot dog with the rest of the common folk.

"I understand, but I would feel much better if you were in the suite. Plus, Candi will be there."

Great, just who I want to spend my night with.

"I'd prefer to sit in the stands, Dad," I reiterate with a little extra firmness.

"What?… Oh, I'll be right there. I'm talking to your sister. She's going to the game Monday night and is insisting she sit in the stands." He's quiet for a second, the deep rumble of my brother's voice vibrating through the line. "You do?" Again, my brother talks. Dad sighs. "Your brother thinks you'll be fine in the stands. I still don't like it. Promise me you'll go up to our suite if you have any issues."

I sag with relief against my mattress. "I promise. No one ever bothers me."

"Yes, but this is Monday night in Chicago. I don't trust any of them with my baby girl."

I can't stop the eye roll. "I'll be fine, Dad, but I promise to go up to the suite with Candi if needed."

"Good. Now that that's settled, I'll get you a room. Candi will email you the details. Oh, and you'll fly on the team plane with us. End of story."

I exhale loudly, realizing it's best not to argue too much. I already won on the separate room and sitting in the stands. I don't want to push my luck on travel plans.

"Fine. Thank you."

"I'm needed up front, Josephine. I'll talk to you later."

I throw my phone to the side and close my eyes as Hermione jumps onto my bed and curls up at my side. I did it. I'm going to the game this weekend. I have my own room, far away from the team—and most importantly, my dad and brother. I get to sit in the stands and wear the number eighty hanging in the closet. And hopefully, later that night, well after the Monday night lights have faded, I'll have him in his bed.

———

Once upon a time, there was a woman who had an exciting secret to share. She was going to travel with the handsome football player this weekend for his game. She booked a room in the same hotel and thinks of nothing else but sneaking into his room long after everyone has gone to bed. She pictures him there, naked, and hovering over her moments before he enters her for the first time. It's all she can think about now. Time seems to slow, the seconds taking longer to tick by in anticipation of what's to come. The only thing that's certain is the woman knows one night will never be enough.

To be continued…

With a smile on my face, I quickly slip into Brock's room and place the note on his pillow. Before I leave the way I came, I can't help but bend down and sniff his pillow. It smells just like him, a mixture of his body-wash and aftershave. It sends warmth racing through my veins, pooling between my legs.

"God, I'm hopeless," I mutter to myself. Hermione jumps up onto his bed, spins around a few times before dropping into the space between the two pillows. She plops her head down and closes her eyes, snuggling into the pillow I know Brock lays his head on at night. "Yeah, I'm not jealous or anything."

With a sigh, I turn and leave the room and head downstairs. The guys should be home any moment now and it's Brock's turn to plan dinner. The least I can do is go down and see what options he's got in the fridge.

I'm barely there a few minutes when I hear the alarm being disabled and the door open. "Honey, we're home!" my brother bellows with a chuckle, making me shake my head. "Why are you filling the dishwasher? It's Brock's turn to cook, and we all know dishes afterward is a part of that."

I glance over his shoulder and find the man in reference smiling widely. "Hey, if Joey wants to help do dishes, who are we to stop her?" he teases, knowing full well I often leave all the dirties for Caleb to clean.

"You never help fill the dishwasher when it's my turn," my brother grumbles, looking like a toddler about to throw a temper tantrum.

A bubble of laughter erupts from my lips. "Well, the difference is you insist on using every single dish and utensil you own while cooking."

He throws up his hands in defeat. "You don't understand perfection."

"No, what I don't understand is using four spoons to stir a pot of noodles."

Caleb laughs and throws his arms around me. "I'm just messing with you. I hear you're comin' to the game this weekend."

I notice Brock perk up, his eyes meeting mine.

"Yeah, I thought it would be nice to get out of the house for a few days before my interviews start. I have a few lined up next week, and I realized if I start a new job, I won't be able to travel with you for a while."

A huge grin spreads across Brock's face, one he struggles to hide from my brother. "I'm gonna run upstairs and change real quick before I make dinner," he says, taking off from the kitchen and leaving me alone with Caleb.

"You know you don't have to rush to get a job, right?" Caleb says, giving me a pointed look.

"I know, and I really do appreciate it, but we've been over this. I want a job. I actually like working. I'm not here to freeload off you, okay? I want to contribute, and not just to the house. I'm good at what I do and want to keep doing it."

Caleb exhales and leans against the counter. "All right, I get it. Just know that you don't have to be in a hurry to find one."

I step forward and kiss his cheek. "I know. Thank you."

"So, you're coming to Chicago, huh? Dad says you're coming with the team on Sunday morning."

"I am. I'd prefer just to fly myself, but you know how he is."

Caleb laughs. "I'm familiar. Listen, I'm gonna run upstairs and return a call to my agent. I'll be down later."

Nodding, I throw him a wave as he exits the kitchen, leaving me alone to finish filling the dishwasher. After about fifteen minutes, I hear footfalls on the stairs. When no one joins me a few minutes after and my task is finally complete, I turn to head to the living room to catch up on that new rock star's documentary I recorded.

Turning around, a scream slips from my lips as my hands cover my racing heart. "Jesus, Brock, you scared the shit out of me."

He just smiles, the softest, sweetest smile, as he pushes off from the doorjamb he's leaning against. "Sorry, not my intention."

"Were you watching me?" I ask, trying to recall if I did something really embarrassing like pick my underwear out of my ass or do a weird little dance while I was loading the dishwasher.

"Yes," he answers, pointblank. "The view was incredible." He reaches for me, gently pulling me into his arms and kissing my lips. "How was your day?"

"Good. I sent out a few résumés, scheduled another interview for next week, and made a few phone calls."

He nods. "I hear you're taking a little trip this weekend." Brock pulls a mangled piece of paper from his pocket and holds it up. "I think someone tried to snack on it, but I'm pretty sure I was able to get the gist of the story." His blue eyes dance with fire as he scans over the words.

Clearing my throat, I run my hands up his chest. "What did you think? Of the story."

Brock reaches for my hand and places it over his hard cock. "I say I more than liked it, don't you think, Sunshine?"

My hand flexes over the bulging crotch of his shorts, cupping him and sliding my hand along his length. "I do think you liked it."

An animalistic growl slides from his throat. "We only have one little problem," he whispers, nipping at my earlobe. When he meets my gaze, he drops the bomb. "I'm bunking with Caleb for this trip. We're all sharing rooms."

My lungs deflate, my heart dropping to my toes. "Really?"

He nods in confirmation. "But… I think I can make it work. It won't be my bed you're in, but what if I'm in yours?"

My ears perk up at his suggestion. "You can do that?"

He shrugs. "Well, it'll be a bit more challenging, but yeah, I can do that. It may not sound like the best plan, but when I tell your brother I'm not sleeping in our room, I can say I met someone." His Adam's apple bobs as he swallows hard. I can tell he doesn't like the idea.

"That doesn't sound so bad."

His eyes dance with desire once more. "Or I could just tell him about you."

Resting my cheek against his chest, I exhale. "Not quite yet. Not on our first night away. I don't want to cause any problems between you two right now, especially if you'll be rooming together."

He sighs and wraps his arms around my back. "I get it."

"We'll tell him soon."

"Promise? I don't think I can keep this casual appearance up much longer, Sunshine. Not when I see you and want to hold and kiss you. I want us more than my next breath, and I don't give a shit who sees or what they think about it."

I nod in understanding. "After the Monday night game, you have a bye week. We can tell him then. This way, if it causes any problems, we have time to try to fix it."

"Deal," he says, kissing my lips soundly. "Next weekend, I'm telling your brother I'm in love with you."

I can't help but smile. Hearing those words never gets old.

CHAPTER
SEVENTEEN

BROCK

At last week's away game, I was away from her for three days. Three days of text messages, phone and video calls when we could squeeze them in, and I thought it was torture.

I was wrong.

This is torture.

I had to watch one of my teammates hit on her during the entire plane ride. By the time we landed, I was spitting nails. I was so pissed off. It's not his fault, I get that, but she's mine. Mine to touch, mine to kiss, mine to love, and mine to flirt with. Not his. Mine. My anger doesn't do any of us any good, certainly not me, because I can't tell him she's mine. Like I said torture.

That was early this morning, and the day has just gone downhill from there. Coach has had us in this fucking conference room since the moment we got to the hotel. Hour after hour, we watch play after play. Normally, I don't mind it. It's part of the job. I love the game and learning, and watching our opponents is part of that, but today, it's all different.

Today, I know that somewhere in this hotel is my girl. She's sitting in her room waiting for me to come to her, or is she? Is she out roaming around the hotel? The city? That just ramps my anger up for the second time today. She shouldn't be out roaming a strange city all on her own. Yes, I know she's a grown woman, but dammit, I need her safe. The thought of her not being safe is affecting my ability to concentrate. The thought of her in her room waiting for me, that's pissing me off.

"What's up with you?" Caleb leans into me and whispers.

"Nothing," I reply, trying not to bite his head off.

He taps his pen against my balled fist that sits on top of the table. "Keep telling yourself that," he says, sitting back in his seat.

It's on the tip of my tongue to blurt out the truth. That I'm so blindly in love with his little sister that I can't even fucking function when she's close and I can't be with her. I know now is not the time for my confession, especially since their father is sitting in the front of this conference room as well.

"You know what you need, don't you?" he whispers, keeping his eyes focused on the giant screen.

"Enlighten me, ol' wise one," I mumble.

"You need to get laid. You've been living with me for a couple of months now, and I have yet to see you go out. You need pussy, my man. That's the cure-all." He smirks. "You need to let go of all of that tension."

Only if it's your sister's. "Fuck off," I grumble. If he knew that I was committed to his sister, I can guarantee he wouldn't be suggesting this. I'm going to go out on a limb and guess that talking about our sex lives going forward is going to be a forbidden topic. Although, that could be a good way to get under his skin. I file that away for another time. It hits me that I've been racking my brain around how to get out of our room tonight. "I have a date tonight." I blurt it out before I have a chance to fully process what I'm saying.

"Oh, yeah? A regular from town?" he asks, his interest piqued. "Does she have any friends?"

"I don't kiss and tell."

Not anymore.

"Since when?" He raises an eyebrow.

"Since now."

"Oh, I get it. You like this one." He nods in approval.

I can work with this. "Yeah, man. I really do. In fact, I'm pretty sure that I'm in love with her." The words slip past my lips before I can think better of it—Caleb full-on turns to look at me, not even pretending to be watching the game tape. At least I had enough sense to say with absolute certainty that I'm in love with her, because I am.

"Come again?" Confusion is written all over his face.

"She's different." I shrug and break his stare, turning my attention back to the screen.

"Different how?" I can still feel his eyes on me, but I don't turn to look. I'm too afraid of what he might see that I won't be able to hide the fact that I'm talking about Joey.

"She's just different."

"Not good enough, my man. I'm going to need you to spell this shit out for me."

"Let it go." My voice is stern.

"How is it that my best friend who has been living with me for months is in love, and I have no idea? Have I even met her?" he questions.

I'm kicking myself in the ass for even saying anything. I should have known he wouldn't just let it go. He's like a fucking vulture and will keep picking and nagging until I give him something. The problem with that is I don't want to lie to him. Not anymore, but I have to. I don't have a choice. I made a promise to Joey, and I intend to keep it. I won't turn into just another person she's not able to rely on. I want to be at the top of her list.

"I've known her for a while. We reconnected, and things are going well." Going well is an understatement. She's my entire life is more accurate.

"Reconnected? When did you meet her?" By this time, he's all but given up on watching the film, and I'm shocked Coach hasn't called him out on it yet.

"College." Not a lie, but it's not what he's thinking. We didn't go to college with her.

"Who is she?"

"Henderson!" Coach calls out his name. "You care to join us, or do you plan on sitting there and shooting the shit?"

"Sorry, Coach, giving my boy here some love advice," Caleb calls back. The room erupts in laughter, and if it were not for the reprieve from Caleb's questioning, I'd probably be pissed off and a little bit embarrassed.

"I got you, Williams," Jefferson says, turning around in his chair to face me. "I have a way with the ladies," he says, bobbing his head and wagging his eyebrows.

"I'm good," I tell him with a reluctant laugh. I'm surrounded by idiots. He might have a way with the ladies, but my guess is it has more to do with his playing for the Ramblers than anything else.

Thankfully, the murmurs settle down, and we go back to watching tape. Caleb surprisingly lets the subject go, but this conversation is far from over. I thought I was being sneaky, letting him know that I met someone who I truly care about. Instead, I opened a can of worms, and instead of planting a seed that I'm committed, I've planted suspicion.

Joey is going to be pissed.

———

"You're wearing a hole in the carpet," Caleb comments.

I stop pacing. Hell, I didn't even know I was doing it to look at it. "I have too much nervous energy."

"Are you that excited to see this girl?" A look passes over his face that I can't decipher before it's gone.

"Yeah," I admit. "I'm that excited to see her."

"Do I get to meet her?"

"No."

"Why not? I'm your best friend."

"She's not ready yet." Not a complete lie.

"What?" he asks, confused.

"She's not ready yet," I repeat. "She's not really one to be in the limelight, so we're keeping her out of it for now."

"When have you seen her? You've been home every night. You

don't go out after the games, and you're in bed most nights before Joey and me."

"Things have been… distant. But we're getting there." Fuck, this is hard. I hate lying to him. I'm trying to give him answers that are as close to the truth as I possibly can.

"So, what? She's from here? Or she traveled to the game? You buy her way here?"

"No. I didn't buy her way here."

"Where is she from?"

"Not far from us." I'm being vague, and we both know it.

"Jesus, it's like pulling teeth to get any kind of information out of you." He runs his fingers through his hair in frustration.

"Listen, man. It's not that I don't want to tell you. It's that I'm respecting her wishes. She doesn't want all the hoopla that comes with what we do. She asked me to keep us under wraps until she was ready, and that's what I'm going to do."

"That's a big ask."

I nod. "She's worth it."

"All right," he relents. "I won't push you on this, but when she's ready, I'm the first in line. You hear me? It's not every day that your best friend falls in love," he says, just as his phone rings. "Yeah?" he answers. "I'm on my way." He ends the call and stands from his bed. "That was the guys. We're going down to the bar to eat. You sure you don't want to come with us?"

I glance down at my phone at the text that Joey just sent.

Joey: I'm ready when you are.

"Nah, thanks, though. She's almost back to her room. We're probably just going to order some room service."

"So what you're telling me is that I have the room all to myself tonight."

"Yes." There is no doubt in my mind that I'll be waking up with her in my arms. Consequences of getting caught be damned.

"Nice." He holds his fist out for me, and we bump knuckles. "Don't do anything I wouldn't do." He winks and shuts the door behind him.

I immediately text Joey back.

Me: Caleb just left to meet the guys for dinner. I'm giving it a few minutes, and I'll be right there.

Her reply is sent with nothing but a number. Her room number. My heart rate kicks up seeing her room number. She's on the same floor as the team, but she's on the other end of the hall from the rest of us. It's a little trickier sneaking into her room, but once I'm there, I don't plan on leaving. I know the guys will sleep late, so as long as I set the alarm on my phone to sneak out before the team starts to rise, we should be good to go.

After ten minutes I can't stand it any longer. I make sure that I have my room key and grab the hat and sunglasses from my carry-on and slip out the door. I keep my head down to ensure I don't make eye contact as I make my way to the opposite side of the floor. Luckily, the hallway is empty, so my disguise was for nothing. I tap once on her door, and it immediately opens. Joey grabs my hand, tugging me inside, before slamming the door shut.

"Did anyone see you?"

"No." I reach for her, but she steps just out of reach.

"What about Caleb? What did you tell him?" She bites down on her lip. I know this is bothering her, and it bothers me too. But this was her choice to wait until we are home to tell him.

"I told him that I met someone. I told him that I was pretty sure that I was in love with her. I told him that she traveled to the game and got a room and that I was staying with her tonight."

"Brock!" she scolds.

"I'm sorry, Sunshine. What was I supposed to do? He was grilling me. He's my best friend, and I tell him everything. *Everything*," I reiterate. "When I wouldn't give him the information he was looking for, he pushed harder. I had to give him something."

"Shit," she mumbles, and finally lets me pull her into my embrace.

"I missed you."

"What else did you tell him, Brock?"

"I told him that you were not about being in the middle of the celebrity that comes with this job and that you asked me to wait. I was trying to tell him as much of the truth that I could. I'm hoping that will make this easier when we tell him what we've been up to."

She nods. I can feel the tension in her body, and I hate it. I've had a shit day from watching my teammate hit on her the entire flight to hours of tape and the grilling from Caleb. I just need her right now. Just Brock and Joey hanging out in a hotel.

"Can we forget all of this?" I ask her.

"Forget what?"

"Caleb. Hiding. Can we just be us? Pretend we're at home and we have the house to ourselves?"

Finally, I feel her shoulders start to relax. "I like that idea."

"Me too." She tilts her head back, and I lean forward, pressing my lips to hers. "And I'm starving," I say against her lips.

"Thank God. I was afraid you had already eaten with the team, and I was going to have to sit here and have you watch me pig out on my own."

"Order us one of everything." I reach into my back pocket and pull out my credit card. "You can't bill it to the room, your dad knows damn good and well you can't eat all of that."

"I'll put it on mine. I don't want them to ask for the name on the card."

"Fine. When you get the bill, I'm paying it."

"I can treat you to dinner."

"This is more than dinner, Sunshine. This is the entire room service menu. No arguments or I call them and put it on my card myself."

"We can't do that." She places her hands on her hips.

"Then I win." I hand her the card, and after about a minute of her trying to change my mind with her mean stare, she relents and takes my card. "Fine," she grumbles.

"Love you, Sunshine. I'm going to shower off this fucking day. I'll be right out."

"You didn't bring clothes with you." She points out the obvious.

"Baby, we're not going to need clothes." I toss her a wink and head to the bathroom. I strip out of my sweats and pull my shirt over my head. My underwear and socks are next. I take my time folding them into a neat pile since I'll have to wear them out of here in the morning. The last thing I need is for the paparazzi to pass me in the hall, rumpled in yesterday's clothes. I'm sure that would make headlines. If I'm put together, I can simply tell them I'm running out for coffee or some other bullshit excuse I can come up with on the fly.

Ten minutes later, with a towel wrapped around my waist, I run and jump on the bed where she's lying. I smack her ass for good measure and then turn to lie flat on my back, angling my head to look at her. "Kiss me."

She doesn't hesitate to lean over me and press her lips to mine. Her taste wraps around me like a warm caress. I need her closer. With my arms wrapped around her back, I pull her to me, never breaking our kiss. I kiss her until our lips are bruised.

"B-Brock," she says against my lips. "The food will be here soon."

"Change of plans. Why don't I just have you for dinner?"

"As enticing as that sounds, I've already ordered, and we're both starving, remember?"

"Fine," I concede. "But once the food is here, there is no talking me out of having you for dessert."

"I ordered dessert."

"Then you can enjoy it while I enjoy you," I say as there's a knock at the door.

"Make sure you check to see who it is," I whisper as I climb off the bed and move to the bathroom. With her dad and her brother both in this hotel, I'm not taking any chances. Part of me wants them to catch us so this game of hide and seek can be over. The other part of me worries about how they will react and what it will do to the bubble that we've been living in.

———

"I'm stuffed." Joey pushes her chair back from the small dining table and moves to the bed. "Why did you let me eat so much?"

"Me? I wasn't about to tell you that you had to stop eating. You're hungry. You eat. It's as simple as that." That's actually one of the things I love about her. She's real. She's never trying to put on a front to impress me.

"So, the night is still young," she says, glancing over at the clock on the nightstand.

"Whatever shall we do?" I play into her game.

"I have a few ideas."

"Yeah? Care to share them with the class?"

"No." She shakes her head. "Not the class. Just with you."

"I'm listening."

"Make love to me." She holds my stare, and I can see it in her eyes. She wants this. Wants me. And honestly, I can't keep holding out anymore. We have the room to ourselves, and she already talked to her dad, letting him know she's turning in early. The door is securely locked, and my willpower is no longer present.

"Oh, this is the good part of the story," she says when I stand and remove the towel from around my waist.

"Sunshine, every part of our story is the good part. Now, get naked."

CHAPTER
EIGHTEEN

Joey

Feeling braver than ever before, I keep my eyes focused on his and stand. He's directly in front of me, tall and proud in all his naked glory, and my mouth goes dry at the desire swirling in those sapphire orbs.

His eyes follow my movement as I reach down and unfasten my shorts. They slide easily down my legs, pooling at my bare feet. Then I reach for my shirt. Grabbing the hem, I slowly lift, hearing only his hiss as I lift the material over my head and toss it on the floor.

He devours me, drinking in my body from head to toe. A part of me wants to cover up my stomach, especially the part in the middle that's a little flabby from too much late-night ice cream. But seeing the intensity in his eyes has me standing still, letting him appreciate what's in front of him.

"Fuck, you're beautiful," he murmurs, sounding awestruck. Brock takes a step forward, his big hand wrapping effortlessly around my hip. "This is sexy," he adds, running one finger from my jaw down between my cleavage and to my belly button.

"It's new," I reply, referring to the sheer black bra and panty set I found online last week and had delivered.

"I think you should wear it every night."

I reach up and slip both straps down my arms, exposing my breasts as I release the front clasp.

"On second thought, as incredible as that view is, this one is just a bit better," he says the moment I drop my bra on the floor at my feet. "Fuck," he mumbles, scrubbing his hands over his face. "Come here."

Taking a step forward, I meet him halfway. I slide my hands up his bare chest. He's like a work of art, something that should be on display in a gallery or temple. His chest is hard, sculpted muscles beneath warm flesh, and even though this isn't the first time I've touched him, it's the first time I know it's leading to more, and I can truly explore his body without reservation.

Brock just stands there, one hand gently gripping my hip and the other balled at his side. "I'm barely hanging on by a thread here, Sunshine," he whispers through gritted teeth.

I continue my slow examination of his physique with my palms and meet his gaze. "What will it take to make that control snap? This?" I whisper, reaching down and running a single finger down his very long, very hard shaft. When he hisses, I wrap my hand around and squeeze. "Or maybe this?"

He grabs my hand, halting my movements. "Enough," he growls. "Get on the bed."

With a smile, I keep my hand right where it is and carefully pull him with me as I move. Brock plasters his mouth to mine, reaches down, removes my hand, and then tosses me on the bed. I laugh as I bounce on the mattress, but the sound falls silent immediately when he crawls on top of me.

We come together with greedy hands and eager mouths, and I have to admit, having him kiss me the way only he knows how is the head-iest feeling in the world. Brock runs his mouth across my jaw and down my neck. "I can't get enough of your sweet skin," he whispers, his mouth continuing its trek downward.

He places open-mouthed kisses across my collarbones before finally reaching my breasts. He takes one long swipe at one of my hard nipples with his tongue, pulling a deep groan that feels like it comes from my soul. All I can do is lie here, with the amazing sensations of his mouth on me coursing through my blood. Brock adds his hands, gently squeezing and kneading each nipple before sucking them deep into his mouth.

I rock my hips upward, hitching my ankles over his hips, and sliding my clit against his hard length. My body is on fire, heat pumping through my veins and trailing along my flushed skin by his touch. It's almost too much, yet not enough at the same time.

I need more.

"Please, Brock," I murmur, thrashing my head to the side as he nips at my nipple and soothes the sharp ache by licking it.

"I'm not done loving on you yet," he informs me, kissing across my not-so-flat belly.

"Later. I feel like I'm going to combust."

He chuckles, warm breath tickling my skin. "Well, we can't have that, can we?"

I shake my head as he kneels between my legs, just staring down at me. "Let me grab my pants."

"No," I reply, reaching for the nightstand drawer and grabbing the box of condoms I slipped inside earlier when I arrived in my room.

"My girl is prepared. I like that," he says with a laugh, ripping open the box and removing a strip of protection. "We'll just set these aside. Something tells me we're going to need them all."

I take the single foil packet and pull it open. Brock hooks his fingers beneath my panties and shimmies them down my legs, tossing them over his shoulder. My hand wraps around his cock once more as I grip the base and give it a little tug before positioning the protection at the head.

"Your hands are magic."

"Funny, I say the same about you," I say, slipping the condom into place.

Brock returns to his position between my thighs, reaching down and sliding the tip of his cock against my clit. "Ready?"

"More than ready. Make me yours."

Something dark flashes in his eyes as he presses the tip against my body and slowly pushes inside. Brock Williams isn't a small man, and no I'm not referring to his imposing six-foot four body. His cock is large and thick, and I can feel the stretch and slight discomfort of him invading me. "Fuck, Sunshine," he groans, not even halfway in yet.

When I tilt my hips up, he's able to slide the rest of the way in, burying himself completely. "Oh, God," I groan. I swear he's pushing against the back of my uterus.

Brock claims my mouth, yet remains completely still, seated deep inside me. "Mine."

"Yes, yours. Only yours."

"Damn straight," he declares, propping his hands on the mattress beside my head, getting into position. "Ready?"

I barely have time to nod before he pulls out and pistons forward, the mattress slamming against the headboard bolted to the wall. Over and over again, he fills me completely—mind, body, and soul. Brock grips my hips, gently lifting me to meet his thrusts. All I can do is close my eyes, too overcome by the amazing sensations, the utter rightness of this moment.

He leans down, taking my lips with his, our tongues sliding together in perfect harmony. "I don't think I'll ever get enough of you, of how fucking amazing you feel," he mumbles, rocking his hips to the same silent rhythm.

"Me either," I groan, unable to fight off the overpowering desire for release. "I'm so close."

"Yeah? Tell me what you want."

"I need to come. So badly."

He chuckles, nuzzling my ear, and slowly rocks forward once more. "How many times do you want to come, Sunshine?"

"Just once. Now."

Again, he laughs, the sound low and dirty. "Oh, no. Never just once. There will always be the first one, and then another one. You ready?"

Unable to speak, I simply nod, trying to hold on for dear life. Brock jerks his hips at the same time I rock, and the result brings stars to my eyes. I'm overcome with desire, the tip of my orgasm just out of grasp. "Again," I demand, reaching and gripping his ass.

I feel the muscles beneath my fingers tense as he thrusts, rolling his hips at the same time and caressing that magical spot deep inside my body. The result is a mind-blowing orgasm, a release so hard I can't breathe. I can feel my muscles clamping down on his cock, but he never slows. Brock keeps pace, drawing out the euphoria until my body feels boneless and completely sated.

When I open my eyes, his gaze is both soft, yet determined. "That was the most beautiful thing I've ever witnessed." He brushes his lips across mine, but only for a second. "Now, let's go for number two."

Before I can even comprehend his words, he moves, changing up his position between my legs and thrusting deep. I clench, my muscles screaming in both protest and for more. He goes to his knees, hitching my ankles around his neck and gripping my hips in his big hands. The result causes my body to fire to life once more, need filling me with renewed focus.

"You're so fucking wet." Thrust. "Tight." Thrust, thrust. "So fucking perfect." Thrust and grind against my pelvis. All I can do is grab the pillow beneath my head and hang on for dear life.

Brock reaches down and slides his thumb over my clit. The sensations are almost too much, and when I try to close my legs—impossible because of our position—he meets my gaze with determination. "One. More."

All I can do is enjoy the ride as he expertly works my clit and pumps into me, as I climb higher and higher. Just when I think I can't take any more, another orgasm slams into me like a tsunami. Tidal waves of pleasure sweep through me as I cry out, his name falling from my lips.

"Jesus," he grunts, slamming forward, chasing his own release. It only takes a few pumps before he curses and whispers my name. Not Josephine or Joey, but the nickname I hope he never stops saying. "Sunshine."

My heart is pounding so loudly, I'm sure Brock and everyone on this floor can hear it. As we try to catch our breath, he releases my legs and turns us on our sides, facing each other. Rough fingers glide gently over my cheeks, my lips, as he just stares at me. "You make me fall harder every moment we're together."

A shy smile spreads on my lips as I close my eyes, encompassed by his strong arms and the thundering in his chest. "I don't ever want to move," I whisper, snuggled against him as he holds me close.

"Yeah, I think we should stay just like this. At least for the next few minutes. Then, I'm going to need you on top of me, watching you move."

The palm of my hand rests against his heart as I close my eyes, my whole body more relaxed than ever before. "I think I'm going to need more than a few minutes," I reply through a yawn.

Brock chuckles. "Let me get rid of this condom and grab a wash-cloth," he says, placing a kiss on my forehead before extracting himself from the bed.

I miss him instantly, but I'm so tired, I don't even have the energy to open my eyes and enjoy the view of him walking away.

A few moments later, Brock returns from the bathroom with a warm wet cloth and moves it between my legs. "I can do that."

"I know, but I want to." He's gentle as he wipes away the evidence of our lovemaking. The moment he throws the cloth on the bathroom floor, he climbs back into bed, pulling me into his arms, my back pressed to his front.

I've fallen asleep in his arms before, but this feels different. More intimate. After what we just shared, it feels deeper and more meaningful.

"I'm going to have to leave before you wake up in the morning," he mumbles, holding me tightly against him and kissing my shoulder. "We have a team breakfast early and then we head to the field for some walk-throughs and warm-ups. I'll be there all day, until kickoff."

"I understand," I whisper, hating that he has to leave so early, but mostly because he has to go before everyone wakes up and starts moving about. There's too much at risk if we're caught.

"We're still telling your brother later this week, right?"

I nod, feeling more settled about the idea of talking to Caleb. "I'm ready to tell him."

"Good," he murmurs, gliding his lips across my bare skin. "I don't want to hide us anymore."

We stay in complete silence and contentment for a while, the only sound in the room the rumble of the air conditioning unit and the steady beat of his heart. "Brock?"

"Yes, love?"

"Tell me a story," I whisper through another yawn.

"Once upon a time, there was a man. He fell so hard, so fast for the most beautiful woman in the world, he was completely blindsided by it. But now he has felt it, now that he knows what true love feels like, he can't imagine his life any other way. He wants nothing more than to fall asleep beside her every night. But the man is also scared."

I open my eyes, my heart clenching with worry, and can't help but ask, "Why was he scared?"

He sighs and nuzzles my hair with his nose. "Because his job won't make it easy on them. He's gone a lot and is often the focus of paparazzi and tabloid bullshit."

It makes me think back to the story I read weeks ago about him on the beach with Gisele Sorenson and the conversation we had in the pool about it. The photo, however, was taken out of context, something I'm probably going to have to get used to dealing with.

Again.

My life seems to always be front and center when it comes to selling dirt. The drama of my parents has consistently been something to help sell magazines. However, even though I know I could potentially deal with more crap, it's not enough to keep me away from him.

He runs his finger up my arm. "I don't ever want to hurt you, Sunshine. Promise me we'll talk before you ever believe anything you read or hear, okay?"

Gosh, is this amazing man for real?

Turning in his arms, I press my naked chest against his. "I promise."

Brock flashes me a quick grin. "Good. Now, tell me a story."

I press my cheek to his chest and yawn. "Once upon a time, there was this ordinary lady—" I start but am interrupted.

"You're anything but ordinary."

"Hey, this is my story," I tease, taking a playful swat at his shoulder.

"Sorry, sorry. Please continue. But... if you could refer to the lady as extraordinary, I'd appreciate it."

Sighing, I shake my head and smile. "Fine. There was an *extraordinary* lady who was very excited to go to a football game the next night."

"Yeah?"

"Definitely. Especially since she's going to be wearing a special jersey to the game. One for the man she loves."

He looks down, fire dancing in those dark blue orbs. "I can't wait to look up in those stands and see you wearing my number."

I relax, my cheek returning to his chest. "The lady was happier than she'd ever been and excited to tell her family about the handsome prince she was seeing."

"Nope. Nuh-uh. They're way past seeing each other," he states, interrupting me once again.

"Is this your story or mine?" I joke, hitching my leg up onto his.

"Your story is missing the facts, love."

"Fine, the lady couldn't wait to tell her family about the handsome prince she was in love with."

"Better," he croons, the deep, rich timbre of his voice like a caress down my spine, igniting my desire once more. He runs his fingers across my back, leaving a trail of fire in their wake.

"Anyway," I start, wiggling just the slightest to help alleviate the sudden ache between my legs, before I pause. "I forgot what I was going to say."

He chuckles, dropping his hand down below the blanket and gripping my ass. "Let's see if I can help you remember."

CHAPTER
NINETEEN

BROCK

Monday night's game was the best of my professional career. Hell, maybe the best game I've played my entire life. I don't know if it was the fact that I fell asleep with Joey in my arms and woke up with her still there? Or maybe it was the fact that I finally made love to her? Maybe it's because I'm in love with her? Then again, it could be that I knew my girl was in the stands cheering me on, wearing my jersey. It's probably a huge combination of everything, but there is one thing in common with each scenario.

Joey.

She's never far from my mind, which is why as I start dinner, even though it's her night, I have a smile on my face. We actually got dismissed early today, and when we got home, she was still at her interview. I decided to start on dinner. Nothing fancy. Spaghetti and meatballs since Caleb and I always need the carbs. Sure, it's our bye week since we played Monday, but we need fuel for practice too. I might be using it as an excuse to pig out on carbs, but whatever.

"Damn, that smells good," Caleb says, entering the room.

"I think you're just hungry," I joke.

"I stand behind the smells good comment, but I'm also starving." He slides onto a stool at the island.

"It's almost ready. I'm going to wait until Joey gets here to put the garlic bread in the oven. It only takes a few minutes to heat up." The words are barely out of my mouth when the front door opens, and footsteps carry down the hall.

"Hey," Joey greets us.

"Hey." I smile at her. Probably bigger than I should for just seeing my best friend's little sister come home from an interview, but I can't seem to stop it. She's my everything, and it's getting harder and harder not to show it. Besides, I haven't laid eyes on her all damn day. Too long in my book.

Caleb furrows his brows at me but turns to his sister. "How did it go?"

"Good!" she says excitedly. "The manager who interviewed me was really nice, and we hit it off. I think I got it," she says optimistically.

"That's great, ba—badass," I say, faking a cough like a fool. I almost slipped and called her baby. "We knew you would kill it." I said we, hoping Caleb thinks my enthusiasm is just me being supportive.

"Congrats, Joey," Caleb tells her, pulling her into a hug.

I ball my fists at my sides to keep from reaching for her. I want to hold her. I want to hug her close and congratulate her with a kiss on her sweet lips.

Just a few more days.

He releases her, and she steps around the island to stand next to me. Unable to resist, I give her a one-armed hug. "Congrats." My voice is softer than it should be, but it's too late now.

"Something smells good." Joey smiles up at me.

I'd give anything to be able to kiss her. "Just spaghetti and meat-balls. I need to pop this into the oven." I grab the baking sheet that holds the garlic bread.

"Thanks for cooking. It was my night," she reminds me.

"You took her night?" Caleb blurts.

I shrug, playing it off. "Yeah, I thought maybe she might have good news about the job, and it wouldn't be fair for her to have to make dinner after that."

"We could have ordered something." He points out the obvious.

What I can't say is that I wanted to make dinner for her to celebrate. That's what a good boyfriend, training to be a husband, would do, but I clamp my mouth shut. I count to five before I reply. "It's not a big deal. You get my night tomorrow," I tell Joey.

"Fine." She sighs as if it's a big inconvenience. I know she's putting on a show. I just hate that we have to.

The words are on the tip of my tongue. I want to blurt them out. Confess to Caleb that I love her, and my world revolves around her. He can't be mad about that, right? I mean, come on. I'm his best friend. Pulling out of my thoughts, I focus on not looking at Joey and stirring the spaghetti. Anything to keep me busy so that Caleb will stop giving me those looks.

Finally, the timer dings alerting us that the bread is done. I continue to look busy, wiping down the counter while they make their plates. Finally, once they are seated, I make my own, grab a bottle of water from the fridge, and join them at the table. I avoid eye contact, knowing I've fucked up enough tonight. I've lasted this long. I can handle a couple more days.

With my fork, I pierce a meatball, and it's almost to my mouth when Joey blurts, "I have to tell you something."

Immediately I drop my fork to my plate and glance over at her. She's not looking at me, though; she's looking at her brother.

"Is this about that dickhead boss of yours?" Caleb asks, sitting up straighter in his chair, his own food now forgotten on the plate in front of him.

"No. It's something else. Something I didn't tell you when it happened." She worries her bottom lip, and it takes everything I have not to reach across the table for her hand.

"Before I tell you, I want you to promise that you won't get mad and fly off the handle."

"I can't do that. I don't even know what this is about. No dice, sister. Spill the beans." He makes a motion gesture with his hand, telling her to get on with her confession.

I will her to look at me, so I can give her a smile of encouragement or at least a nod, but her eyes are locked on her brother's. "Brock and I are dating." Her words spill out, and even though it's like ripping off a Band-Aid, I feel nothing but relief that the truth is out there. That I can hold her and kiss her anytime that I want.

"Repeat that?" Caleb shakes his head.

"You heard me, Caleb. Brock and I are dating." She finally looks across the table at me, and her eyes soften. "I'm in love with him."

"I love you too," I tell her, because I can't not. When the love of your life says the words, you say them back.

Caleb looks across the table at me and then back to his sister, who is sitting in the seat next to him, much to my dismay. "You"—he points at Joey—"and you." He points at me. "Are dating?"

"Yes," we say in unison.

He shakes his head as if he can't believe what he's hearing. "How long?"

"We've been dancing around it since the day I got here," Joey confesses.

"Fuck!" Caleb's chair screeches against the hardwood floor as he pushes back from the table. "Months?" he asks, running his fingers through his hair as he begins to pace the dining room.

"Yes." Again, we reply at the same time. It's almost been two but feels like a lifetime yet still not long enough.

He mumbles something I can't decipher under his breath when he all of a sudden stops pacing and turns his glare my way. "My baby sister? Really, Williams? She's my fucking sister!" he roars. He turns to Joey. "And you. In my own home? How dare you?" he asks, his voice raised in anger.

"I know that. She's also the woman I love, so I would appreciate it if you could keep all that anger pointed this way."

"You—" He points his finger at me as he steps closer. "Don't get to tell me what to do."

"If it comes to Joey and her being upset, then damn right I do."

"How do you figure?" he seethes, taking another step forward. He's now leaning with his hands on the table, his eyes locked on mine.

"Because I love her, Caleb. Not just for today, but for all of her tomorrows. This isn't a game. It's real life, and she's my number one priority. So, if you feel like spouting off at the mouth some more, that's fine. I can take it, but you point that shit at me and leave her out of this."

"Brock—" Joey starts. I turn my attention to her, where she's still sitting across the table.

"No, Sunshine. I get it. He's pissed we didn't tell him. I get that, but I will not have him talk to you like that. I don't care that he's your brother, and I don't care how mad he is."

Joey surprises me when she stands from her chair and walks around the table toward me. I automatically move my chair back, ready to stand with her, but she surprises us all when she sits on my lap and loops her arms around my neck.

"What do you think you're doing?" Caleb asks, this time with less heat in his tone.

"I love him, Caleb. I know not telling you was wrong. It was my idea. Brock wanted to tell you and asked to do so several times, but I wasn't ready. I wanted to be in the little bubble that we had created. I wanted us both to have time to flesh out our feelings. To have a chance to feel them and explore them before anyone else got involved." She turns to me, her lips so close I can practically taste them. "Thank you for giving me that. Thank you for giving me this." She places one of her hands over my heart. "I'm sorry for asking you to lie to your best friend, but it was time I needed."

"I told you anything you need."

"Holy shit," Caleb blurts, as he falls into the chair he vacated just moments ago. "You two are really in love?" It's coming off like a question for us and a statement for himself as if he needs to say the words for them to sink in. "Hold up," he says, eyeing me. "This weekend? At the away game? You were talking about Joey?"

"Yes."

"And you were gone all night." He's finally allowing himself to logically put two and two together, and I'm suddenly glad I said the things I did to him that day.

"I was."

"You were with my sister."

"I was with my girlfriend, who also happens to be your sister, yes."

"You told me you met someone and that you were in love with her."

"I was telling you the truth. As much of the truth that I was able to do and still respect her wishes. I also told you that she flew in to see me and watch me play."

"You." He moves his attention to Joey, who is still snuggled up on my lap. "You wore his jersey that day. I remember seeing it and was going to give you shit for not wearing mine but decided against it."

"The first game this year that I went to, I wore yours." She looks at me and grins. "I wanted to wear his, but we weren't there yet. Everything was new, and we were still fighting this crazy, intense pull that we have with one another."

"You broke the bro code." His eyes are once again on me.

"I did. And I know it's a dick move, but I'm telling you, man, I'd do it all over again if it meant at the end of the day she'd be mine."

"That's my little sister you're talking about."

"I'm also talking about the love of my life. Look, I know this is hard for you to understand. I know it's a lot to take in. If you want me to leave, to go to a hotel, I can do that—" I start, and Joey stops me.

"No. If you go, I go."

"You're choosing him over me? Over your brother?" He's no longer yelling. His voice is more defeated than anything.

"It's not a choice, Caleb. You are my brother. I will love you no matter what. But the way I love Brock, it's different. He understands me on a level I never thought possible. He's burrowed his way so far into my heart that it's no longer my own."

My heart feels like it trips over in my chest as I process her words. Unable to help myself, I lean in and press my lips to hers. It's a quick kiss and my first from her today. Caleb groans, and I have to bite back a smile.

"Do I have to watch that"—he points at us—"all the time now?"

"Yes," Joey and I say at the same time.

"I love him, Caleb. Please understand that we didn't go into this lightly. We fought our connection until we just couldn't fight it any longer. I hope one day you find a love like ours. I want you to find someone you feel like you can't breathe without. Then and only then will you understand what he means to me."

"What she means to me," I add.

"Fuck," he mumbles, resting his elbows on the table and covering his face with his hands. No one says a word as we give him time to process what this is. It's not a fling. It's forever. I'm not sure how much time passes. I'm too focused on the woman in my arms who's resting her head against my shoulder. I have my arms around her, and to be honest, I'd be content to just sit here with her like this for the rest of the night.

"Okay," he says, lifting his head. "This is how this is going to go. First, I'm still pissed. No, I'm hurt that you kept this from me, but I understand why you did. It doesn't mean that I like it." He looks from me to Joey and back again. "Second, we need to set some boundaries. Dude, I can't see you mauling my little sister twenty-four seven. So, when we're all hanging out, the PDA needs to be kept to a minimum."

"I'm going to touch him." Joey makes her own demands. "And I'm going to kiss him. You can't keep us from that. However, we will agree to keep it PG in front of you."

"Fine," he begrudgingly agrees. "Third, you—" He points to me. "Are still my best friend. So just because you're all in love and shit doesn't mean our guy time is over. That is nonnegotiable."

I didn't realize how worried I was about losing his friendship until he spoke his third demand. "Always." I lean forward, offering him my fist, and he bumps his into mine.

"And fourth," he says, "I don't want to hear you two knocking boots. So you find time to do that shit when I can't hear you."

"Like when you're asleep?" Joey offers.

"La la la la la," he says, placing his hands over his ears, making us laugh. He shudders as if he's repulsed and drops his hands. "Fifth," he says, with a gleam of mischief in his eyes. "You—" he points at me and then at Joey. "Are going to have to tell Dad."

"I can handle Dad," Joey assures him.

"You sure about that, little sister?" he asks, with a raise of his eyebrow.

"He's just going to have to deal. If he wants to be in my life, then he needs to accept that Brock is now a huge part of it. Otherwise, he can pretend he no longer has a daughter. Mom does a fine job of it."

I squeeze her tight, hating her bitch of a mother for treating her the way that she does. "Babe, this is your family."

She turns to look at me, her hands landing on the sides of my face. "You're my family, Brock. We're in this together, right?"

"No question."

She turns back to her brother. "Dad will just have to deal."

Caleb grins and picks up his fork. "This I've got to see."

Just like that, all is well again in our world. I admit I was expecting a far worse outcome, but he must see it. He has to see the way we gravitate toward one another and the way we look at each other. There's nothing but love in my heart for the beautiful woman sitting on my lap. Now that we've jumped this hurdle, I can't wait to see what the next sixty-plus years bring us.

CHAPTER
TWENTY

Joey

Playboy Williams Seen Leaving Hotel Room

That's the leading headline on every major online tabloid site on the internet, and the one I woke to this Thursday morning.

With a deep sigh, I toss the covers off and grab one of Brock's T-shirts left on the chair and slip it on. It's huge but brings a smile to my face. Plus, it smells like him, which is my favorite part about stealing his clothes. Once I'm covered, I head downstairs to find some coffee. I'm certain there's a pot sitting on the counter, waiting. Brock would make sure of it.

The kitchen is quiet as I pour myself a tall mug and splash in my favorite creamer. Only after my first sip do I open back up my phone and read the article. The photo is grainy, but clearly shows Brock exiting the room. *My room.* It was taken Monday morning after our night together, when he had to slip out before everyone was up and moving.

The article speculates over who was in the room. They suggest everyone from Gisele Sorenson to Ivana Donte, who Brock was rumored to have dated a handful of times two years ago. My only saving grace is the fact his head is blocking the room number. Otherwise, it would be easy for someone to figure out it was linked to the team, and specifically to me.

I click over to another site, which contains the same photo. This article comes with a quote from "someone close to Brock," who confirms the room belonged to a group of five women he met at a club that Sunday night. That one makes me snort.

Just as I'm reading the third claim, a message notification pops up.

Brock: Don't go online.

Me: Too late.

Brock: Can you believe that bullshit?

Me: You mean you weren't enjoying a five-girl orgy that night?

Brock: Fuck no. I was in bed with the woman I love that night. The orgy happened the next night. *insert winky face*

Me: *snorts laugh* That must explain why you were so tired on the flight back home. You slept soundly for an hour, like you didn't get enough sleep the night before.

Brock: I didn't get any sleep. I was up all night.

• • •

Me: Orgies are pretty demanding, or so I've heard.

Brock: *insert laughing emoji* Fuck, I love you. Thank you for being so cool about the bullshit that goes with dating me.

Me: And I love you. Don't let the stuff online get in your head.

Brock: I should be saying that to you.

Me: We're a team. In this together.

Brock: Hell yes, we are!

Brock: Also, Caleb thinks they'll keep digging until they hit pay dirt. If there's anyone you want to tell before our relationship potentially goes public, might want to do that soon.

I know he's referring to my dad.

Brock: I can go with you to talk to him. I don't think you should do it alone.

Me: I'll call his assistant and see when he has some free time.

When he doesn't reply, I set my phone down and take a few sips of coffee. I know they have meetings mixed in with their practices, so the last thing I want to do is bother him when he's busy. His job might be to play a game, but there's so much more than just showing up on Sunday and playing. There's a whole new level of commitment that comes with professional sports, and Brock is one of the most committed I know.

After finishing my coffee, I grab my phone and call Marcy. I know my dad is busy today, so I decide not to even bother him with my invite.

"Richard Henderson's office, how may I help you?"

"Hey, Marcy, it's Joey."

"Oh, hi, Joey! If you're looking for your dad, he's in a meeting right now," she starts, always so pleasant and friendly.

"I figured he was. Actually, I was wanting to know if he has some free time coming up that I can steal a few minutes."

I can hear her clicking on her keyboard. "Let me look. Actually, how does Saturday night sound? He was supposed to have dinner with the mayor and a few council members, but it got pushed back. I haven't changed the reservation yet, so I still have a table reserved at Harper's Point."

Knowing all I have to do this weekend is sunbathe by the pool and snuggle with Brock, I accept. "That sounds fine. Was Candi going?" I ask, really hoping this wasn't a dinner party with my stepmom.

"Actually, no. I believe Candi is out of town this weekend."

I actually let out a sigh of relief. "Perfect."

She doesn't hide her laughter. "Six o'clock at Harper's. I'll change the reservation to two."

"Actually, can you make it three?"

"Of course. I should have known Caleb would be attending too."

I don't correct her that it'll be Brock going, not Caleb. Once she confirms the details of our dinner, I sign off. Before I can even set my phone down, it rings with a local number. "Hello?"

"Is this Josephine Henderson?" a woman asks.

"This is she."

"Josephine, this is Francie Baxter human resources director for Premier Advertising. How are you this morning?"

My heart rate jumps up in anticipation. "I'm doing well, thank you."

"I'm happy to hear. I'm also happy to offer you the position of junior advertising executive. After your meeting with Mr. Pascal, he insisted we make room for you with the junior team, as he felt your experience was better suited there."

"Wow, I'm... honored. But he didn't have to create a new position for me. I'm more than happy to start at the bottom and work my way up."

She chuckles. "He thought you might say that. Mr. Pascal was actually considering expanding in a few areas prior to your interview. He just moved up his plans to create new positions in light of your brilliant interview."

She goes on to lay out the details of the position, compensation, and benefits package. It's an incredible offer, one I'd be silly to refuse. "Then you accept?"

"I do," I reply eagerly, the biggest smile on my face.

"Excellent. You mentioned in your interview you could start soon. Is Monday too soon?"

Nothing pressing crosses my mind, except I'll need to go to my storage unit and retrieve my professional wardrobe. "Monday is perfect."

"Excellent. We're so glad to have you as part of the team. Oh, before I forget, you'll be working directly under Jennifer Gooding. She wasn't at the interview yesterday because of a family vacation, but she is aware of the employment offer and your potential hiring. She will be your direct contact point and handle your training. Fair warning, however, she was planning a small team-building retreat next weekend. Her entire team will be off Thursday and Friday and then traveling to Lake of the Ozarks for the weekend. This is an annual event Jennifer does, and it just so happens to fall right after you start. If you're not comfortable going, we can certainly continue your training in-house without Jennifer or the team, but I know they'd welcome your attendance if at all possible."

I already know the answer to her question. Of course I'll be attending. What better way to get to know my new team than join them on

their weekend retreat? "I'd love to go, and don't foresee any sched-
uling issues for next weekend."

"Excellent. I'll let Jennifer know, and I'm sure she'll want to discuss
it more in greater detail next week. Welcome to the Premier family,
Miss Henderson. Expect an email confirming our offer to arrive in your
inbox within the hour."

"Thank you. I look forward to starting."

When she signs off, I'm left with an overwhelming feeling of anticipation and gratitude. I feel like I'm truly starting to pave my own
journey in my new city. Up next is going to be to secure my own place
to live. As much as I like hanging with my brother all the time and as
generous as his offer is to let me stay here indefinitely, I'm ready to
have my own place again. One where Brock can come and go as he
pleases.

One without family ears just a few thin walls away.

The past is the past, and all I see now is the future.

A future with Brock.

———

Saturday night proves to be anything but typical. As I swipe an extra
layer of mascara across my lashes, I can't help the nerves that bubble in
my gut. Sure, I was anxious to tell my brother I was dating his best
friend, but now I have to tell my dad I'm dating one of his players. Not
just any player either. Brock Williams, legendary playboy. The fact that
I'll be sharing this news with my father, a legendary playboy in his
own right, doesn't go unnoticed. In fact, I think it's what contributes to
my anxiety over tonight's dinner. Plus, we'll be in public, which means
the likelihood of being photographed and ousted to the rest of the
world is pretty great.

Any chance of continuing our quiet existence will most likely be
out the window this evening.

A knock sounds on my door moments before I hear it open and
close. As I secure the tube of mascara, I catch movement in the
doorway of my bathroom. Brock leans against the doorjamb, his eyes

taking a lazy perusal of me from head to toe. "Jesus, Sunshine, you're stunning."

I glance down at the simple black wrap dress. It's not the most seductive or revealing dresses, but it makes me feel pretty. Add in the heat I see pooled in his blue eyes and I know I made the right choice for this evening. "Thank you," I reply, trying to hide the blush creeping up my neck by lowering my chin shyly.

He steps forward, resting his hands on my forearms and pressing his lips to my own. "Are you about ready?"

"I am," I reply with a sigh, checking my appearance one last time in the mirror.

Brock takes my hand and leads me through my bedroom. I get my first glance at how delicious he looks in his black trousers and a red button-down. He's not wearing a tie and has the top button opened. The sleeves are rolled up a bit, exposing tanned skin and corded forearms.

Talk about arm porn.

We find Caleb sitting in the living room, watching coverage of a college game. "You sure you don't want me to go too?" he asks the moment we descend the stairs.

"No, thank you. We can handle it," I reply, glancing at Brock, who gives me a reassuring grin.

"All right, but holler if you need me. I'm gonna head over to Jones's place in a bit to watch the fight on pay-per-view. If you guys get done early and want to come hang out, you're welcome."

I bend down and give my brother a quick kiss on his cheek. "I'm sure we can think of something else to do, Caleb. You know, with having the house to ourselves and all."

A look of horror crosses his face as he practically jumps up from the chair, one that makes Brock crack up. "Baking cookies. That's what I'm going to think you're doing, okay?"

Brock slaps my brother on the back. "Oh, there is definitely a *cookie* involved in what I have planned, man."

Caleb punches Brock in the arm before turning his attention back to the television. "I hope you can't get it up later."

Brock laughs. "Are you kidding me? Have you seen how hot your sister is? Getting it up is never a problem."

Caleb groans and closes his eyes, as if in physical pain. "Get out of here before I rethink my entire stance on letting you live here, Williams."

"Good night, Caleb," I sing, taking Brock's offered hand and walking toward the door.

"Night," he grumbles, muttering something about horrible best friends who sleep with his sister.

The night air is perfect as we head to Brock's car. He opens the door for me, but before I can slip inside, I'm spun against the side and kissed soundly. "There. Now we can go," he whispers the moment he lets me come up for air.

The ride to the restaurant takes a little longer than usual. Thanks to a charity event at the museum, there's extra traffic downtown, so by the time we arrive, I'm feeling extra nervous. Brock senses it and has kept the conversation light and his hand on mine the entire time, but as we stop in front of the valet stand, I can't help but sense impending doom.

"Hey," he says, taking my hand and bringing it to his mouth. "It's going to be okay, Sunshine. We got this."

I nod and give him a quick smile. "I know." I take a deep breath and add, "I don't know why I'm so uneasy about tonight."

He ignores the valet standing outside of his door and turns to face me. "Have you ever brought a man home to meet your parents?"

I swallow hard, recalling the one instance I did. It was my senior year in college and my then-boyfriend, Kobie, came home with me for Thanksgiving. It had been a train wreck from the beginning. My dad and his then-wife fought the entire meal, and when we left to go have dessert with my mom, she kept hitting on him and talking about whipped cream. The next day Kobie broke up with me, stating we weren't really compatible. But I knew the truth.

He couldn't deal with my crazy family.

Not that I blamed him.

"Once. It didn't go well."

He offers me a small, reassuring smile. "This time it'll go better. Do you know why?" When I shake my head, he continues, "Because I'm not going to be scared off by either one of your parents. I've known your dad since college, remember? And even though I've only met your mom on one other occasion, I've heard all the stories from Caleb. There's nothing you can tell me that'll make me change my mind, okay? So, try to relax. Let's go inside and have a nice dinner and try not to worry. I'm not going anywhere."

I offer the best, most reassuring smile I can muster. "Okay. Let's go."

Brock flashes me that panty-melting grin I love before climbing out of the driver's seat and handing his keys to the valet. He waves off the second man, opening my door himself and helping me out. We walk side by side, while I try to appear as confident as any woman would, being on the arm of Brock Williams, but deep down there's still a touch of dread.

When I don't spy any cameras pointed our way, I start to relax just a bit. Inside, a pleasant man in a suit greets us. "Good evening. Do you have a reservation?"

"We're meeting Richard Henderson."

"Ahh, yes, Mr. Henderson has just arrived. This way to your table," he instructs, walking through the dimly lit restaurant and heading for the back corner table. I'd expect nothing but the best, most private table for my dad.

He spots me coming, and the moment he sees Brock behind me, a surprised look crosses his face. "Josephine," Dad says, standing up and kissing my cheek. "I assumed you were bringing your brother with you tonight."

"Sorry, I didn't think to clarify with Marcy when she scheduled our dinner," I state.

"Brock, good to see you," my dad says, extending his hand.

Brock takes my dad's hand and gives it a firm shake. "And you as well, sir."

"Well, shall we?" Dad says. He reaches for my chair at the same time Brock does, and the result seems to be a slight stare down, with neither of them making the initial move to release their hold on my chair. Finally, my dad lets go and steps back, his eyes watching and assessing our every move.

When I take my seat, the other two do the same. There's a slight awkwardness hanging over us, and I know it's only a matter of time before my father asks what's going on. I glance over and notice a fourth place setting, and my heart instantly drops. I really don't want to add Candi into the mix.

Clearing my throat, I say, "I thought Candi was out of town this weekend."

My dad glances at the seat, his face not giving anything away. "Yes, she is. I ran into someone else today and invited her to join us for dinner."

My interest is piqued instantly. "Her?"

"Joey."

My jaw drops when I hear her voice behind me. Slowly, I turn and find my mother directly behind me in a skin-tight dress, barely containing her largely enhanced boobs. She flashes me a wide smile, her lips painted the same color of red as the dress she wears. "Mom."

And just like that, my heart drops into my shoes.

No way will this night go as planned.

Not with both my mother and father seated at the table across from me, and poor Brock stuck in the middle of the chaos.

If I ever deserved a stiff drink, it's definitely tonight.

CHAPTER
TWENTY-ONE

BROCK

I can feel the tension radiating from her body in waves. Her wide eyes find mine, and I hate that there's nothing I can do short of grabbing her and hightailing it out of this restaurant. However, this needs to happen. With the pictures of me sneaking out of her room going viral, it's only a matter of time until the vultures discover whose room I was in.

Unable to stop myself, I reach over and place my hand over hers that's resting in a tight fist on the table. I lean into her, lowering my voice so only she can hear. "You tell me when and I'll get you the hell out of here." I know we don't need their blessing. That's not why we're here. With her dad's connection to the team, it's a courtesy more than anything. The fact that he tossed her mom into the fold of our evening was a dick move on his part.

"What's going on?" Richard asks. I turn my gaze to him to find his eyes locked on my hand that's covering hers.

Joey picks up her glass of water and takes a hefty drink before placing the glass back on the table. "Brock and I are dating," she blurts, which with this crowd, at least now that her mom is here, that's really the best way. We need to get this conversation over with, so I can get her out of here.

"What?" Richard asks, his face turning red as his eyes move to me. "You're sleeping with my daughter?" he asks.

"Dad. I said we were dating. How did that turn into sleeping together?" Joey defends.

Sure, he's not wrong, but the assumption again shows how big of a prick this guy is. "I'm in love with your daughter, sir." My voice is strong, and my shoulders are squared as I hold his stare.

"The hell you are," he spits out. "Josephine, I forbid you to see him. He's one of the league's biggest players."

"I'm aware of the fame that comes with dating a professional athlete, Dad," Joey replies.

He points a meaty finger at her. "That's not what I meant, and you know it. He's a playboy," he sneers.

"Oh, well, there's nothing wrong with playing the field," her mom speaks up. Her hand reaches out as if she's going to touch me, and the glare I send her way stops her, but her manic laugh tells me she's enjoying this little charade.

"I know his type," Richard drones on. "Football players are not the type of man you give your heart to."

"Tell me about it," Lucinda quips.

"Stop!" Joey says, raising her voice. "Enough. This isn't a decision either of you get to weigh in on." She flips her hand over and laces her fingers with mine. "Brock and I are both adults. We make our own choices. I would like to think that you, as my parents," she stumbles over the word, "would be happy for me. I've found a man who treats me the way every woman dreams of." She turns those big brown eyes to me. "And he loves me."

I want to pull her out of that chair and onto my lap. I want to kiss the hell out of her right here in front of her parents and the crowd that I'm sure has caught on to the tension at our table. I want to show the world that she's mine and that she's right. I do love her. I want every person in this room to know that.

"Are you sure you want to date our Joey?" Lucinda asks. "She's more, how should I say this...?" She taps her chin, pretending she doesn't know what she wants to say. I've heard enough stories about her from both Caleb and Joey to know she's a snake, and she's never cared about her daughter. She was simply a pawn, a meal ticket, so to speak. "Reserved, and well, I'm sorry, dear, but boring," Lucinda finally says. "You would be much better suited with someone not like our Joey here."

"Who, Mom? You?" Joey says. There's venom in her voice, and if looks could kill, Lucinda would be lying out on the floor right now.

Instead of disputing her daughter's claim, Lucinda grins and takes a sip of her wine. Her eyes flash to me, and she winks. I roll my eyes at her letting her know her games don't work with me.

"You are not dating him," Richard grates. "I forbid it."

"Well—" Joey lets go of my hand and places hers flat on the table. "When you decide to act like a mature adult and accept that I am no longer a little girl and can make my own choices, we can talk. Until then, don't bother." She stands from the table, and without being asked, I stand with her. "I'm in love with him." She looks at her dad, and then her mom. "You can either accept that and be a part of my life, or you can pretend you don't have a daughter."

My gut twists at her declaration. I hate that she's tossing out ultimatums. I hate worse that it's my past that put her in that position. I wasn't a saint, but I wasn't as bad as the media made it out to be either.

"Josephine." Richard's tone is cold. "Don't you dare walk away."

"Sorry, Dad, you don't get to call the shots in my life."

"I'm paying for your apartment," he counters.

"An apartment that I didn't want, but you insisted I live in," she fires back.

The entire room is watching this scene unfold, and I know by the time we make it home, speculations that it was her room I was leaving will be out there. I'm not upset about it, and I hope she's not either. She said that we were in this together. I just hoped we could have announced our relationship on our own terms.

"And for your information, I no longer live there. I quit my job and moved here. I don't need your money."

"I can give her anything she needs." I move closer to her and place my hand on the small of her back. "You ready, Sunshine?"

She smiles up at me. I can see the stress of the night is weighing her down, but there is still a sparkle in her eyes when they're trained on me. "Yes. Take me home."

With that, we turn and walk out of the restaurant. Murmurs follow us, but we both keep our heads held high and ignore the huffing and puffing Richard is doing behind us. We let it all fade into the background as we make our exit.

Once outside the restaurant, Joey exhales a deep breath. I don't say anything, knowing there are too many prying eyes lurking in the shadows. I give my ticket to the valet and when my car pulls up, I open the door for her and wait for her to settle in before closing it. Once I'm inside with her and behind the wheel, I still remain quiet, letting her process things.

Pulling out of the restaurant, I take a few back roads, making sure that no one is following us, before turning into the parking lot of another restaurant. I leave the car running but unbuckle my belt, then hers, and pull her onto my lap. It's a tight fit, but I need to hold her. "I'm sorry."

"You have nothing to be sorry for. My parents never cared about me. Especially my mom. Can you believe her? It's not like it would be the first time she took a boyfriend from me."

"She's vile for the way she treats you. I'm sorry. You deserve better."

"And my dad. Who in the hell does he think he is? I'm twenty-five years old. A grown-ass woman. He can't dictate my life. He can't tell me that I can't love you." She turns to look at me. "I can't imagine a world where you're not mine, and I'm not yours."

"You don't have to," I assure her.

"I mean, I get it, though, if you wanted to jump ship because of my crazy-ass family. It's a lot to deal with and a huge ask for you."

"You didn't ask me. I love you, Joey. Not for just the good times but for the bad times too." I push her hair back out of her eyes. "This is a forever kind of love, Josephine Henderson. I can take anything your parents or the press dish us, as long as I know at the end of the day it's you who will be lying in my arms at night. That's all that matters to me."

"You want to know the worst part?" she asks.

"What's that?" I'm preparing for a deep discussion in my head, but she surprises me when she finally speaks.

"I'm starving."

I throw my head back against the seat, not able to contain my laughter. "Tell me what you want, baby, and I'll get it for you."

"Mexican."

"Done. Are we eating in or picking it up and taking it home?"

"Taking it home. I want to get out of this dress, eat, and then snuggle with you." She kisses me softly on the lips before maneuvering herself back to the passenger seat. "Your car's too damn small for this." She giggles as she struggles to get settled back into her seat.

I smack her ass that's currently in my face. "I don't know. I like the view it provides," I tease.

"Brock!" She laughs, and the sound washes over me, doing wonders to wash away the drama of the night.

Pulling my phone out of my pocket, I hand it to her. "Call us in some food, Sunshine. I need to get you home, get you fed, get you out of that dress, and we have some snuggling to do."

"I love you, Brock. So much."

I reach over and give her thigh a gentle squeeze. "I love you too."

———

This week has been rough. Joey's dad, when not glaring at me from the sidelines, is being a dick. He rips me apart after every single play. Nothing I seem to do is good enough. Well, in his eyes anyway. Coach even got on Caleb a little after practice. At least that's what Caleb said. I keep my head down, shower, and get the hell out of there. He doesn't seem to care who sees him rip my ass for no good reason either.

My teammates don't comment, but they all see it. Caleb's pissed at his dad, but Joey and I have both asked him to leave it alone. This is our fight, not his. Eventually, Richard's going to have to see that his daughter means everything to me. And if he doesn't? Well, I guess we will cross that bridge when we come to it.

That's not the worst of the shit creek and no paddle this week has dished out. We have an away game this weekend, and Joey has to go to some kind of team-building retreat for her new job. So yeah, this week sucks balls.

"What time does your flight leave?" Joey asks me as we're standing in the kitchen. She's making a pot of chili, and I'm soaking up as much of her time as I can before we're both heading off in separate directions this weekend.

"We fly out tomorrow afternoon." This season is the first ever that I've dreaded an away game. I never had anything or anyone holding me at home before. Now that I do, I never want to go.

She nods. "The retreat is only a couple of hours away, so I'm going to drive. I plan to leave early tomorrow afternoon as well. We have to be checked in by tomorrow night to start the team exercises first thing Saturday morning."

"I hate being away from you." I'm well aware I sound like a whiny bitch, but it is what it is. I want to be where she is all the time.

"It's only for a weekend. I wasn't planning on traveling to the away game anyway, so even if I wasn't going to the retreat, you still wouldn't see me."

I hate that she's right. I hate even more that this is a part of my job, and there is nothing that either of us can do about it. Well, unless I can convince her to travel with the team. "We should discuss you traveling to all of my games."

"Right," she drawls. "Do you actually think my dad is going to let that fly?"

"We don't need his permission."

"Brock, I can't afford to fly to all of your away games."

"I can afford it." That's something else I love about her. She couldn't care less how much money I have in the bank.

"It's a waste of money."

"That's where you're wrong. I'd pay just about anything not to have to be away from you."

A slight blush coats her cheeks from my words. "That's your future children's inheritance you're spending," she teases.

"Our future children. And I've invested well, add in the endorsement deals, and our kids will never have to work." I adjust my stance. The thought of her growing round with our babies is hot as fuck.

"But they need to work. These hypothetical children that you speak of. They need to know what it means to work hard for something and accomplish it."

"I agree with you. You were the one worried about their inheritance," I say, pressing a kiss to her lips.

"We talked about this," Caleb groans, stepping into the kitchen.

"What? It was a simple peck on the lips."

"My sister's lips," he challenges me.

"The love of my life's lips," I fire back with a grin.

"Leave him alone." Joey smiles up at me.

"Fine." I kiss her again for good measure.

"That smells great, Joey." Caleb comes to stand on her other side and leans over, getting closer to the pot.

"Well, it's ready. Grab a bowl." She points to the bowls I set out for us earlier on the counter beside Caleb and takes a step back. I immediately pull her into me, her back aligning with my front, and wrap my arms around her.

"Thanks for dinner, Sunshine."

She tilts her head back, and I kiss her nose, making her giggle. "You're welcome."

The three of us sit down and have dinner together. We keep the topic light, steering clear of anything football or related to their dad or Joey's mom. I enjoy these moments, but as I sit here, I realize it's time for me to find my own place. Joey and I can't live with Caleb forever, and I want to start making those memories with her in our home.

"Your night to clean," Joey tells me.

"Yes, dear."

"Ah, man. She's already got you toeing the line. You sure you want to be all in love and shit?" Caleb teases.

"Wouldn't change it for anything." I stand and grab our bowls. "Go relax. I'll take care of this and be right there."

"I'll help. I was just teasing."

"Nope. This is my last night with you before Sunday. I need you to go get changed and do whatever it is you need to do. Because once I'm done in here, I'm not letting you out of my arms." I drop a kiss to the top of her head.

"Okay."

"Love you," I say softly, but Caleb is sitting so close I know that he can hear it.

In the kitchen, I rinse the bowls, load them into the dishwasher, and move the pot of chili to the refrigerator. I'm wiping down the counters when Caleb walks in. "Of course, you show up when the work is done." I chuckle.

"You really love her, don't you?"

Tossing the sponge into the sink, I give him my full attention. "Yes."

He nods. "It's not that I didn't believe you. I did, but it's just not a side of you I've seen before—however, tonight, I could see it. The way you hovered by the stove when she was cooking, the soft kisses, and the constant touching. Hell, you were eating and could barely take your eyes off her, even when her attention was on me."

"I wish I could explain it to you, Caleb. I really do. I just don't have the words to tell you what she means to me. She's a part of me," I say, tapping my fist over my heart. "Right here."

He nods. "I'm sorry Dad's being a dick."

"As long as she's still smiling, I can handle it. It's when her smile fades that you need to worry."

"Let's hope that doesn't happen."

"Now, if you'll excuse me I'm about to spend the weekend away from my girl, and I need to get my fix."

Moving to the living room, I don't see her, so I make my way upstairs. I find her in my bed, with her Kindle. Once inside the room, I close the door and lock it. After stripping out of my clothes, I turn off the overhead light but leave the small bedside lamp on. I grab a condom from the nightstand and toss it at her before sliding under the covers. "I'm going to need that," I say, pointing to her Kindle.

"You said we were going to cuddle."

TELL ME A STORY   189

"We are, but what I should have also said is that we get to sleep in tomorrow, so I plan on spending my night buried deep inside you. At least until we're both too exhausted to keep going. I need something to hold me over until I come home on Sunday."

"Why didn't you say so?" She smiles, powers off her Kindle, and hands it to me.

"All night, Sunshine," I remind her as I move to settle between her thighs. I make quick work of suiting up, tossing the wrapper on the floor.

"Promise?" she asks.

My answer is to push inside her. She should know by now. I never break my promises.

CHAPTER
TWENTY-TWO

Joey

"Joey, over here!"

I turn and find Mia and Nathan over by the refreshments table and head that way. "Hey, guys. How was your trip?"

Nathan replies right away, "Good."

"Uneventful. Isn't this place gorgeous?" Mia asks, glancing around at the lodge we're all calling home for the next two nights.

"It is. Crazy to think I've never been here before," I reply, referring to Lake of the Ozarks.

"Me either. This is my third retreat with Jennifer, and she always picks a different place. Last year, we stayed at a big spa in the city. Two full days of massages and body treatments between our meetings. It was heaven."

I pull out the agenda for the weekend, and while I don't see massages on the schedule, I do see group activities like fishing and enjoying s'mores around the campfire, which sound fun. "I haven't been fishing in probably two decades," I confess, watching as the rest of the team gets checked into the lodge.

Nathan gives me a look full of skepticism. "I've never been. I don't even know how to cast or bait the hook. We can be partners."

"I'm thinking you'd probably want someone with a little more experience," I reply with a chuckle.

He shrugs. "We can fumble through it together." Nathan offers me a quick smile, but I don't see anything that might indicate he's flirting with me. He's about seven years older and has been with Premier for almost ten years now. I've been told he was offered one of the senior advertising executive positions years ago, but he turned it down because he didn't want to lose evenings and weekends with his family.

"I appreciate it." I chuckle, just as Jennifer calls our attention to gather together.

"Once everyone has checked in, you can get settled in your rooms. We'll meet back down here in the lobby at five to six. The restaurant is expecting us at six for dinner. After that, you're free for the rest of the evening. You can explore the lodge and the grounds, take advantage of the pool, or whatever you want. Then, we meet down here at seven sharp to begin our weekend," Jennifer announces to the seven other team members in the lobby.

I've only been with Premier for a few days but I feel right at home. Instantly, I liked Jennifer. She displayed all the right attributes as a leader, and that opinion has only been reinforced since that first day. I'm truly looking forward to getting to know my coworkers better this weekend.

"See you guys in a bit." With my keycard and luggage in hand, I head for my room. We're all on the ground floor, our rooms situated together down one entire hall, probably to encourage continual communication and togetherness.

The rooms are exactly as I'd pictured, in light of the décor in the lobby. The bed is king-sized, with rustic bedposts and a bedspread featuring bears, deer, and other wildlife. The walls are painted your standard beige color, and the furniture is different hues of brown wood. Even though it's not my taste, I'm super excited to be here. It's all about the experience.

However, I do still miss Brock like crazy.

Even though I saw him just a handful of hours ago, I feel like a part of me is missing, which is silly, considering we've been together for such a short time. But he's different than anyone I've ever known or dated. I'm not dependent on him, but I feel more complete when we're together.

I also know these absences are good for us. His job will take him away too many times to count, and if I can't get by without him, that's a problem. However, it doesn't feel like a problem to me. Sure, I miss him, but I'm anxious and excited about this trip. I love my job. It's a part of who I am, and even though Brock has mentioned me not having to work, he's not pushed it. I think he knows how much I truly love doing what I do.

Just as I start to unpack my suitcase, my phone chimes with a text.

Brock: Just landed in Seattle. Miss you.

Me: Glad you made it safe. I'm unpacking now. We have a group dinner at six.

Brock: I'll be at practice until then. Talk after?

Me: I'll call when I get back to my room.

Brock: FaceTime. I want to see your gorgeous face.

Me: Deal. Love you.

Brock: Love you more.

· · ·

I can't stop smiling. We'll both be back home Sunday evening. The Ramblers play the early game on Sunday, so they'll be flying back home afterward, which is why they left on Friday instead of Saturday. Just over forty-eight hours until I can kiss those lips again.

I barely set my phone down before another message pops up. This one from my best friend.

Taylor: You couldn't at least smile a little? You look like you sucked on a lemon right before this shot was taken.

A moment later, the photo pops up. Yeah, it's definitely not a flattering one. My face is slightly puckered and my eyes squinty. I recognize it immediately. It's one similar to those already published after our disastrous dinner with my mom and dad last Saturday night. It only took approximately two hours before the first photos went viral. Fortunately, the previous photo wasn't nearly this bad. This one, however, makes me look angry, sad, and disgusted, all at the same time.

Me: Jeez, that's a terrible pic! I swear they only post the most unflattering shots.

Taylor: It's the downside of being famous.

Me: I'm not famous.

Taylor: Maybe not to you, but your dad is pretty famous, your mom the field bunny who had an affair with a famous player, and you're shagging one of the most famous current players on the roster. I'd say that makes you famous too, sweet cheeks.

. . .

I groan, hating her logic. Mostly because it's true. I've had cameras focused on me since I was in diapers. Everyone tried to get pictures of the daughter of pro-footballer Richard Henderson. Especially when said daughter was born from an affair. The public scandal still gets notoriety. In fact, I remember once in junior high, I overheard another mom call my mom Monica. It took me years before I realized she was referring to Monica Lewinsky, infamous White House intern who had an affair with President Clinton.

Me: I don't like you anymore.

Taylor: LOL! Anyway, don't get too worked up over the pic. Paparazzi are scum-sucking, soulless creatures who feed on misery and Taco Bell.

Me: What did Taco Bell ever do to you?

Taylor: Don't ask.

Me: Thanks again for taking care of Hermione for me. I hope she doesn't give you too much trouble tomorrow.

Taylor is going to the house to feed and water my cat. It's one of the plus sides to having your bestie close by.

Taylor: No problem. Besides, it gives me another chance to snoop around your brother's bedroom. I bet I find porn in his nightstand drawer.

• • •

Me: *insert gagging emoji* If you do, I don't want to hear about it.

Taylor: Anyway, have fun at your retreat. Let's plan dinner when you get back.

Me: Sounds good.

Taylor: Bye!

I toss my phone to the side and finish unpacking my suitcase. Only when I have everything where it needs to go do I finally take a few minutes to relax. Even from the ground floor of the resort, we have a beautiful view of the lake, as well as the popular Osage Beach area off in the distance.

Staring at this sight gets me thinking about the views I hope to enjoy someday with a house of my own. In Springfield, I was in a fancy apartment, and the view was of other fancy buildings nearby. At my brother's, the houses are far enough apart that you don't really see your neighbors' houses, especially with the privacy fences.

But staring at this has me thinking about water, like a running creek or a pond, and lots of trees. Maybe a rope swing or a swing set out back, where kids can run and play. Quiet. Tranquil. Peaceful.

A sudden question flashes in my mind.

I wonder what Brock wants to see when he looks out his back window.

————

"Tell me all about dating a professional athlete," Mia asks from across the table, her eyes alive with excitement.

We're all sitting together, the eight of us enjoying a drink before the appetizers arrive, and right now, all eyes are focused on me. "Oh, well, it's not any different from dating anyone else," I say, trying to brush off the attention, but of course, no one is having it.

"Not any different? You're dating Brock Williams! He's crazy hot and makes like fourteen million alone on his endorsements," she replies, sipping her fruity cocktail drink.

I feel my cheeks blush as I reach for my glass of wine. "I do agree with the handsome part," Pat says from the far end of the table. She's the oldest member of our team, a grandma of three young grandkids, who has been married since she was eighteen.

The women all nod, while the guys just seem to be more interested in the football part. "How does he like his new team? They're doing well this year. I don't think the Ramblers have gone three and oh since the nineties."

"Ninety-four," Dwayne confirms.

"He seems to like it," I reply awkwardly, shifting a little in my seat.

"He's doing well. Six receptions in nine passes last game, with one TD. Twice he ran for more than twenty yards per carry. I think it's safe to say, if he keeps this up, he's looking at Pro-Bowl contention," Dwayne confirms, clearly above par on football stats.

"Yeah, that touchdown against Chicago two weeks ago was money," Nathan adds, lifting his drink. "Nothing like scoring against your former team."

"Plus, he's dated Gisele Sorenson," Tyler says with a low whistle. As the only single guy in the group, he quickly turns the conversation toward that part of Brock's life that was always front and center in the media. "Talk about a babe. Did you see that swimsuit spread for that lingerie company?"

I flash him a quick grin, not really knowing how to reply or if one is really required at this point. Fortunately, I'm saved from answering when he continues.

"I bet it's tough dating someone of his stature. I mean, the man is followed with cameras and has women throwing themselves at him, literally, everywhere he goes. You're a very brave and trusting woman," Tyler throws out there with a laugh.

I force another smile as I reach for my glass of alcohol. I down almost half the contents, wishing we were talking about anything other than Brock. No, that's not true. I love talking about Brock. I hate the doubt that just crept into my mind at hearing the comments.

But that's all they are.

Comments.

I trust Brock, even when he's several states away. We may not have been dating very long, but I know he's one of the good guys. I don't have to worry about Gisele, or any other woman for that matter.

"Let's leave poor Joey alone," Jennifer chimes in. "We don't want to scare her off her first week with too many questions."

I throw her a grateful smile and feel myself start to relax as the conversation quickly turns to a recent ad for tires published in a newspaper by a competitor. I listen to the ideas thrown out about how we would have done it differently, making mental notes about the dynamics and chemistry of the group as a whole.

The rest of the dinner goes well, as we try not to talk about work, but fail miserably. In fact, if anything, this dinner did wonders for sparking a few new ideas for upcoming campaigns our team is scheduled to work on. By the time we all leave the restaurant and head to our rooms, I have the biggest smile on my face and can't wait to get to work on some of them.

When the door finally closes behind me, I toss my purse and phone down on the bed and head for the window. Out back, I spot several sitting areas for guests to use and one under the stars is calling my name. I head over and grab my tablet, letting it power up while I change my clothes. Once I throw on an oversized long-sleeved shirt, one I found in Brock's closet this morning with the Ramblers' logo on the front, and a pair of black yoga pants, I'm all set to check out the property I've been hearing about since I arrived. Grabbing my tablet, I head for the door.

Just before I open it, my phone chimes with an alert. The screen shows a voice mail notification, sent fifteen minutes ago. I glance at the top and notice I have only one bar of service. Something tells me coverage out here is on the spotty side, and I make a mental note to check into the free Wi-Fi.

Clicking on Brock's message, I press my phone to my ear as his message begins. "Hey, babe, we're taking a quick break at practice. I found out we're doing a team dinner down in the hotel restaurant after we leave here, so I probably won't be able to call you right away. There's some talk about—"

"*Oh, Brock Williams, you're so hot. Will you have sex with me?*" The question is followed immediately by laughter, as if whoever the teammate was who was trying to impersonate a woman could barely hold it together long enough to get the words out.

"Jesus Christ, Jones, knock it off! I'm leaving her a damn message," Brock says absently. "Sorry, babe. Jones was just busting my balls and being an asshole. Anyway, after the dinner, most of the team is talking about staying down at the bar and watching a game for a bit. We can't drink, but the coach is encouraging it as team building. I may have to stay a while, but I promise to call you as soon as we're done. I love you and hope your dinner went well. Kick ass, Sunshine."

"*I love you!*"

"*Love you, Sunshine!*"

"*I'm such a loser!*"

"Fuck you all!" Brock hollers to a chorus of laughter, hanging up the phone and making me shake my head and chuckle. His teammates are seriously the craziest.

Pulling up the message app, I fire off a quick note.

Me: Have fun with your teammates tonight. That's an order! *insert winky emoji*

Me: We can talk in the morning before you leave for practice. Besides, I have a date with a book, a margarita from the resort bar, and a lounge chair out by the lake. I love you!

I slip my phone back into my purse, grab my tablet, and head for the door. Sure I'm going to miss our video chat later tonight, but knowing he's with his team, continuing to strengthen those relationships, is more important right now. I've heard it for years from my dad, and later, my brother.

He has a job to do.

It's best to give him the space to do it.

CHAPTER
TWENTY-THREE

BROCK

"I can't believe you're wifed up, man," Jones grumbles. "When I heard you were joining the Ramblers, I was stoked to have a new wingman. I feel like I got juked," he says, taking a long pull of his Dr Pepper.

"You think you got juked?" Caleb speaks up. "He's my"—he points at his chest—"best friend. I thought I was getting my wingman back. But nooooo, do you know what I got instead? This guy—" he jerks his head at me "—all lovey-dovey with my little sister." He pretends to shudder at the thought.

"You're just jealous," I say, pointing out the obvious. I let their ribbing roll off my shoulders. There is nothing they can say that can make me change my mind about being, as Jones put it, "wifed up." Joey is my entire world. They would be so lucky to find what we have.

"Pfft." Jones leans back in his chair. "No jealousy here, brother. You're stuck with one pussy while I get the buffet," he says. At the exact moment, a group of jersey chasers walks by our table. They giggle and wave and exaggerate the shake of their hips in their too tight, too short dresses.

"I can't believe you're letting him live. Hell, you didn't even give him a black eye," Jeff Rogers, our starting left tackle, speaks up. "When she was in town a couple of years ago, you issued death threats. What gives?"

I take a sip of my water and pretend like I'm not interested in Caleb's answer when in fact, I'm hyper-focused on the sound of his voice, waiting to hear how he's going to respond.

"He's my best friend." He shrugs. "If I'm going to trust my little sister with anyone, it's going to be him."

My shoulders instantly relax as I lean back in my chair. I don't know what I expected him to say, but that wasn't it.

"And what are we? Chopped liver?" Jones calls him out.

"You're friends and teammates, but Brock and I have been friends a hell of a lot longer." He offers no further explanation, and thankfully the guys let it go.

We spend the next hour just sitting in the hotel bar, shooting the shit. We're all stone-cold sober, but it's still been good to hang out with them. I've not spent much time outside of practice with my new team, and I'm glad we did this. We've had several groups, both men and women, walk past our table in the back of the bar, but so far, everyone has left us alone. It's been nice. I hate that I missed talking to Joey, but I plan to text her when we get back to the room. Maybe she'll still be up.

"I'm out," Rogers says, standing and throwing some cash on the table.

"Hell, we might as well all go." Jones stands, and he too tosses money on the table. Caleb and I and the rest of the team who showed up do the same. I don't know what their hurry is, but for me, I want the chance to at least say goodnight to my girl.

"How's Joey doing at the retreat?" Caleb asks as we're walking through the hotel lobby back to the elevator that will take us to our rooms.

I turn to look at him. "Good, she really likes her boss, and the rest of the te—" I stop talking when I bump into someone. "I'm so—" I start to apologize until I see who it is that I bumped into.

Lucinda Gordon.

Her hair is twisted up on top of her head. She's wearing way more makeup than a woman her age, hell any woman should be wearing, and the mix of her perfume and the liquor wafting off her is making me sick. To top it off, she's dressed like a hooker.

My hands are on her shoulders as I try to steady her. It was a knee-jerk reaction that I'm very much regretting as she moves in, wrapping hers around my waist. She smells like a damn brewery. "What in the hell are you doing here?" I ask, removing her arms from around my waist and taking a step back.

She advances again, but I step back, moving away from her, holding up my hands. "Don't." There is a stern warning to my tone. I don't want this woman near me. She might have given birth to the woman I love, but she was never a mother to her. Some of the stories I've heard from both Caleb and Joey make me sick. I hate the shit she put Joey through growing up.

"You're drunk, Lucinda," Caleb spits. "Go sleep it off."

"Oh, are you offering to come with me?" She winks, or at least I think that's what she was trying to do. She is well and truly wasted. "What about you, big man?" She turns her glassy eyes back toward me. "You know you want the older, more mature version. I can show you things my daughter never thought about," she slurs. "I know men like you. You can't resist a wet pussy, and mine is ready for you." She grips the hem of her dress as if she's going to lift it and stumbles toward me. I take a step to the left, and she falls to the floor. I make no move to help her up. Instead, my eyes find Caleb's.

"Piece of shit," he grumbles. "We need to get out of here before a crowd starts to form." He looks around, and thankfully, there's not another soul in sight. How we managed that in this hotel when the entire team is staying here, I'll never know.

"Sounds good to me." I purposely step around Lucinda, ignoring her pleas to let her show me how good we can be. Bile rises in my throat when her words replay in my mind. She has no regard for her daughter's feelings whatsoever. She is the epitome of a jersey chaser. It's hard for me to process my sweet, loving, sexy-as-hell girlfriend came from the piece of trash we left lying in the middle of the hotel floor.

"Thank fuck Joey isn't here this weekend," Caleb seethes as we step onto the elevator. "Lucinda wouldn't have given two shits if she was standing next to you. She still would have pulled that stunt. Worthless." He shakes his head.

"No shit. She's going to be pissed when I tell her what happened." Not only is she going to be pissed, but I know she's also going to be hurt. There's no way can I keep this from her, though. These kinds of secrets are what destroy relationships, and that's not what's going to happen to us. With me having to travel so much for my job, she needs to know that she can trust me, and that means having hard conversations like the one we're about to have, no matter how bad neither of us really want to. I hate that I can't be there to hold her when I tell her, but I think it's best to get it out now.

"You're going to tell her?" Caleb questions. "While you're both out of town?" He raises an eyebrow.

"Damn right. I don't hide anything from her, and I don't intend to ever start. That kind of shit kills relationships, especially with our career. I hate to be the one to tell her, but at the same time, I want it to be me too. I wouldn't put it past Lucinda to run to the press, or hell, they could have been lurking in the shadows, and we didn't see them. I want her to hear it from me."

He claps a hand to my shoulder. "You're a good man, Brock Williams. I meant what I said tonight. If it had to be anyone, I'm glad it was you."

Not gonna lie. I have to swallow back some emotion welling in the back of my throat. "Appreciate that," I manage to say as the elevator doors slide open.

We stop outside our doors. Our rooms are across the hall from one another. "You want me there when you talk to her?" he offers.

"Nah. I've got this. I'll see you in the morning," I say, scanning the keycard to my room.

"Not too early." He points his index finger at me, wearing a grin before scanning his own card and disappearing into his room.

Kicking off my shoes, I plop down on the bed and pull up her number. I listen to it ring, but there is no answer. Instead, it goes straight to voice mail. Son of a bitch. I really wanted to talk to her tonight. "Hey, Sunshine. It's me. Something happened tonight that I wanted to tell you about. Call me when you get this. It doesn't matter how late. I love you." I end the call and toss my phone on the bed. I can't believe Lucinda and the nerve of her actions. I'm her daughter's boyfriend, and she knows I am. For her to come on to me like that... to say the things she was saying to Caleb and to me, I'm repulsed. But it's not just that. My heart hurts for my girl. I know what this is going to do to her, and I hate I have to be the one to deliver the hurtful news.

I feel gross after having her hands on me. Stripping out of my clothes, I head to the shower. The hot spray does wonders for my tired muscles. Too bad it does nothing for my mood. I'm dreading this phone call with Joey, but it's the right thing to do. Turning off the water, I quickly dry off and slip into some sweats before turning off the bathroom light and making my way back to the bed.

I settle back against the headboard and check my phone—nothing from Joey. My nerves can't take waiting, so I call her again. Only to get her voice mail for the second time. "It's me again. First, I want to tell you I love you and I miss you, and if I don't happen to get to talk to you tonight, I hope you sleep well. I called earlier to tell you that Caleb and I ran into your mom here at the hotel. It was... an experience. Let's just leave it at that until I can talk to you. I love you, Sunshine."

I sit here scrolling through my phone for the next hour, waiting for her call, and it never comes. Worry tries to settle in, but I push it away. I'm sure she's sleeping, and her phone is probably on vibrate. She wasn't expecting to hear from me tonight, so I'm just going to have to wait until in the morning to talk to her. I'm exhausted and need to get some sleep. Before I do, just in case she's not sleeping and forgot her phone or something, I decide to give her a story, one she can either come home to or wake up to. Either way, both are going to be with thoughts of me.

Me: Once upon a time, there was a man who was living his best life. He had the career he always wanted, and he recently found the love of his life. Although his career takes him away from his love, there isn't a moment she's not on his mind. He can't seem to think of anything else.

In fact, all he can think about is coming home to her and showing her how much he's missed her. He plans to spend a lot of time wrapped up in their bed making love to her.

Me: To be continued…

———

I wake with a start to the sound of fists pounding on my door. My eyes squint at the alarm clock to see it's just after six. Holy hell, I feel as though I just closed my eyes an hour ago. It's too damn early for whatever it is Caleb thinks he's going to drag me along to.

"Williams! Wake the hell up." I hear Caleb say through the door. He sounds mad, even upset, and that's when panic begins to take root.

Joey.

I couldn't reach her last night. What if something happened?

"I'm coming!" I call back as I scramble out of bed and to the door. Pulling it open, I step back to prevent being run over by a fuming Caleb as he enters the room uninvited. "What's going on? Is it Joey? Is she okay?" I'm suddenly wide awake as worry grips my chest. I should have tried harder to get a hold of her last night. "Tell me." It's a demand.

"It's Joey, but not how you think. Physically, she's fine. Mentally, I don't know." He runs his fingers through his hair, which already looks like he's made that exact move a hundred times this morning.

"Explain."

"It's easier to show you." He pulls his phone from his pocket, and his fingers fly across the screen. My stomach drops because I know I'm not going to like whatever it is that he's about to show me. "Here." He thrusts his phone in my face.

Taking a deep breath, I look down at his phone and cringe. It's a picture of Lucinda and me in the hotel lobby. I'm looking down at her, with my hands on her shoulders, and she's staring up at me. It looks intimate, but it wasn't.

"Son of a bitch," I seethe. "How in the fuck do they hide where we can't see them? This isn't at all what happened," I rant as I read the headline.

RAMBLERS TIGHT END DATING MOTHER-DAUGHTER DUO

"What the fuck?" I look up at Caleb. "Has she seen this shit?" I ask him. I silently beg him to tell me no.

"I don't know, but she probably has by now. I got woke up from a raging phone call from our dad. He's pissed as hell. Fuck, man, he was going on about you not being good enough for his daughter and how a tiger doesn't change its stripes or some shit. He even dropped the word trade in there. He might not be able to make the trade, but he has the influence on the team to make it happen. This is bad, Brock. Real fucking bad."

"You were there," I say, my voice rising. "You witnessed the entire fucking debacle of a nightmare it was. You can tell them the truth. Call your dad and tell him the truth."

"I did tell him. He didn't want to hear it. He said I was defending you because you were my best friend. I'll try again once he cools down. What you need to worry about is Joey."

"Fuck!" I roar, placing my hands behind my head as I pace the room. "I tried to call her twice last night, and she didn't answer. I texted her too," I say, rushing to the nightstand by the bed to check my phone. Pulling up the message I sent, I see there's no reply waiting for me. She loves our stories. If she's seen this, she would have replied. Right?

Dialing her number, it goes straight to voice mail. "Voice mail," I grit out, calling her again. And again. And again. Each time I get her voice mail and fear takes over. I'm split down the middle with fear that something has happened to her, and the other half is scared to fucking death. She's going to see this before I get a chance to talk to her and think that what she's reading is real. I've never been more scared in my entire life as I am in this moment. Either side of the fear that I'm facing could mean that I lose her, and I'm not okay with that. I'm not me without her.

I call her again. "Joey, it's me. Baby, I need you to call me as soon as you get this. Please, Sunshine. I need to talk to you. Call me, please," I say, tossing my phone on the bed. "What the fuck do I do?" I ask Caleb. "I can't lose her, man. I can't." I shake my head as the thought of her ending what we have has my stomach rolling.

"There's nothing we can do but keep trying."

"You call her." I point to his phone in his hand. He nods and dials her number. "Hey, Joey. It's me. I'm with Brock, and we're worried about you, and we need to talk to you. Call one of us back as soon as you can. Love you, sis."

I have to fix this. I need that fucking article axed. Immediately. Reaching for my phone again, I pull up my agent's name and hit Send.

"Brock?" he asks groggily.

"Miller. We have a problem." I go on to tell him what's wrong, and he's going to get the agency's publicity team and lawyers on it. That's the great thing about working with him. His agency offers full service to their clients. He's basically my one-stop shop, and right now, I need him to earn every fucking penny of the cut he gets from my contract and endorsements.

"Why isn't she answering her phone?" I ask, my voice cracking, when I've finished talking to Miller.

"I'm going to do what I can. Maybe we can call the resort and have them track her down," Caleb suggests, already typing on his phone before placing it to his ear. "Yes, I need to be put through to Josephine Henderson's room, please," he tells whoever answers. He pauses. "Thank you."

I stand from the bed and walk toward him, but he holds up his hand to stop me. "Joey," he greets, and I sag in relief that he finally has her on the line. "Hey, don't cry," he says, and I feel my world shatter as I drop to my knees. I never wanted to hurt her. I never wanted my career to cause her pain and to think that it's all at the hands of her mother.

"I need to talk to her," I say, climbing back to my feet and reaching for his phone.

"Brock." This time it's Caleb's tone that's a warning. "I know, Joey," he says, his voice softer. "You don't have to talk to him, but you do have to listen to me."

CHAPTER
TWENTY-FOUR

Joey

I sniffle. Again. I hate crying, and ever since I got up this morning, I feel like I've been doing just that. I can't even imagine what my face must look like right now. I'm supposed to be downstairs with my new team, having breakfast before our first round of team-building events, but here I am, crying over tabloid drama once more.

"Are you listening to me?" my brother says gently.

Sniffle. "Yes."

"It's all bullshit, Joey. Every word. I was there. I watched it happen and heard everything said."

I close my eyes, relief filling my entire being. Not because I believed what was printed. I simply don't trust the woman who gave birth to me, the one who has used me as a pawn to get more from my dad my entire life, to do whatever she can to keep herself front and center in the prying eyes of the media.

The one who has made it more than clear she takes what she wants and screw who she hurts.

"Why is she there?" I voice the question I've had since I woke and saw that horrid photo on my screen.

"I don't know," he replies honestly. "She was drunk and stumbling near the elevator. She practically fell into Brock and then started hitting on us. It was vile."

I can't even process the words he's saying. "She hit on you too?"

Caleb snorts. "Like a groupie backstage at a Whitesnake concert."

I close my eyes, embarrassment washing over me. "I'm sorry."

"No," he practically demands. "You don't apologize for her behavior. I've heard it my entire life, Joey, and I won't hear it anymore. You did nothing wrong. You're not responsible for how she acts, what she says and does. Your whole life, you've done everything you could and should to make that woman happy, but enough is enough. I don't want to hear any more apologies from you, you hear me?" His tone is much softer as he asks that last question.

"I hear you."

"Good. Now, are you okay? Really?"

I take a deep breath and flop back on the bed. "I think so. I'm just sad that this is my life, you know?"

He doesn't say anything for a few moments before he finally replies, "I know. This isn't what you've ever wanted."

"I don't want to be in the news, Caleb. I don't want to have my picture taken everywhere I go. This is too much." I feel the tears welling up again, but I quickly blink them away.

"I know, sis. I know."

We don't say anything for a few minutes, but it doesn't matter. I'm comforted by having my brother on the other line. "Listen, I need to get downstairs. I have a whole day's worth of activities I'm supposed to be a part of, and I'm sure they're wondering where I am."

He sighs. "Do you want to talk to Brock?"

Do I?

Yes. I need to hear his voice more than I need my next breath of air, but isn't that the problem? I've become completely focused on him. A man. Something I swore I'd never do, not after witnessing my mom's antics growing up.

"Not yet. Tell him I'm okay, but I really need to get down to my meeting. We'll talk when we get home."

"Joey," he says, getting ready to argue.

"Please, Caleb. I just need… a minute. To think. To breathe. If I talk to him right now, I'll be crying and sad he's not here, and I just don't have it in me right now."

"I understand."

"Just tell him… tell him I love him, and I'll see him tomorrow night when he gets home." My throat is thick with emotions and unshed tears.

"I'll tell him."

"Thanks, Caleb. I'll talk to you later. Good luck tomorrow, okay?"

He snorts. "Thanks. You gonna watch?"

"I don't think I'll be able to. Our retreat ends at noon, and then I have to drive home, so I'll be on the road while you play."

"Just promise you'll call if you need anything, all right? Me, Brock, whoever. We'll be tied up all day with practices and meetings, but we'll get back to you as soon as we can."

"She can call me anytime for anything." I hear Brock state adamantly in the background. It puts a smile on my face.

"I will. My phone doesn't get the best reception here, just so you know."

"Okay, sis, I'll let you go. Kick ass in your team building shit," he adds, bringing a smile to my face.

"You know it."

"I love you, Sunshine." His words come through the phone loud and clear, making me close my eyes and just feel the power of his statement.

"I love you too," I whisper, even though he's not holding the phone.

"All right, we need to get ready to head to the stadium."

"Kick ass, Caleb."

"Kick ass, Joey."

Before I hang up, I hear Brock in the background, throwing a barrage of questions at my brother. I feel guilty I didn't just talk to him, but I wasn't lying when I said I needed time to think. And my mind is a jumbled mess right now.

Getting up, I run to the bathroom to survey the damage. Yeah, I look like I went two rounds with Mike Tyson. I place a cool rag over my eyes, praying it takes some of the puffiness away, and change my shirt into one that isn't wrinkled and tear streaked. I throw on a thin layer of mascara and grab my stuff. Even if I don't feel one-hundred-percent, I'm at this resort for a reason. Time to put my thoughts of Brock and the drama that seems to be surrounding me out of my mind.

I'm here for a reason.

Time to get to it.

———

I don't know how I made it through the day, but I managed.

When I finally arrived for breakfast, thirty minutes after everyone else, the looks they gave me confirmed any question I may have had about them seeing the tabloids. After I ordered a cup of coffee and a toasted bagel, I told them the story was fabricated, most likely in an attempt to discredit me or Brock, and that I was focused on the reason we were all here.

Hardest thing I've ever done, but I pushed Brock and my mom out of my head and did what I came to do. Together, we hiked one of the Lake of the Ozarks' most famous trails, fished, and completed exercises to encourage our group to work as a team. It was effective, honestly, and all things considered, I truly enjoyed my day.

Now, after sitting around the campfire out back and indulging on s'mores, I'm headed back to my room for the night with the promise to reunite with the team for breakfast in the morning.

The minute I step back inside my private space, the weight that's been silently accompanying me all day starts to settle on my chest once more. The moment I woke and found a link to the latest tabloid story on my phone comes back to me with the force of a hammer to the chest. I don't always get my texts and phone calls, but *that* particular piece of information had no problems getting through the technology barrier of our secluded location.

Figures.

I slip into the bathroom and take a quick shower, desperate to wash the smell of the outdoors off me. As much as I've enjoyed the day, I'm even more excited to grab my tablet and curl up on the bed.

I go ahead and plug in my phone, even though it was barely used today. I had it off while we went through our team-building activities, but now that I'm alone again, I should probably power it up and see what nightmares await.

Several messages do pop up, which is surprising. The first one I click on is from my brother.

Caleb: Hope you're having a good day.

A smile crosses my lips, and I go ahead and fire off a reply, letting him know I did have a great day. Then, I click on the next message, the name that makes my heart skip a beat. I see a whole slew of messages, all received at some point throughout the day.

Brock: I love you.

Brock: I hate this. But I understand.

Brock: I get why you didn't want to speak to me. I just want you to know I'm here.

The next one comes midafternoon, most likely during a break in his practice schedule.

Brock: Once upon a time, there was a man. He was sad and didn't know what to do. See, he led a charmed life, getting paid to play the game he loved. However, with that love comes a price. He found that out the hard way when the media went after the woman he loves more than football. They set out to discredit him and make his love doubt the man he is. That tore him up inside. So much so, he vows to spend the rest of his life telling her how much she means to him. To be continued…

Brock: Her smile could lighten up even the darkest nights.

Brock: Her laugh fills my soul with fire and happiness.

Brock: She's the most hardworking woman I know, and I love and respect the fact she wants to forge her own way in this world.

Brock: She's a loyal friend and a caring sister.

Brock: Her heart is pure and filled with goodness, even though it has been broken in the past by those trusted to protect it. To protect her.

Brock: I'll never forget that first time I saw her in the elevator. She was wearing a yellow bikini, and from that moment on, I've thought of her as sunshine. Bright, cheerful, a ray of hope in this dismal and stressful world we live in.

Brock: I fell in love with every part of her, including her flaws. She pours entirely too much creamer in her coffee. She's a touch grumpy first thing in the morning. She has a cat, for crying out loud, when I've always considered myself to be a dog man.

Brock: But despite all of that, I'd choose her. Every second of every day. I'd always choose her.

. . .

The last two messages arrived about thirty minutes ago.

Brock: I'm going to bed, alone. Because my heart is halfway across the country doing her thing. I'm so fucking proud of her, and to be honest, I've asked myself more times than I can count... what did I do to deserve her? I'm not sure I'll ever be able to answer that question, but I do know I'll spend every ounce of energy I possess to making sure she never feels less than the amazing woman she is. She's my heart, my reason for living. And I love her more than I ever thought possible.

Brock: I don't want her to reply tonight. I want her to focus on her job. I want her to crawl into bed, hold onto the pillow, and know that if I were there, it would be my arms wrapped around her. Holding her tight. Good night, my sunshine. Sweet dreams, love. And know you'll be in mine too. I can't wait to see you Sunday. I can't wait to hold you in my arms once again.

"Good night, Brock. I love you too."

With tears in my eyes, I set the phone down and grab the pillow. As instructed, I close my eyes and dream of Brock, of his arms wrapped around me once again.

———

The drive home seems to take forever. Traffic heading into Kansas City is backed up from an accident on the expressway. I've tried listening to nineties pop music, but nothing is really helping calm this anxiousness I feel inside me.

I'm thirty minutes from home, and all I want to do is get there, unpack, shower, and get ready to welcome the man I love home. Sure, it's not our home, but maybe soon we'll have a space of our own, one for just the two of us.

And Hermione.

I was up most of the evening, thinking. I considered my life from every angle and came back to the same conclusion: I want him. It doesn't matter what job he has, what the rag mags say. Every relationship takes work, as long as you're willing to put in the time and effort.

I'm willing.

And ready.

Just as the line of traffic I'm in starts to inch forward, I flip the station, hoping to catch coverage of the Ramblers game. I find it right away, and a smile instantly spreads across my lips.

"It's been a rough game for Ramblers fans today. Down by twenty late in the fourth, we're anxiously waiting for a status update on Ramblers' tight end, Brock Williams. He was injured in a vicious hit near the end zone, which resulted in a fumble from Williams."

"No," I gasp, my heart pounding as fear grips my chest. My hold on the steering wheel tightens.

"We'll report more as soon as we find out the status on Williams, but also when we hear about the trade rumblings that began prior to kickoff. Rumors arose mere hours before the team took the field, and speculation is it has something to do with the stories surrounding Williams and his girlfriend, Ramblers' offensive coordinator, Richard Henderson's only daughter."

I close my eyes briefly, as worry makes it hard to breathe.

"Whatever the reason for the trade talk, we hope the rumors aren't true. Since Williams joined the team, we've seen a new life breathed into this team, including an impressive three and oh start on the season.

"What we do know is today's team is a far different one than the Ramblers who have played the first three games of the season. And I'm sure Ramblers fans everywhere are just praying we can get through the rest of this game without any more injuries or turnovers.

"We'll be back after this."

CHAPTER
TWENTY-FIVE

BROCK

My head wasn't in the game. Neither was my heart, for that matter. They're both with Joey. She should be driving home about now, and that means as soon as these damn doctors clear me, I can head home to her. I still haven't talked to her, and it's killing me. I can't concentrate, and all I can think about is her. She knows I'm innocent, but that's not enough for me. I need to get my arms around her. I need to hold her and kiss her and tell her how much she means to me. I need to feel her in my arms.

I can't breathe without her.

"Williams." Dr. Stern, the team doctor, snaps his fingers. "Can you follow my finger?" he asks. I follow his finger and manage to be present enough to answer his array of questions he deems necessary to put me through. I get it. It's concussion protocol, and the league takes this shit seriously. I understand why, and I agree with them, but I can't concentrate for shit, and it has nothing to do with the hit I took out there on the field and everything to do with the one that blasted my heart.

"All good, Doc?" I ask. I need to get to my locker and see if she's called or texted me. I don't really expect her to have done either since I know she's driving home, but a man can hope. I sent her so many messages that have all gone unanswered. My anxiety level is through the roof. I'll fight for her. For us. I won't lose her over this. I won't. If she can't handle the press, I'll give it all up. What I won't give up is Joey. Never my Sunshine.

"You have a mild concussion. You'll have to sit out from practice for at least a week."

"Okay." I move to get off the table.

"And you can't stay by yourself."

"I have roommates."

"I can't guarantee that you'll be able to play in next week's game. You need to be symptom-free and must be able to pass the baseline tests. I have some dynamic stretches and balance training you can do, but I don't want you to start them for at least forty-eight hours."

"Fine." I move to stand and sway a little.

"You need to just lie here for a few."

"I can't do that," I tell him.

"You're not going back out there, Brock," he says, exasperated.

"I know." I try to stand again, this time, I'm successful, but the room spins.

"What in the hell are you doing?" This comes from the doorway, from a voice I recognize as my best friend.

"I need to get to my phone. I need to check on Joey."

"Fuck, Brock. You just took one hell of a hit. Sit your ass down," he grumbles.

"Have you heard from her?"

He holds up his helmet. "Game just ended."

"Right." I nod, and the move only makes my head feel as though it might explode.

"Sit down," Caleb hisses.

"I need my phone."

"Fine. I'll get it. Just sit the fuck down." He turns to the door, pushes it open, but steps back when the phone in his hand rings. He grins as he strides back to where I'm leaning against the bed and shows me the screen. Joey. A sob breaks free from my chest when I see who it is.

My Sunshine.

"Hey, Joey," Caleb greets.

"Caleb!" She sounds frantic. "I just heard. How is he? Please tell me he's going to be okay."

"I'm right here, Sunshine," I call out, already feeling better just hearing the sound of her voice.

"Brock." Her voice cracks. "Let me see him," she says, and Caleb hands me the phone.

"Hey, you." I sigh, resting back against the table. I can see the tearstained streaks on her cheeks, her eyes are hazy with tears, and her face and neck are blotchy, but to me, she's never looked more beautiful.

"I need to see you," she says. "I need to be there." Her eyes roam over what she can see of me in the camera, looking for injuries. "Are you okay?" She places her hand over her mouth, but it wasn't soon enough. I saw the quiver of her lips as tears well in her eyes. "Tell me you're okay," she whispers.

"I'm okay," I assure her. I wish I could reach out and slide my arms around her waist. I need to hold her next to me. "Just a mild concussion."

"Just?" she scoffs. "That's serious, Brock Williams," she scolds.

"I know, baby, but I'm going to be just fine."

She ignores me. "Have you seen the doctor?" she asks. "What are they saying?"

"I have seen." I turn the phone so that she can see Dr. Stern.

"Tell me what he needs to do and not do. I'll make sure it happens."

Relief washes over me. She's not leaving me, not yet at least. She's going to stay and make sure I'm okay. That counts for something, right? That means that she still loves me, and she's not going to hold this media shitstorm against me. Not that I did anything wrong, but it is my career that had the press seeking me out, and more than likely her mother too. Then again, it could just be the twisted fuck that she is, and she wants what her daughter has. I use the word mother lightly. More like an egg donor.

It's not until Dr. Stern stops talking and I hear her sweet voice again that I will myself to focus on their conversation. "I'll be with him," she tells Dr. Stern. "I'll check on him regularly and make sure he doesn't start any of this for forty-eight hours."

"Sounds like you're in good hands." Dr. Stern nods at me, smiles at my girl, waving at the phone, and leaves us alone.

I turn the camera back to face me. "I'm sorry," I say before she can.

"You have nothing to be sorry for. If anyone needs to be apologizing, it's me. I avoided you, and then there's my mom...." Her voice trails off.

"I love you, Josephine Henderson."

Her brown eyes soften, and once again well with tears. "I love you too." She huffs out a breath, looking up at the ceiling. When her eyes find mine again, she's composed herself. "I'll be at the airport. Is that okay? If I wait there for you?"

"Yes." There is nothing that I want more.

"Are you sure you're going to be okay?" she asks again.

"You heard the doctor. I'll be just fine."

"Have a safe flight. I'll see you later tonight."

"We're wheels up in three hours later." Caleb tells her. That's if everyone showers, and gets through their press interviews in time. I hope it's sooner than that so I can get to her.

"I'll be there."

"Love you, Sunshine."

"I love you too."

———

The flight did nothing to ease my headache. It didn't help that Dr. Stern, Caleb, and Coach Matthews all kept checking on me, as well as some of the other guys. It didn't go unnoticed to me that Coach Henderson wasn't one of those people. Hell, I'm not even sure he was on the plane. I took a seat in the back and closed my eyes, willing the flight to be over.

I see her before she sees me. She's sitting outside the Starbucks with her Kindle in her hand. I know she's engrossed in whatever book she's reading. My girl loves her stories. With my suitcase wheeled behind me, I take a seat next to her. She turns to smile kindly, but as soon as she sees that it's me, she launches herself into my arms, only to pull away just as quickly.

"I'm sorry. Did I hurt you?" Her eyes take me in once again, looking for injuries now that she can see me in the flesh.

"It hurts me that you're not still in my arms."

She smiles through her tears. "I'm so sorry," she says, her voice cracking.

"None of that," I tell her. "We're good, Sunshine. I promise you. We're good," I repeat.

Caleb stops next to us. "You two ready to head home?" he asks.

"Yes. I took an Uber here so I could ride with you." She stands and slides her Kindle into her purse.

"Take me home."

She helps me stand from the seat, and I place my arm around her shoulders, leaning some of my weight on her but careful not to give it all to her. Slowly we make it toward the exit.

"Which one of you drove here?" Joey asks.

"I did. Let me help," Caleb offers, taking my suitcase so I can hold onto his sister a little better.

"I'm fine. Just got my bell rung. I'm better now. You two can stop fussing."

"Oh, so you can walk on your own?" Joey tilts her head to look at me.

"Yeah, the dizziness has passed, but I'm not letting go of you." There is no room for argument in my tone.

"I didn't ask you to," she sasses.

With a smile on my face for the first time in days, we make our way to the parking garage. As soon as we push open the doors to the parking lot, we're swarmed with media. Cameras flash and microphones are shoved into our faces.

"Brock, what do you think about the trade rumors after only a few games with the Ramblers?"

"Brock, is she worth it?"

"Brock, how can you compare mother and daughter?"

The three of us ignore their questions as we push forward to Caleb's car. He opens the back door, and Joey and I both climb inside. He rushes around and slides behind the wheel, locking the doors. Thankfully he has dark tinted windows.

"What in the hell was that? Why are they talking about a trade? Am I being traded?" I ask Caleb, meeting his eyes in the rearview mirror. I know there were rumors, but I thought that's all it was. Rumors.

"Fuck, man, I don't know what's going on."

"It's our sperm donor," Joey speaks up. "He not only wants to control my life he wants to ruin it."

"Let's get home, and we can figure this out. We need to get away from these leeches." Caleb puts the car in Drive, and slowly, we move through the swarm of media.

———

"I can't believe him," Joey seethes as she tosses her tablet on the couch next to where she's curled up next to me.

"This is low, even for him," Caleb agrees.

"And the bastard won't answer his phone," Joey hisses.

When we got home from the airport, Joey got me settled on the couch, and ran upstairs to get her tablet. It didn't take her long to find an interview from her dad that was given after today's game. He tried to play it off that my performance was lacking, and if it continued, there could be another trade in my future. The reporter called him out, reciting my stats. His face turned bloodred. It wasn't until he asked him about me sleeping with his ex-lover and his daughter that I truly thought his head might explode. He huffed out a "No further comment," and stalked off toward the locker rooms.

"Hey." I pull her into my chest. "It's fine. My stats on the field speak for themselves. It's going to be fine."

"Other than today, the team has been killing it, and Brock filling the tight end position has a lot to do with that. The team owner and Coach Matthews know what's up. He's not going to let the highest-ranked tight end in the league go because our dickhead of a father tells him to.

He might have pull in the league, but trust me, he doesn't have that much," Caleb chimes in.

I shrug. "We'll deal with whatever comes our way."

Joey sits up and turns to look at me. "How are you so calm about this? This is your career, Brock."

Reaching out, I push her hair back out of her eyes. "Yeah, but there are some things that are more important."

"What? You've worked your ass off for your career. You can't mean that."

"Let's just take it all one day at a time," I tell her. "Now, I could use a shower. I need to wash off the travel."

"You good to get upstairs?" Caleb asks.

"I got it. I'll take it slow and be sure to hold onto the handrail," I assure him.

"I'm coming with you."

"Good." I lean forward and press my lips to hers. "I need my back washed." I wink at her, but she doesn't smile as I had intended. "Baby, I'm fine. I promise. It's a mild concussion. I'll be back on the field in no time." She eyes me suspiciously but helps me stand and follows me upstairs.

———

"I needed that," I say, taking the towel that Joey offers me. She showered with me and insisted I sit on the bench while she washed me from head to toe. I should shower at home after a game more often.

She holds out her hands, helping me step out of the shower. I don't tell her that I can do it on my own. I let her have this, taking care of me. To be honest, I'll take whatever she's willing to give me. After the silence between us this weekend, I'm ready to soak up anything and everything she has to offer.

"You hungry?" she asks once we are both dressed and in bed.

"No. I just want to hold you for right now."

"I like this plan." She snuggles closer, resting her head on my chest.

"I missed you." Those three words are the best I can do, but they don't even touch the surface of the last few days without her.

"I missed you too. I'm sorry I went radio silent. I just needed to wrap my head around all of this madness and the fact that it's mostly because of my... because of Lucinda."

Did you hear that crack? That was my heart breaking for her. This woman in my arms has so much love and light to give. My Sunshine deserves so much better than what she was born into. Sure, she never wanted for anything. But to never feel loved by your mother and have a father who tosses around orders and money like it's a good substitute for his time and love, causes an ache in my core for my beautiful girl.

"Can I ask you something?"

"Anything."

"How are you so calm about all of this? What my dad said, my mom and her vile actions. My parents are tearing your world upside down, and yet you're eerily calm about it all."

"They're not tearing my world upside down, Joey. You are my world. You're here next to me where you belong. My arms are holding you close, and I know we're going to be okay. That's all that matters to me."

"You could be traded. Of all the things I thought might tear us apart, I never imagined it would be my parents."

"They won't."

"How can you be so sure?"

"Because I'd give it all up first."

She lifts her head to look at me. "Tell me you're kidding."

I cradle her face in the palm of my hand. "I'm not kidding. I never kid when it comes to you and how much I love you."

"This is your career. Your livelihood."

"Sunshine, I'm twenty-nine. I have a handful of years at best before I retire. This game is taxing on your body, and well, it's not all I have to live for anymore. I have you," I say, lowering my voice. "I want to build a life with you. Buy a house, a ring, have some babies. I want to be there for all of it. I meant it when I said I've invested well. I could walk away today with no regrets and no financial strain."

"I can't let you do that."

"It's my decision, and if that's what it comes down to, I'll walk away without a second thought." Tears well in her eyes as she shakes her head. "You're my everything, Sunshine."

A sob breaks free from her chest, and she buries her face in mine. "I-I love you."

My hand traces up and down her back, soothing her. "I love you too," I assure her, over and over again.

Eventually, her cries quiet, and when her breathing evens out, I know she's fallen asleep. Only then do I close my eyes, holding her a little tighter than needed. She's back in my arms where she's meant to be, and I'll do anything, give up anything to see that she stays there.

Josephine Henderson is my happy ending.

CHAPTER
TWENTY-SIX

Joey

"Tell me a story, Sunshine," he whispers.

I'm curled up on his side in my bed, and even though I know he's supposed to be sleeping, he's not. He's just lying here, holding me close and absently stroking my arm.

"Once upon a time, there was a woman madly in love with a football player, who just so happened to be the most handsome player in the league."

"I like this story already," he mutters, pressing a kiss to my forehead.

"The world went crazy, lies were told, lives were disrupted. The football player was thrust into the limelight, taking the woman with him. At first, she hated it, despised the havoc it created in her life. Until she realized, he was her life. What happened to him, happened to her. Even though she had the choice to walk away, she knew it wasn't an option for her. Their love, her love for him, was too great, too powerful. She wanted a life with him, even if that life was one of chaos."

I glance up, meeting his gaze. "Even among the chaos lives a beautiful story. *Our* story."

Brock grins and places another kiss on my forehead. "You are the most incredible woman I've ever known, Josephine Henderson."

I sigh, resting my cheek on his bare chest once more. "We have a long road ahead of us, and I'm not just talking about the next few days while you recover from your concussion. There're the trade rumors we'll have to deal with, and I'll have to confront my mom."

"You don't have to do that alone."

I take a deep breath. "Yes, I do. I need to have this conversation with Lucinda Gordon on my own, face-to-face. Calling her mother at this point makes me sick. I need to look her in the eye and tell her how much she has hurt me, and I'm not just talking about what happened in Seattle. For years, she's used everyone around her, bled them dry, myself included. It's time I told her how I feel, how badly she has hurt me. Then walk away. Because at the end of the day, I don't think my words will affect her. She'll never change, and it's time I cut the toxic from my life."

"And I'll be right there with you. If not beside you, nearby, waiting to take you home."

I move my hand, reveling in the feel of his hard, muscular chest beneath my palm. "What are we going to do about the trade?"

"I don't know." Brock sighs, his arm getting a little tighter around me. "When I signed my rookie year with Chicago, I thought that's where I'd stay my entire career. Sure, I knew deep down the chances of that actually happening were slim, but I had faith in my ability, my game, and my team."

Another sharp inhale as his heart thunders in my ear. "When I was traded to Kansas City, I was grateful for the opportunity to play with Caleb again. Eager to move to my new city and get back to work. Then I saw you again, and nothing was the same.

"When I signed, it was a one-year contract, with the option to extend up to four years. Negotiations were to begin at week seven of the regular season, not week four, so why there's trade talk now, I'm not sure. And why Miller, my agent, hasn't heard a word is beyond me."

"I bet he's not happy," I whisper, running my fingers through the dark hair on his chest.

"Oh, he's fucking pissed. The first time he heard anything was on Twitter before the game. He started making calls to the Ramblers' office, but no one was available. Last we talked, he was waiting on a call from the GM to find out what's going on."

"What will you do? If you're traded?"

"Depends where it is. If I don't like it, I'll retire early."

"What if I go with you?" I ask, without giving it much thought. But the truth is, I would. I'd go anywhere with him in a heartbeat.

"I can't ask you to do that. I won't, actually."

My heart practically bursts with love and appreciation for him. "You didn't ask. I offered."

"And I appreciate that more than you'll ever know," he says, sliding his lips across my forehead. "Let's cross that bridge when we get there, okay?"

"Okay," I reply through a yawn.

"Sleep, Sunshine."

"Brock? Tell me a story," I mutter, closing my eyes and feeling the weight of the day starting to lull me into sleep.

"Once upon a time, I met the strongest, most remarkable woman in the world. She changed my life from the very beginning, and all I want is to create a life with her. Someday, I'll ask her to marry me, but until then, I'll settle for showing her how much she means to me..."

————

I steel my spine, raise my fist, and knock on the door. The homes I grew up in gradually got bigger and better each time we moved. Once my mom figured out how to get more child support from my dad and how to find more wealth with each new boyfriend or husband she found, the houses grew to support her lifestyle.

Mom opens the door and gives me a wide, white smile. "Joey! What on earth are you doing here? Aren't you supposed to be working?" she asks, stepping aside and letting me cross the threshold.

"I am, yes. I took an extended lunch today so I could speak with you."

Once she closes the door, she follows me into the formal living room, the sound of her expensive high heels echoing off the white walls. "You know, if you find yourself a rich man, you would never have to work again. Like Brock Williams. His endorsement deals are key to you getting anything and everything you want. Trust me on this, darling," she says, taking a seat in one of the wingback chairs.

I sit across from her on the uncomfortable sofa, which was clearly bought for its price tag and not for its coziness. "Actually, that's why I'm here. I wanted to speak to you about Brock."

Mom holds up a martini glass. Where in the hell did she get that from? "Oh? What about him?" she asks, playing coy.

"I think you know. You were there, in Seattle, if I recall."

"Oh, that," she says, waving off my concern. "A few friends and I hopped a plane and went to the game. Marcia Davidson has the biggest crush on that quarterback. We decided to go watch him play in person."

I don't need to mention the fact the quarterback is married. Everyone knows that. What I do decide to mention is my knowledge of her presence at the hotel. "Tell me about running into Caleb and Brock at the elevators."

My mom looks at me, puzzled. "Are you referring to what happened when that photographer snapped the picture of Brock and me? Brock approached me while I waited for the elevator. He invited me up to his room," she replies matter-of-factly.

And even though I'm expecting something similar to this reply, hearing it hurts more than I anticipated. "Really? So, he hit on you?"

"He did. I couldn't believe it, honestly. I'm your mother!" she states with a sneer on her painted lips.

Hearing all I need to hear, I stand up. The movement seems to catch her off guard. "That's right, you are my mother."

"I told him no, absolutely not was I going to his room. Not when he was linked romantically to you."

"Okay," I reply, turning and walking toward the door. Before I reach the foyer, I stop and turn back to face her. "That is interesting, though. Considering I heard it was the other way around."

Mom laughs, a dry, uncomfortable noise. "Well, of course he would say that. No man likes to be caught with his pants down, sweetie. They lie."

I nod, as if considering her words. "Funny, it was actually Caleb who told me it was the other way around. He witnessed the entire exchange."

Mom snorts in disgust. "You mean Brock's best friend? Not only would that man cover for him, but he clearly hates me. He blames me for ruining his parents' relationship."

"You *did* ruin his parents' relationship."

She rolls her eyes. "I only reacted to an invitation, Joey, which is exactly what happened in Seattle. Except this time, I didn't go up to his room."

"Because you weren't invited."

"Because I knew it was wrong."

"Right. It was wrong. And yet you still came on to my boyfriend, knowing full well we were in a relationship. We both know you did, but what I really want to know is why?"

Mom's eyes are wide as she realizes she's cornered. I'm not backing down this time, and I think she knows it. "Listen, sweetie, I had been drinking—" she starts, but I cut her off.

"Yes, you had. That still doesn't excuse you coming on to my brother *and* my boyfriend."

She rolls her eyes and takes another sip of her drink. "Okay, Josephine, stop being so dramatic."

"Dramatic? I think I have a right to be a bit dramatic when I find out my mother tried to seduce my boyfriend. And maybe I wouldn't be this *dramatic* if it were the first time, but you and I both know it wasn't."

Mom's mouth opens, like a fish out of water, but no words come.

"Camden Lenz."

That grabs her attention. A look of panic crosses her face.

"You remember him, right? The guy I was dating three years ago, right out of college? You met him a few times over the nine months we were together. In fact, I'm pretty sure you met him several times on your own, right? *Without* me being present?"

"I-I-I..."

I close my eyes, hearing all the confirmation I needed. Even though I suspected they had slept together, I didn't have proof. But in my heart, I knew. *I knew she had slept with him.* Camden had told one of our mutual friends he was seeing an older woman on the side. There was only one older woman who fit the equation. It was in the way he always wanted to invite my mother to dinner and then found some excuse to step out of the room when she was also out. I didn't want to believe it then, and I hate hearing the confirmation now.

"I can't believe you," I whisper, closing my eyes and fighting off the tears.

"It's not what you think, Joey."

"No? It's not my mother sleeping with my boyfriend while we were together? Or my mother flying out to Seattle to try to seduce my current boyfriend when she knew I was out of town? It's not like that?"

She just stares at me, refusing to reply.

"I'm tired of letting you hurt me." Standing up straight, I face her head-on. "I want nothing to do with you. A real mother doesn't try to hurt her own child intentionally, which is what you've done my entire life. I'm no longer your pawn, a toy you can play with when you're bored. Stay away from me, Lucinda. I mean it. Stay away from those I love. If you don't, I know there are plenty of skeletons in your closet you'd hate to have exposed."

She gasps as I turn to head toward the door. "You're blackmailing me?"

I turn and meet her wild gaze. "I am. You should know how it works. It's a play I took from your playbook."

"Josephine!" my mom hollers as I open the front door. "Why on—"

"No," I reply, cutting her off. "As of today, you no longer have the power to hurt me. Stay away from us, or all of your secrets will be shared with the world."

"You wouldn't," she cries, her eyes welling with tears.

"Try me." I hold her eye for several long seconds before she looks down, finally breaking eye contact.

Without another word, I walk out the door, leaving it standing open, and head for my car. Once inside, I set my shaking hands on the steering wheel and take several deep breaths.

I did it.

I can't believe I told my mom off.

With a smile on my lips, I start my car and pull out of the driveway. With each second that passes, I feel lighter, freer than ever before. A huge weight has been lifted off my shoulders, and I, for one, can't believe how amazing I feel.

Like my whole life is before me.

A path I get to forge.

Freedom has never tasted so sweet.

––––––

"Hey, where's Brock?" I ask the moment I step into the kitchen and find only Caleb.

He diverts his gaze, a sign that he's keeping something from me. "He ran a few errands after practice."

Brock received the all-clear yesterday to begin practicing with the team again. It's been just over a week since his mild concussion during the Seattle game and the media shitstorm that followed. He put in his time, did what the team of trainers and physicians said, and is finally back out on the field where he wants to be. He had to miss the San Francisco game on Sunday, but only because the lead physician felt it was better to be safe than sorry.

During his time off, his agent and he met with the general manager and head coach. Both assured him they had no knowledge of any trade and said any talk of it was clearly a rumor. They even insinuated it was started on social media and had nothing to do with the comment my dad said during the post-game interview. I think they're covering for him—hell, everyone thinks they're covering for him—but Brock says there's not a lot we can do about it. We just have to see what the negotiations bring in a few weeks.

"Errands? What kind of errands? I thought you went to practice together," I press, staring at my brother and watching him squirm.

Caleb shrugs and gets up to grab a bottle of water. "He said he had a stop to make and dropped me off. That's all I know."

I'm pretty sure he's lying. I can tell by the way he refuses to look at me, and how the tips of his ears are turning red. "You sure?" I hedge, pressing the envelope.

He turns around, ready to argue, but it falls flat on his lips. I start to get a little worried, that maybe Brock is in trouble and my brother doesn't know how to tell me.

"What's going on?"

He growls and starts to pace. "He went into a meeting after practice today."

My mind starts processing. "Was it with the physician? Are they worried he isn't ready for Sunday?"

"No, nothing like that," my brother insists, running his hand through his hair. "It was another meeting. A coach."

I blink a few times, glancing around as I think. "But his contract says the negotiations aren't until after week seven. That's two more weeks yet," I argue.

Caleb closes his eyes. "It was another coach. He went to see the offensive coordinator."

Realization sets in and my throat is suddenly Sahara dry. I turn, worry and fear gripping my chest. This can't be good. Not at all. Especially since we both agreed that when this conversation happened, I'd be there too.

Now, he's dealing with this alone, and there's nothing I can do to help him, except sit back and wait for him to get home.

From a meeting with my father.

CHAPTER
TWENTY-SEVEN

BROCK

As soon as I drop Caleb off, I head back to the stadium. Richard doesn't know that I'm coming, and that's exactly how I want it. I have the element of surprise on my side. My agent and the GM have both assured me that the trade rumors are, in fact, that, just rumors. They claim they were started on social media, and that may be true, but it's still from Richard's asinine comments.

I'm done playing games with him. He needs to know that nothing he says about me and no amount of trade rumors or hell, even a trade, is going to keep me from his daughter. I know that my past was somewhat promiscuous, but it wasn't anywhere near as bad as the tabloids made it out to be. The past is in the past, and meeting Joey changed me. She's all I see, and it's time he understands that.

Pulling back into the players' lot, I grab my keys and phone and make my way back inside. The security guard, John, tilts his head in acknowledgment as I pass him, making my way to the locker room. Pushing inside, I walk through the empty room and back toward the offices. Coach Matthews is already gone, but I knew he would be. His kid had something going on today, which is why practice actually ended on time for once.

My feet carry me a little farther until I reach Richard's door. Ramblers' offensive coordinator, followed by his name, is stuck to the wall beside the doorframe. I like to think Dick is more fitting. At least it's an appropriate nickname for him, and I won't get called out on it if I slip and call him that to the media. A smile tilts my lips. I might just have to do that. It's a name I know from both of his children that he loathes.

Without knocking, I step inside of his office. He looks up when he hears me enter and scowls. "What the fuck are you doing here?" He crosses his arms over his chest and glares at me.

"I'm here to talk, and you're going to listen." I don't stop moving until I'm standing in front of his desk between two chairs. I won't be sitting because this won't take long.

"I have nothing to say to you."

"I don't really give a fuck." I shrug. "You're going to sit there and listen to me. Because I do have something to say to you."

He opens his mouth to argue, but I hit him with a glare, similar to the one he just gave me, and that shuts him up.

"Item number one." I hold up one finger. "You're a dick. Dick." His forehead scrunches up, and the tops of his ears turn red. Both give me immense satisfaction.

"Item number two." I hold up two fingers. "You, sir, are shit for a father. When Joey and I have kids, I swear to you I'll be the opposite of every fucking thing you are to her."

"I've provided for her," he counters.

"She didn't need your fucking money or fancy-ass apartments. She needed you. *You*. Her father. She needed one fucking adult in her life to love her and to listen to her. She needed a dad, not a football superstar to toss money her way. Sure, you might have given her the best that money can buy, but all that girl ever wanted was love. Your love, and you denied her."

"I love my daughter," he says, sitting up straighter in his chair.

"Yeah? You love her? Then why do you never listen to a damn

thing she has to say? She was so nervous to tell you about us because she knew you would fly off the handle. And let's be real, Dick, it's not my past that you're afraid of. It's your own. You know how so many in this league live with a woman in every city. In fact, that's how Joey got here. You, a married man, sleeping with a jersey chaser."

It's no longer just the tips of his ears that are red, but his entire face. "Fuck you. You don't know anything."

"Item number three." I hold up three fingers. "Your jersey chaser was never a mother to Joey. She manipulated you to get more and more money, but none of it went to Joey. Not a single penny. She had you hook, line, and sinker." I pause for just a few seconds, letting that tidbit of information sink in. "Ah, I see the shocked look on your face. This takes me back to item number two. If you were any kind of father and had built a relationship with your daughter, this wouldn't be new information. Instead, all you wanted to do was parade your trophy wives around and toss money at her. You tried to buy her love, Richard, but you didn't need to. She loved you regardless."

"I-I didn't—" he starts, but I cut him off.

"Of course you didn't. I believe both items one and two both apply here."

He scoffs but remains quiet.

"Piggybacking on item number three. Your jersey chaser, the one you invited to the dinner that your daughter wanted to have with just the three of us, hit on your son and me." I drop that little nugget of information into his lap. His eyes grow wide, and for once, he's not disputing my claim. That's because he knows that bitch just as well as we do, and nothing is out of her jurisdiction if it gets her what she wants. I go on to give him the gory details of the night we ran into Lucinda in the hotel lobby.

"Bitch," he mutters under his breath.

"She is. I'd love to tell you that you should never have touched her because you were married and all that, but I can't find it in me to do so. You never having gotten your dick wet with Lucinda would have led to a world without Joey, and that's just not something I can even fathom at this point in my life."

He tilts his head to the side, studying me, but I don't let it get to me. This man is nothing to me. He's hurt her too many times, and I won't stand for it. I know Joey was going to see her mom and that she's done with her. She wanted to be with me today, but regardless of how this little information session goes, I want her to make her own decision about keeping her father in her life. I'll deal with him. For her. If that's what she wants. I don't want her losing the only parent who obviously cared about her, even if it was in his own fucked-up way.

"And finally, item number four." I smirk, holding up four fingers. "I love your daughter, Richard. It's not just a passing fling. I feel as though I can't breathe when she's not near me. There is not a single second of the day that I'm not thinking of her. I'll take our nights curled up in front of the TV at home over a night out with the guys any day. Right here." I tap my fist over my chest. "She lives right here, and it's her permanent residence."

He surprises me when he doesn't comment, instead letting the silence hang between us. That's okay because I've got more to say, and then I'm out. He can take the information and do whatever the fuck he wants to do with it. I'll be there for Joey, no matter what the end result may be.

"She's my future. You can toss out rumors of a trade, you can pull strings to make that trade happen, but it's not going to tear us apart. No, you see, when you love someone, and I mean really love them from the depths of your soul, you do what you have to do to be with them. Joey can come with me, which she's offered to do." I watch as shock registers on his face. "And I'm not above giving it all up for her."

"Bullshit."

I shrug. "I don't need you to believe me. I know in my heart there isn't anything I wouldn't do for her. If it means retiring once my contract is up this year, I'll do it. She's my entire world. I know you don't understand that... hopping from woman to woman, and you're what... on wife number four? It must suck to be you. I can promise you with every breath inside my body that the day that Joey and I say our wedding vows, they're for life."

"You're getting married?" he croaks. Finally showing an ounce of emotion other than anger at my ambush.

"We're not engaged, but it's coming. Soon. I can't imagine a day of my life without her in it. So, we're at a turning point here. You have the chance to decide what kind of father you want to be going forward. Either way, she's going to have two men." I point to my chest. "And her brother to give her all the love and support she could ever need. Besides, that's how it's always been, right? Caleb has been the one to show her unconditional love until me. Now there are two of us." Making a fist, I rap my knuckles against his desk. "I hope you do the right thing." With that, I turn and walk out of his office. I feel lighter, having had the opportunity to say my piece. There is just one thing nagging at me, and I'm going to fix that now too. I'm marking both of these things off my list, and then it's forever with my Sunshine.

———

I made the drive to Springfield in two hours. Joey called me five times on the drive, but I ignored her calls. It was hard to let each of those calls go to voice mail, but this is something I have to do. As soon as I'm done, I'll call her, but I'm afraid if she finds out what I'm doing, she'll talk me out of it.

The call I did answer was my mother's. I made sure to tell her that Joey was the love of my life, and that she would—if I had my way—have those coveted grandbabies soon. At least I hope she will. She laughed, and if I'm not mistaken, shed a few tears, but told me that I needed to run that promise past my future wife before making it.

My future wife.

That sounds damn good. I have to force the smile off my face as I pull open the door to *his* office.

"Good afternoon, may I help you?" the receptionist greets me.

"I'm here to see Skylar Davis."

"Do you have an appointment?"

"No. I'm Brock Williams from the Kansas City Ramblers. I was hoping to have a few minutes of his time." I offer her my most charming smile.

"Of course, Mr. Williams. Let me just check to see if his last meeting has ended. Please have a seat." She points to the chairs in the lobby.

I nod, but I have no intention of sitting. I know everyone has seen the headlines. This woman appears to be in her early sixties, so maybe she doesn't follow social media or the sports scene and gossip sites, but I know damn good and well, when Skylar hears my name, he's going to know why I'm here.

I'm here for Joey.

When she turns to head down the hall, I follow along behind her. I get curious glances, but she doesn't seem to notice. When she stops at his door and announces my arrival, I hear him tell her no. He's too busy. *Fuck that.* I step up behind her. "I'll take it from here, Cindy," I say, repeating the name he just called her.

"Get out of here," Skylar demands.

I ignore him and stalk toward his desk. "I'm going to cut to the chase. I know you know who I am." My voice is low and lethal. "And that tells me that you also know why I'm here." He stares at me, trying to keep a neutral expression, but I can see the fear written all over his face. He's five-ten, maybe five-eleven, and what, a buck fifty? I have several inches and at least a hundred pounds on the guy. Thankfully for him, he's smart enough to see my rage and keep his mouth shut and listen.

"I know what you did, Skylar. I know that you put your hands on the woman I love. I know that you threatened her, and you can imagine I don't take that kind of thing lightly."

He shakes his head, as his hands tremble at his sides. He's scared. Good. This is nothing compared to what I'll do if I find out he even breathes her name or touches another woman inappropriately.

"Do you know who I am?" I ask him.

He nods.

"So you know that I have money. Lots of money and lots of connections."

Another nod.

"If you so much as breathe Joey's name, I'll end you. If I ever find out that you touched a woman without her permission and then threatened her afterward, I will dismantle this company piece by tiny piece, until there is nothing left. Your name in the industry will be shit. You should be thanking your lucky stars that Joey didn't want to press charges against you. She just wanted it all to blow over, but you see, I can't live with that. You hurt the most important person in my life, and for that, you need to have consequences."

"Consequences?" he asks, his voice shaking.

I nod. "Joey gets a severance package. Six months of pay, as well as a glowing recommendation from you and the other partners here at the agency. I don't care how you go about getting them, but you have a week to make this happen. A week, Skylar." Reaching into my back pocket, I pull out a business card for my agent. "The check and the letters can be sent here. I don't want you in contact with Joey. Ever." Placing my hands flat on his desk, I lean over so that we're close, so close I can smell his fear. "Do you understand?"

"Y-Yes, sir."

"Mr. Davis. Is everything all right here?" I turn to look over my shoulder to see a security guard with his hand on his gun strapped to his waist. Cindy must have called him.

"Mr. Davis?" I prompt, ignoring the security guard.

"Everything is fine, Sam. Thank you," Skylar squeaks.

"I was just leaving. Skylar." I point at him. "You have a week." With that, I turn and push past the security guard, who seems to be starstruck once he realized who I was. I nod at him, offering him a smile, and make my way back out to my truck.

I immediately fire off a text to my agent, telling him what he should expect to see in a week's time before hitting Joey's contact. The call rings through the speakers as I pull out onto the lot.

"Brock?"

"Hey, Sunshine." Just hearing her voice makes me smile.

"Where are you?"

"I had some errands to run."

"What kind of errands?"

"The kind that you probably aren't going to like," I confess.

She sighs. "Tell me."

"I went to see your father."

"I told you I wanted to be there."

"I know, but this was something that I needed to do."

"How did it go?" I go on to tell her about my visit with her dad.

"He was quiet when I left."

"Oh, Brock." She sniffs. "I-I don't know what to say. Other than Caleb, I've never had this kind of love and support. 'I love you' just doesn't seem strong enough for how I feel about you."

"I know, baby. I know," I assure her.

"So, that took all this time?" she asks, changing the subject.

"No. I'm in Springfield."

"What are you doing in—No. Please tell me you didn't."

"You made Caleb promise, but not me," I remind her.

"What did you do?"

"Nothing. I just made it known that if I ever found out about him touching a woman inappropriately, I'd ruin him and his company."

"Brock! He could call the press or worse, the cops."

"Oh, security showed up. He sent them away. And you should be getting a check for six months of severance pay and letters of recommendation from all the partners. I know you don't need either, but it was the principle. He wronged you, and this is a small way of helping to make it right. Granted, nothing will make him putting his hands on you or threatening you okay, but this at least makes him uncomfortable. He's going to have to go to accounting for the check and his partners for the letters. He's going to have to be the one to explain why he's doing what he's doing. I gave him a week."

There's silence on the other end, and I'm afraid I might have fucked up. I'm going to have to do some major groveling when I get home. However, when her laughter rings through the speakers, I realize I was wrong.

"I wish I could have seen his face," she confesses.

"Damn, I should have taken a picture for you," I joke.

"I miss you."

"I miss you too. I should be home in a couple of hours."

"Brock?"

"Yeah, Sunshine?"

"Tell me a story."

I don't have to glance in the rearview mirror to know that I'm grinning. Joey is everything I never knew I wanted or needed.

"Once upon a time, there was a man who fell madly in love with a beautiful woman. Loving her changed him. Her love made him want to be a better man. The love they shared had him thinking about weddings, and babies, and a house full of love, laughter, and sunshine."

EPILOGUE JOEY

Joey

I've never experienced a more electric energy in my entire life. The entire stadium is on their feet, screaming and cheering for their team. The score is tied at seventeen with two minutes to go in the fourth. The winner of this matchup wins a trip to Miami, to the biggest game of the year.

Championship game.

I don't think I've ever been this nervous in my entire life. I'm on my feet, standing alongside legions of Ramblers fans, my hands gripping those of my friends around me. Taylor is on one side, while Mia, my coworker and friend, is on the other. Sure, we could have watched from a suite upstairs, but this is where I want to be.

This is where I want to watch the game.

I tighten my hold on my friends' hands and hold my breath. The line gets set. The quarterback takes his position. He calls out the play, glances from his left to his right. There's a moment I swear I can see his eyes when they connect with Brock's. Brock gives him a slight nod, and I know it's coming.

My eyes widen as the ball is hiked. Brock takes off, running ten yards out before cutting hard to the left. He holds out his hands, the ball thrown his way. He reaches and has to adjust his pace to catch it, the ball thrown almost out of his grasp. But Brock has it, his big hands securing the football at the five-yard line.

I watch as a defender comes from out of nowhere, driving his shoulder and helmet into Brock's side and knocking him off his feet. The momentum of the hit carries him toward the goal line, and all I can do is watch in horror as he spins through the air, landing hard on his side.

But something else happens in that moment.

As he's spinning through the air, Brock holds out the football, reaching for the white line of the endzone. I feel my own air woosh from my lungs as he falls against the turf, the linebacker who drove into his side falling on top of him.

The whistle blows.

The referee holds his hands up in the air.

Touchdown.

The crowd goes wild, the stadium erupting into an ear-piercing roar of celebration. I don't even realize I've joined in, screaming and jumping up and down, until Taylor pulls me into a hug. "That was amazing!" she yells, though I still struggle to hear her. "I can't believe he caught that! It was way overthrown."

A proud smile breaks out on my face. Of course he'd catch it. My man can perform under pressure better than anyone I know. He's the number one tight end in the league this year for a reason.

The celebrations in the stands continue as the field goal team takes the field. I watch as my brother counts out his steps, lines up the kick, and waits for the snap. The moment the ball is in the air and positioned in front of him, he drives it up and over the goalpost, securing one final point in the game.

Brock is the first one to run out onto the field and throw his arms around Caleb as he's walking back to the sidelines. I can see their mutual smiles, even from the stands, and I've never been prouder of both of them.

The final minute winds down, and the crowd lets out a mighty roar as the visiting Thunder is unable to score any points on their final drive. The Ramblers have won.

They're going to the championship game.

In his first year with Kansas City, Brock and the team have not only punched their ticket to the biggest game of the year but have rewritten the history books too. They've only lost one game this season, the one in Seattle where Brock got his concussion, having the best Ramblers regular season record in franchise history.

Brock also secured a four-year extension to his contract. In fact, it was my dad who pushed for the terms, making sure the main office realized what they had with his addition to the team. He signed that contract quickly, knowing it was going to keep us here for what he suspected were to be the final years of his career.

When the crowd on the field grows, I lose track of Brock in the mix. I know he's down there, celebrating with his teammates, coaches, and management. It isn't until I see someone push through the crowd, heading toward the stands, that I realize Brock is on the move.

I stand up on my seat, Taylor reaching out and gripping my shirt so I don't fall. We make eye contact, matching smiles on both our faces. He holds up his arm, raising his helmet high above his head, and that's when I see it.

The tattoo.

The sun he had done a month or so back on the underside of his arm. He positioned it there because that's his favorite place to have me rest my head when we fall asleep at night. The burst of bright yellow sunshine no one knows the meaning of except us.

I wave like a lunatic, throwing my own arms high above my head.

When he lowers his arm, he taps his chest, something he's started doing after every game. He says it's for me, where he keeps me tucked during his times of victory and tribulations, in his heart.

Media surrounds him and our moment is lost, at least for the time being. I know there will be much celebrating later tonight when we're finally alone in our own home. My thighs clench together just thinking about it.

Tonight, I'll get to hear one hell of a story.

EPILOGUE BROCK

Brock

This has been the best fucking year of my life, and if all goes well tonight, that declaration will be sealed forever. I don't need the outcome of the championship game to make the declaration official. I just need my Sunshine and one three-letter word.

Pulling into the driveway of our home, I smile, knowing that my girl is inside waiting for me. When this place came on the market in the same gated community as Caleb's, I knew it was going to be our forever home. I called the realtor, and that night, as soon as Joey was home from work, we went to look at it. She fell in love immediately, and so did I. Not just with the house, but with the future I could see playing out as we live here. We made an offer that night and never looked back.

We've lived here for a few weeks, and we're finally getting settled, but that's not good enough for me. I want the vision. I want the house full of laughter and love and the pitter-patter of little feet. I want the welcome sign on the front porch to say welcome, with our last name. Not just mine, but ours. I'm ready to take the next step toward making that happen. I just hope she is too.

Pulling into the garage, I leave my bag. I'll get it later. Right now, all I want to do is wrap my arms around her. That is definitely priority number one. Pushing open the door from the garage to the house, I kick off my shoes in the mudroom and call out, "Honey, I'm home."

"In here," she responds.

I follow her voice to the living room. There's a pizza box sitting on the table with a couple of bottles of water and a box of breadsticks that my girl has already started on. Hermione is hanging out on the back of the couch, snoozing away. While our rescue dog, Fable, who is a mixed breed that I surprised her with the day we moved in, is curled up beside her, eyeing the pizza. She knows my girl is going to give her a bite. Who am I kidding? I can't say no to either one of them. Fay, as I like to call her, knows damn good and well I'll be giving her a bite of mine as well. But first...

"Sunshine." I breathe out her name as I bend my head to kiss her lips. "Missed you."

"Missed you too. Great game today. That was one hell of a catch." I flash her a grin before sitting next to her and reaching for a breadstick. "I know this goes against your diet, but it's a celebration, and I didn't want to waste time cooking. I just wanted to spend it with you."

This couldn't have worked better in my favor. "We're going to the championship game. I can afford a cheat night with my girl." We spend the next fifteen minutes eating and talking about the game.

"I'm telling you, I was gripping their hands so tight I don't think they'll be regaining feeling in those fingers anytime soon, if ever." She laughs.

"I'm sure they're fine," I assure her. "You done?" I ask.

"Yes. I'm stuffed."

"I'll clean up. Why don't you go get ready for bed? I'll be right up."

"Deal." She places a loud, smacking kiss on my cheek and heads upstairs.

I gather the now-empty pizza and breadstick box, along with the rest of our trash, and take it out to the larger can in the garage. While I'm out there, I grab the gift that I've been hiding for her from the small safe. It's a large black box, and a smaller one. After making sure the house is secure, and the lights are off, I head toward our room.

"What's that?" she asks immediately when she sees the larger box in my hand. The smaller one is shoved inside the pocket of my sweats.

"I got you something."

Her eyes soften. "All I need is you."

"Well, this is kind of for both of us, and you already have me." I hand her the box. "Open it."

She grins and pulls the lid off the box. I watch as the tears immediately form in her eyes. She looks up at me in question. "What does it say?" I ask her.

"The story of Brock and Joey, and this picture—" She runs her fingers over the black-and-white image. "It's the first one we ever took together."

"I know. Open it." She does as she's told, and she gasps when she sees what's inside.

"H-How did you do this?" she asks, flipping through the pages.

"When we moved, I realized that I wasn't the only one who had kept copies or screenshots of all of our stories. There are a few that are missing—the ones we told in person—but that's okay, because our story is to be continued. Not just with words, but with love, and laughter, and life," I say, kneeling by the bed.

She sits up and wraps her arms around me in a hug. "This is the best present I've ever been given."

"You think so?"

"I know so."

"Well, I added a story that you haven't read yet. Flip to the last page." She grabs the book and does as I ask.

"Brock," she cries, as her eyes scan the page.

"I think I should read it to you." I take the book from her hands and wipe at her tears with my thumbs.

"I don't need you to," she starts, but I stop her by kissing her softly.

Pulling back, I don't bother to look at the last page of the book. I have this part of the story memorized. "Once upon a time, there was a man, a football player, who fell hard and fast in love with his best friend's little sister. He knew that giving in to the temptation of her was a risk, but it was one he was willing to take and would gladly take over and over again, knowing that the outcome was her love.

"With each passing day, the man fell more in love with her, until one day he realized, calling her his girlfriend and living with her wasn't enough. He wanted her to share his name. After all, she already owned his heart and soul. The man decided he was going to ask her to marry him. All he could think about was building a future with her, and he wanted to get started on that future sooner rather than later. To be continued…"

Setting the book on the bed, I pull the small black box out of my pocket and open the lid. "Sunshine," I start, my voice cracking. "Will you do me the incredible honor of becoming my wife? Will you help me write the next chapters of our story every day of our forever? Will you marry me?"

Tears roll down her cheeks, but her smile is as bright as the sun. *My Sunshine.* She begins to nod as she repeats the word yes, over and over and over again. "Yes! I love you so much."

With shaking hands, I pull the ring from the box and slide it on her finger. Just as I hoped, today is officially the best day of my life. "I love you, future Mrs. Williams."

"I love you too, Mr. Williams, and I love our story."

THANK YOU

Thank you for taking the time to read Tell Me A Story.

Want more from Kaylee and Lacey?

Fair Lakes Series:
It's Not Over | Just Getting Started
Can't Fight It

Standalone Titles:
Boy Trouble
Home to You
Beneath the Fallen Stars

Kaylee & Lacey writing as Rebel Shaw
Royal
Crying Shame

ACKNOWLEDGEMENTS

THERE ARE SO many people who are involved in the publishing process. We write the words, but we rely on our editors, proof- readers, and beta readers to help us make them the best that they can be.

Those mentioned above at not the only members of our team. We have photographers, models, cover designers, beta readers, formatters, blog- gers, graphic designers, author friends, our PA, and so many more. We could not do this without these people.

And then we have our readers. If you're reading this that means you took a chance on a new to you author, and we cannot tell you what that means. Thank you for spending your hard-earned money on our words, and taking the time to read them. We appreciate you more than you know.

Special Thanks: Becky Johnson, Hot Tree Editing.

Deaton Author Services, Sandra Shipman, Jo Thompason, and Kara Hildebrand, Proofreading

Just Write Creations – Cover Design

Chasidy Renee – Personal Assistant

Jo, Sandra, Jamie, Stacy, Lauren, and Erica

Bloggers, Bookstagrammers, and TikTokers Tempting Illustrations, and Graphics by Stacy The entire Give Me Books Team

And our amazing Readers

Made in the USA
Middletown, DE
12 October 2022

12487451R00146